CHILD
OF
INTENTION

AMRITA MOHANTY

authorHOUSE

AuthorHouse™ UK
1663 Liberty Drive
Bloomington, IN 47403 USA
www.authorhouse.co.uk
Phone: UK TFN: 0800 0148641 (Toll Free inside the UK)
*   UK Local: (02) 0369 56322 (+44 20 3695 6322 from outside the UK)*

Published by AuthorHouse   11/25/2021

ISBN: 978-1-6655-9317-5 (sc)
ISBN: 978-1-6655-9318-2 (hc)
ISBN: 978-1-6655-9316-8 (e)

PROLOGUE

Sometime in the distant past ...

THE CRACK IN THE marble steps had been left for many centuries. Inlaid into the white marble, were blooms of soft pink and yellow. This one tile still displayed a crack, made by one of her son's god-strengthened knees falling into the stone. The dent was tiny, his infant knee leaving a mark no bigger than an orange, and the gold in the stone sparkled in the radiating cracks.

He had been so rosy-cheeked and happy then, always fighting with his twin brother, a constant swirling riot of wings and laughter. Now he was grown with his own love, his own power—though she still felt she could choose better for him. Her glacier blue eyes were gazing at the stone, recalling the memory of the beautiful little Fae queen that had helped him learn to fly.

It had been a joy to realize that her son had something that none of the other godly children could boast on: beautiful crisp white-feathered wings. Of course, any of them could fashion themselves a pair, but not of the same beauty or with the same gracious movement. She had loved watching him wake and seeing him stretch the long feathers to their furthest limit, loved feeling the tips flick across her face during the dark nights when he snuck into her bed.

But what so few knew of him was that for the first tender years of his existence, Eros had not been able to get himself even an inch off the ground. Only after some negotiation had the little queen of the Oahesa agreed to teach him in the same way that they taught their young how to fly. She did not trust the rest of her own Pantheon to nurture him as he deserved.

In fact, she enjoyed the company of the Beluvial Fae more than most of the other living things in the two worlds. She was after all, a daughter born of the elements, just as they had been. Her origins always cast her out from all the others, the others who came from the Titanomachy. She suspected that she did not come from these people at all. Somehow, she had stepped out of these waters with no memory of anything before the bubbling water.

The goddess pulled a trim and muscled golden leg up, bending her knee as she leaned against one of the great pillars holding up the roof of her Olympian temple. She had chosen a temple with several fruit gardens, laden with apples, grapes and mangoes. Several small turquoise bathing lakes chequered the mountain, private alcoves hidden from celestial eyes. From here, there was a rare portal straight from her world to the ocean depths of the sister world, Beluvial—a collision of dimensions that led to a molecules-thin layer of separation between the worlds. Last night Lir had risen up from the depths of one of those pools. He was a beautiful sight, with his broad chest and long dark green hair. She had paid dearly for the portal, but every time she saw him, it had been worth the thumbnail of ambrosia spirited off of Olympus.

Through the valleys of Olympus she had a clear view of the world below, the human world. She had wanted to be able to look down towards them at all times. Her great canopied bed sat in the middle of the open room that was surrounded by decorated pillars, gossamer cotton streams swaying on the soft, floral-scented breeze. The soft blue sky could be seen through the decorated archways, bright sunlight pouring in. A sleeping man stirred in deep blue sheets on the heavy carved wooden bed. She always chose this colour for him, this indigo that the humans derived from the molluscs of their sea. He always looked so beautiful in it with his light blue skin and dark green hair. Lir was one of them—one of the Fae. She was still married, and in order to keep her husband from scandal and to keep herself in the good graces of Zeus and Ares, she always hid him.

She often wondered why he never questioned the secrecy. He came every seven years and spent only a few days with her. To a god that was a tragically brief time. But she knew that Lir had his own sons, his own wife. He had been kind, loyal, and honest with her and wanted nothing from her but to enjoy her company and please her as much as she pleased him. It was something she seldom got living amongst the petty gods in this Pantheon. She was the goddess of love, and she knew love in all its forms, knew its many manifestations. What made her think of the Fae so much on this crisp morning was that soon

Lir would construct one of the greatest structures conceived by any of the pantheons.

She pictured that sweet Oahesa queen. They had been smaller once, only large enough to be able to sit comfortably in palm of her hand. But the little queen understood the magic that allowed them to fly. She helped patiently through every trip and fall her beautiful blonde boy endured, every time his wings got under him and he stumbled from the air. It was not something she ever remembered doing, stumbling. Just a silken ascent from the warm water onto the sands of the island, a beautiful gold and pink sky and the smell of sea salt.

It was different for her children. With the blood of the Pantheon coursing through them, they all shone and coalesced into this world. As they achieved their godhood, even they began to treat her differently, see her differently. Although Athena, Hera and Demeter all whispered about her, about how many of her children had been born with wings, at least her winged children seemed to thrive here.

She didn't know why she was angry with Lir. She was uneasy, but the Veil would change things. It had been decided for over a hundred years that the Fae would leave Earth. Peace had been bargained for before they destroyed everything, and all the pantheons had agreed to the separation of the worlds, for their own survival. Zeus could not be happier. With the Fae gods and their power and kin leaving, the pantheons left on earth were soon to be some of the most powerful beings on this world. But she was going to be terribly lonely.

No one else had been able to fashion a spell of this kind. It ensured peace. The Fae wanted their world protected from the humans. The humans were scared of their powers. Now that the wars were over the other pantheons were no longer caught in the middle, no longer picking sides. He had delivered on his promise that all creatures both sentient and fae from the smallest to the largest, were innocent of the actions of the high Fae and would not be barred from the magic of either world.

But the gods of this Pantheon would not be allowed to cross, an agreement reached so that the Fae gods would also leave this world. Their gods so often liked to walk amongst them, they even granted the Fae powers in sacred spots. It was a practice she had always feared. Humans were barely above the beasts that roamed the earth; how could they be trusted with fashioning this universe? Sure, a powerful object or a wish granted here or there was amusing. But real power?

When Lir was awake, she would ask him, just as she had asked a hundred times what he thought of this choice. She smiled, knowing they would argue and debate and then enjoy even more passion when they decided to reconcile their differences. She stared at the dent in the marble tile. She would never see any of them again: not Lir, not the pretty Oahesa or the Pes maids and their beautiful tails.

'I can't come with you,' Aphrodite whispered to herself, still watching the sleeping Fae god half naked and draped in indigo sheets.

CHAPTER 1

SHE WASN'T HIS FAVOURITE human, but he had to admit after many years, he found it comforting to watch her crazy habits. Amara was running around her apartment trying to get organised enough to leave. She was a creature of almost neurotic habit, though she fought the label; her life choices had to fit a yet unseen order.

Ribben had been watching her for hours already, saying she had been splashing around in the tide pools on the coast. At least today, she hadn't slipped and fallen in. Keirin had seen it happen once and laughed uncontrollably until he could barely pull air into his lungs. To achieve that was quite a feat for little Amara. He, of course, was a Lord of Air.

Not-so-little Amara, he thought, smiling as he admired the stretch of jeans and how they hugged her hips. He had seen her grow up into such a peculiar woman.

Next to him a small blue creature started to shuffle on the end of the tree branch. The spindly stretch of wood should not have supported both their weights, but then he wasn't sure if Ribben weighed anything at all. He had seen the small blue form walk over snow and not leave any footprints.

'She's about to Awaken, Keirin. I knows it.'

'She is too young and too human.' He pulled his knee against his chest and rested his chin against his leg. He peered through her window, waiting for her to gather her things and get organized enough to leave the house. Seven trips back and forth, and she still had the textbooks everywhere and her wallet was missing in one of her reusable environmentally friendly shopping bags.

Ribben shivered as his skin rippled. It looked moist, though Keirin knew that, touching pixie skin, you would only find a warm velvety texture. Dark blue dots faded and ebbed under his skin. Keirin, with only his thoughts, stretched the space that he was using to stay warm. Around him he churned the air in the sphere of invisible space. The more the thought and effort, the more the molecules moved. It was instinct, and with their constant motion they warmed and caressed his skin. Ribben relaxed and sighed as the warmth enveloped him.

'Thanks, KK.' Ribben slid further towards the thin tip of the tree branch, balancing impossibly.

'She's lost the keys as well,' Keirin said, sitting back down and getting comfortable. He knew that it would be at least another fifteen minutes before Amara left the house for the pub.

'Ribben, this is the coldest time of the year in this country. Why are we here? She's human and only in her twenties. She's probably never going to Awaken. That girl is going to live a long, simple life tracing minerals in fish populations and recycling.'

At a triumphant shout from inside the house, the corner of Keirin's mouth quirked up as he recognized her victory cry. She didn't even know she had one, except she made the same noise every time she had succeeded in even the smallest of tasks. He had never figured out whether it was cute or sounded diabolical.

'Let's go. You've proven me wrong enough times that I can't ignore you pestering me about her. You owe me big though. I had to *beg* for special permission to come over so soon after my last visit. She's not the only reason I'm supposed to be on this side of the Veil. In fact, most of the Mehsari would love for me to forget about her altogether.'

'You never forget about her, KK, nots ever.'

'Not with you around I won't.' Keirin jumped deftly to the ground, landing with a small thud as cold air wrapped around him. The smell of damp grass and woodland air surrounded him as he inhaled deeply. He glanced up, tilting his head and making an exasperated noise to goad his companion into moving. Ribben shuffled on the branch and sniffed, not hesitating to jump down without making a sound.

'Race you? Even though I know nixing is easier for you on this side of the Veil.'

'High praise from big Fae.' Ribben took his hand, smiling. One second later, the tall exotic man and his blue companion vanished.

It was the first time that she had seen him, he sat stretched out like a predator in the booth across from her usual seat. It was impossible not to notice him; he was like a wolf among sheep. Also, he was handsome and young, when everyone else in her local pub on a Tuesday night was upwards of fifty. She was in here because she needed to work and never got anything done at home.

Amara shuffled into her usual booth, tossing the too-heavy set of textbooks and a duffle bag on the seat. Her beige coat was still beaded with water but warm as she went to the bar to make her normal order. 'Sam, I need a mulled cider. It's November and freezing. A girl needs libation to nurse her wounds; bring a girl some seasonal cheer.'

'Haven't got any,' he said blandly, staring steely-eyed at her. She had pestered him with this question every year since she had moved to the coast.

Grey eyes beamed back her best stare. For moments, they cooled the air with their coy game, but Sam's lips finally cracked into a smirk. 'Negotiations? You can have scampi and chips with no mushy peas, but mash and cider for regular people.'

'Chilled cider? The customer is always right, Sam.'

'That or starve.'

'Throw in a brownie, and I won't start a riot.' Leaning against the bar, she rose to her tiptoes and winked at what was her favourite bartender in town. He was also the only bartender in town.

Sam chortled and walked away, his beer belly almost shaking over his belt buckle, the plaid button shirt barely covering his stomach. He had been her first friend in this town. A familiar face, with his crow's feet—the cost of years of smiling—with dirty blonde hair that was thinning on top.

The pub was traditional to a fault, with low ceilings and gold railings that lined a dark mahogany bar. Long wooden tables and booths screamed the theme of old-world farmer. Hunter plaid and brown were patched everywhere. Even the carpets were an ancient 1970s green. It was like time travel, but it had grown on her. The windows held characteristic swirls in the glass, evidence of how they traditionally spun out glass windows in England. She was staring at a favourite swirl over the head of Mr Wolf, she realized. She turned around and leaned against the bar as she waited for Sam to bring her drink.

Beautiful. That was all she could think when she saw him. Well-cut grey slacks covered long legs; elegant loafers made him look well-dressed. Running her eyes up his body she couldn't understand the change to a cream-coloured cotton shirt topped with a black hoodie. A hoodie? With those too-expensive loafers? She rolled her eyes. Why did some men dress like they weren't even trying these days? They needed to spend money to look sloppy in her opinion. She continued to walk up his body with her eyes until she slammed into a set of deep brown eyes looking right back at her. The returning stare was as penetrating as her own. She was being evaluated as well. Poor him.

Amara was not a British rose. She had pale brown skin from her mother and steel grey eyes from her father. Most of her peers were taller; she was not leggy or lithe in appearance. She was petite but with generous hips. Curvy was what she called herself now. Chubby was what she was called in school. It had taken her years to understand that she was never going to look like her friends because of her heritage. The turning point had been when she realized that everyone wanted to be something else, look like something else. 'If you can't please everybody,' her mother always said, 'then own pink things and dance like a lunatic.'

She nervously tucked her pin-straight shoulder-length hair behind her ear. Knocking her knee-high leather boots, she kicked off the bar to slide back into the booth. She tugged at her jeans and pink sweater, and then she pulled off the jacket and caressed the water beading on the outside of it like glittering jewels. She stole a glance at the wolf; he was staring at her now with something of a startled expression, with raised eyebrows under short dark hair revealed as his hoodie fell backward. He leaned forward gripping the wooden edge of the table. Gods, what was a man this handsome doing here? His profile was practically chiselled with the five o'clock shadow he was sporting.

Sure, fine, she thought. *Stare away at the only other not Caucasian person in the pub.* She pulled out the textbooks and let them thud on the wooden table. Studying again at her age wasn't as easy as it used to be. She was trying to complete her PhD, and the field work was amazing. Her days were spent looking at life in tidal pools and the impact of pollution on fish populations. She was being paid, poorly, to do what she loved. Today consisted of obsessively collecting samples from several run-off sites.

She was yanking out an toxicology textbook, to give her some guidance on analysing her latest test samples, when a cider was plunked down in front of her. Sam flashed a rare smile as he winked at her. 'Looks like you have a fan. You cheating on me, A?'

Her glare was all the answer he needed to have him bellowing in laughter as he walked away. A cold draft hit her as she looked up to see Micheal walk in to start the late shift, giving her his typical grin. She had been swooning over that grin for two years since he'd moved back to his hometown. Looking for 'the slow life' he had said, 'to settle down'.

She'd never seen any man move faster from woman to woman. His mother had been Scandinavian and given him blonde hair, blue eyes, and good looks. He was the guy every girl in town wanted to be with. Staring at the table in earnest, Amara started flicking her pen as she tried to focus on the page in front of her. Give her a lecture room full of people and she was a lioness of confidence. Put her in Micheal's gaze and she was a bumbling schoolgirl.

'You have to be joking,' someone scoffed.

Amara turned to see the wolf muttering to himself. He couldn't know; her pining couldn't be that obvious, could it? She stared at the table again and picked up her cider for a sip. The moment it hit her lips, she slumped into her seat and sighed, ran a hand through her black hair, and leaned her head back against the booth.

'Long day, hon? You look like something washed in from sea. Sam said you were waiting for this, so I thought I'd run it out to you.' Micheal leaned in to place the hot, steaming bowl of food in front of her as she nervously moved her paperwork and books out of the way.

She pulled herself together and gave him a smile. 'Thanks, lovely. You know what they say, no rest for the wicked.' Micheal chuckled, and she watched him leave, quite happy with her view.

'This is not happening. I refuse, Ribben. She's not even good at flirting. I am going home, and we won't pursue this any further.' Amara glanced back to see the wolf getting up from his empty table. He was like a storm moving towards the door. He was rolling past her table when she sensed a tickle of wind playing with her hair. The stranger came to a dead halt a few feet from her. She flipped to another page, shovelling some mashed potatoes into her mouth. As she watched from the corner of her eye, his hands clenched and unclenched, and the wolf turned on his heel. Then she was smacked into her chair by a smile that was beautiful. If only it went to his eyes.

'Hi, I'm Keirin. Fae Boron.' Her head twitched as she flinched from a buzzing in her ears, and he seemed to agree with someone as he shuffled towards the table.

'Um ... ah Aahra,' she managed to mumble with potatoes still in her mouth. She got a look saying that she could do better, so she swallowed quickly. 'Oh, sorry. I'm Amara.' The buzzing happened again, and she could have sworn it was a whisper that sounded a lot like a snicker. She really was letting sanity go today.

'Could I sit, ma'am? I need to speak with you urgently.'

Who was he calling ma'am? 'Yeah, the seat's free. I'm sorry, are you ... from the university? If you're a student looking for help on a dissertation, I'm not an adviser; I'm finishing my own degree.'

'No, my student days are long since done. I just wanted ... your name—uh, to get your name. Did your father ever tell you where you came from?'

'Listen, my dad's lived in our family cottage for his whole life, and his whole family is from England. If you're referring to my heritage on my mother's side ... what does it matter to you that she's Indian? Is there something I can do for you?'

Large hands were clasped again, and Amara could almost hear his teeth grinding together in frustration. His eyes darted to the space right next to her. She followed his gaze, wondering for a moment if she could see a shape outlined as well. She blinked several times, but the space appeared empty.

'I apologise for making you uncomfortable. I won't be

bothering you again.' Keirin got up, and as he stormed towards the door, she could almost feel whiplash.

'Damn, A,' Micheal said from behind the bar. 'You didn't tell us that you were seeing someone. But that fellow is a bit moody, isn't he? Or is it some lover's spat?'

Amara sat there absorbing what he'd said. *Why did it have to be in front of Micheal?* she fumed. She closed her eyes and breathed out. Dear god, it was in front of Micheal. 'I don't know him,' she said with a big sigh and pulled the books closer to her, letting the food sit on the side. She let embarrassment wash over her.

Amara spent a couple more hours looking over some statistics and feeding the data into graphing software. After jotting some final notes on a napkin, she motioned to the bar that she wanted to pay her tab and gathered up her things to go home. The parking lot was empty, and her weathered car looked lonely as she piled her things into the passenger seat in an unsteady heap, ready to head home. The flat was no more than ten minutes away, but it might as well have been a universe away, as she felt like a pile of walking lead.

Micheal chose this particular moment to come out of the kitchen back door. Holding the night's garbage, he waved at Amara with a friendly grin. As she tried to wave back, the arm of her jacket got caught on the handbrake; one awkward jerk and an overpowered grin were her only defences. Micheal mouthed, 'Are you OK?' Amara nodded furiously in answer. When he finally walked back inside, Amara stared through the windscreen and whined, *'Perfect. Just perfect.'* Her now freed hands were at the two and ten positions of the pink fur-covered steering wheel. She lifted her gaze to the ceiling of the car and took a deep breath before reversing out.

It had been years since she had been with anyone—three to be exact. She was twenty-eight, and she had started seeking something different in life. Her mother's side of the family found her old and entirely too independent. They were forever disappointed that she had not made every effort to get married and start a family. It was not that she didn't want those things for herself but that it didn't seem to happen. There was no connection when she met men; words were hollowed out before the first casual drink was done, and she was checked out and daydreaming.

She shifted the car into gear and started weaving her way through the lit streets. Amara loved the town for how green, lush, and quiet it was. Especially on winter nights. The streetlights lit the dense trees from underneath, and from these pools of warm yellow ambiance flowed an ocean of green shadows. She would visit the nearest city to see a show or visit a museum, but her heart lay at the coastline and the seashore. Tonight there was a full moon, and the ocean could be seen rippling under the moonlight. The stunning view was why she had rented this place. She liked the freedom of having a high vantage point to look out over the trees and the ocean, only a few miles away. She stood for a minute at the railing to take it in again as if saying goodnight. The wind ruffled her hair into her eyes.

She unlocked the door and welcomed the warmth of her simple flat, a sofa, a TV and a kitchen in one room and a clean bedroom. She started to strip her clothes off in the hallway and strolled naked towards the bathroom. Never again would she be able to go back to sharing a house with people again. She was uncivilised and loved it. The small bathroom was clean and lined with shells and turquoise accents, and she hopped into the shower turned the water on full. She purred under the water pressure. Hot water may be the best invention ever. She let the water ripple over her and leaned against the tiled wall of the shower.

From a distance she heard her phone buzzing. She rolled her eyes, annoyed at anything that penetrated this bubble of water and warmth. Minutes passed that she wasn't counting. She got out of the shower and wrapped herself in a pink bathrobe with white polka dots, fell into bed, and curled up under the baby pink duvet. Things were sparse in her flat. Her bedroom contained a single dresser and some paintings on the walls that were there from the landlord—scenes of British dairy cows in oil paints. The dresser and cupboard were full to the brim with clothes, but she made sure it couldn't be seen.

Along the dresser and through each room were photos of her parents. Her mother was second generation Indian, and her father was English. She'd tried once to go through his family tree but was lost in the tangle of Irish, English, and Polish. Amara didn't look hugely Indian anymore except for the dark hair of her mother and a cream brown to her skin. She had moved out of her family home years ago, but their love had always come with her. Missing her mother's food on tired nights stung the most. Her appearance was deceptive; she could eat a mountain of Indian food.

She looked up momentarily at the windows of her room. Had she seen something? This happened to her so consistently, she thought she was a little mad. She was sure she'd seen a light or a shape out of the corner of her eye, but by the time she looked back, nothing was there. She chalked it up to a trick of the brain. Like when you learn that everyone has a blind spot that your brain fills in for you. Surely her brain was just overactive. The trees moved in the breeze, illuminated by the tree light. She watched the branches sway, hypnotised by them for a while. The deadline for her dissertation was looming in front of her, and she needed sleep. She walked away from the windows and picked up her phone.

Jess was messaging for the third time to ask about plans for getaway weekend. Having just broken up with her boyfriend, for the fourth time, she needed time away from her regular haunts. Why she kept going back to that mess of a man, Amara couldn't understand. Well, that was a lie; she could. Maybe she hadn't done it four times, but she had stumbled down that self-loathing path before. She breathed a sigh, telling herself to be a good friend and wrung out some empathy for her friend. Amara pushed the dial button and called back while falling comfortably into her abundant duvet.

After one ring, Jess snapped straight into conversation. 'Thank god; I need to book the tickets. What is taking you so long to get your crap together? It's a good deal, B&B for two days and one night, and there's a sauna. A Sauna. Please? I just don't want to be the lonely old spinster alone, all on my lonesome.'

'Jess, I'm not sure I can afford it. Can you book it for us, and I will pay you back next month when I've got the money? If that's the only thing, I can definitely do it. Been ages since I've seen you anyway. And you will not believe what happened tonight. I was a twelve-year-old girl in front of Micheal.'

'What? Micheal? That hunk of man? Please tell me you finally jumped on that bartender. Why aren't you naked and rolling around in the proverbial hay with him. What did he say? I'm trying not to explode with processing this. Breathe, woman, breathe.'

'I am breathing.'

'Me, not you.' Of course.

'No hope for Micheal and me I'm afraid.' Why would she be thinking of him? 'Then there was this other weird guy. He sort of had a go at me in the pub. I didn't even know him, but he came up to me wanting to … I can't remember now; help with something? I've never seen him before. Actually he was more gorgeous than Micheal. There was something so solid about him. Broad shoulders and a giant.'

'Well, that's it, you're screwed.'

'Excuse me? Just because I see a guy whose body is mouth-watering doesn't mean I lose all control. Not anymore anyway. I will have you know I blew him off and went home.' Amara's eyebrows pulled together. Why was she bragging about coming home alone? This may have been a miscalculation. 'But not before getting my arm caught in my handbrake and Micheal clearly thinks I've got a learning disability.' This was an emotional facepalm moment, even by phone; her skill clearly was finding ways to avoid attractive men.

'No. I mean as soon as you're talking about a guy's back, you are totally on the hook, bait eaten, line being drawn in. Also, how do you even attach yourself to your handbrake?' Jess began snickering. 'How would I do that on purpose? God, that man—if I didn't live so far away, I would be there every night.'

'That is not true. I like all kinds of men, of all kinds of shapes and sizes.'

'So true. This is exactly how it started with the other one.'

'Yeah, him.' She sighed and stretched her legs under the duvet. 'He did have me on a hook.'

There were a few moments of silence as Jess realized she

shouldn't have brought him up. Amara's ex was the reason she hadn't been with anyone for three years. She had been burned, deeply. For a while, she struggled to just learn to live with the heartache. 'I'm not surprised about Micheal. He wouldn't suit anyway, Ams. You need a deep pool of a man.'

Amara thought about it on the phone. She had been brazen in her early twenties with men. But she did hold back now. Maybe she was looking for something deeper?

'Well, it's no problem for me to book the tickets,' said Jess. 'The firm has been taking on lots of new work lately, so I've got a Christmas bonus coming up. In fact, don't worry about paying it back. It's girl time for us.'

There was a tap on the window. Amara glanced up; instinct forced her to stare again at the trees swaying outside. Nothing was there. A shiver went through her.

She turned towards the dresser and saw a small round pale blue stone. When had she bought that? She got out of bed and picked up the stone and felt it heavy in her hand. It was the size of a large coin, not smooth but rough and comforting to the touch.

Had she brought this here? Maybe it was something she found but she forgot? That must be it. She did like the stone. The heavy weight was somehow grounding to her; it was as if she was sinking downward and being anchored.

She set the stone down and drifted back to listen to the end of Jess's update. 'I'm never going back. I know he didn't cheat on me, and he's not horrible, but how could he just chip away at me because I earn more than he does? Every time he tells me it's not an issue, and every time it is.'

'I think it's complicated being a man in this century. They

haven't figured out how to be the knight in shining armour without offending us, and I think they don't want to. But society hasn't given them a better way to show they care except to provide.'

'So you don't think he's an ass?'

'I'm not saying that, Jess, I'm saying you can't keep asking him to be someone else. And yes, the way he blew up screaming at you in the middle of dinner and stormed out makes him an ass. He's lucky it wasn't me. I would have thrown the wine bottle after him.'

'O.M.G., that time in London when you tackled a man who grabbed your ass. I will never forget it. So glad I got to see that.'

Amara chuckled and then told herself, *Surely I'm a much older and wiser girl than I was then.* Mostly. She had taken boxing in school and archery. She didn't consider herself an athlete these days, but there was a time when she had seen herself as fit. Height was always her downfall. Taller people could overpower her in the ring, so she had learned to be quick and never end up in that position.

'I'm calling it a night, Jess. You going to be OK?'

'I'm always OK after talking to you. Thanks, and so excited about this weekend coming up. I'm going to email you all the details.'

Amara hung up the phone and curled into the sheets. Her eyelids grew heavy, and it didn't take long for sleep to find her. She stretched out, feeling as if she was pulsing from the inside. For a moment, she again glanced out the window and almost expected to see a flash again. Her head sinking comfortably into the pillows, she drifted off to sleep listening to the wind.

CHAPTER 2

MEHKAR GAVE A DEEP sigh, as he looked down on the council floor. The Mehsari were meeting for the second time in two months, which was wildly unusual. They had been called so quickly that half of the nocturnal Fae members could not attend. Judging by the scene of a smug Vitar smirking at a yelling winged Oahesa, it was not going well. He stood alone in the circular viewing gallery that overlooked the chamber, hearing the echoing voices rise up.

It was lost to memory when the Belaphoros Temple came into existence, or even if it was made or simply found. Like the Sithens of the old world, it seemed to have a life force all its own. Sometimes people would wake to find the colour of the Temple had changed, or domes had rearranged themselves. When a new member of the Mehsari was elected by their people, rooms would be resized and rearranged. The changes to the interior were even more frequent, with hallways and rooms shifting position.

Made out of the very stone of the mountains, the pillars framed white and black window and door frames, as round gold domes erupted out of the crevices of the mountains. Huge stone doorways opened up into an intricate underground labyrinth of rooms; some were large enough to hold the Henta beasts of the north, and other small dark spaces could house even the smallest winged Fae that favoured this region of Beluvial. Mehkar used to have rooms in these halls, before his position had been handed over to his successor.

Some had theories that the Evandrus line must have shifted the stones of the mountain, moulding the granite as if it was liquid. Mineral deposits over several millennia shimmered in the warm white Turine lights that lined the floor of the grand room, made of smooth pink and orange stones. The walls began as rough and uneven but would soften to a smooth shiny stone. From the floor there was a defined line where the stone began to smooth and curve into a spiralling ripple, like water rushing towards the ceiling instead of towards the ground. In the centre of the curved dome was a perfect humble open circle that allowed the bright sunshine of the outside sky to pour into the dark room, in a single bright golden beam. The beam currently held a very angry flying Oahesa, one of the small folk.

The small creature only reached the height of Mehkar's knees and looked like a porcelain doll with white skin and jet-black hair. Her wings were pulsing back and forth, which Mehkar recognized as true distress. Reflecting the sunlight, the iridescent purple that was hidden in the black feathers reflected onto the chamber walls. Surrounding her in a circle of chairs and altars were the creatures that represented the Fae life in Beluvial. Mehkar took in a deep breath, smelling the dry earth, trying to steel himself for the performance that he was sure to witness.

'We are being hunted.' The statement reverberated through the open air.

'Peeva, we are all aware of the losses, the missing. But if you have no proof that the Vitar, that any nation is responsible … what would you have the council do?'

'All of the missing are from the same border, from the Vitar's border where the lands nurtured by the small folk begin. Seven flocks have vanished. Is my queen's court to believe that they left everything they owned, left meals on their tables uneaten, left children alone without anyone? The young were left! We demand a response from the Vitar, demand explanation!'

The Vitar, generally secretive shapeshifters, were always the quietest on the council floor. Quiet usually signalled an individual who was trying to construct a clever way to lie through the spell of intention. The Fae had too many languages for any translator to learn, and some of their number did not even speak in words.

Her solid dark eyes drilled across the room, and her wings rustled back and forth, ruffling the simple grey floor-length dress made of rippling taffeta material. The uncontrolled twitch to her wings revealed the depth of the rage that she was containing. The focus of her attention was a tall languid figure, lounging on the stone seats granted to council members. His head rested on his fist, giving him a bored demeanour, but his barely concealed toothy smirk let everyone in the room know he was amused. Blonde curls on the Vitar's head seemed to stay impossibly still as he slowly stood up, something unusual as it was not the custom to speak unless you were on the arena floor.

Mabon cleared his throat, a loud and uncomfortable sound. Speaking within these chambers was an intricate dance of diplomacy. Long ago through old magic, a simple spell was created, the Spell of Intention. Though a form of common magic, it was found to have a useful side effect. Fae of different languages could understand each other. Subsequently, all words that were spoken or telepathic thoughts could be understood, in any language. The wonderful nuance of the spell was that if you tried to lie, all in the room would hear only your true intentions. All eyes rested on Mabon, as the shapeshifter stood ready to choose his words wisely. Of all the creatures in Beluvial, those who shifted between two forms were the least trusted.

'Lady Peeva. The Vitar express our deepest sympathies over the loss of your kin. Let me state with perfect clarity. No Vitar are known to be involved in the disappearance of any of the small folk at the Red border.'

Damn. Mehkar gripped the sandstone railing. The response was more evidence of his immaturity. In fact, both the Vitar and Oahesa had not been on the council for more than fifty years. It was almost infancy. Mehkar shook his head and was looking to the ground in frustration when he heard a screeching cry echo through the chamber. He looked up to see that an enraged Oahesa was inches away from the Vitar. Her powerful wings were beating in arching strokes to keep her against an invisible barrier, her fists beating against it so that each strike reverberated around the domed room. Each blow created vivid bioluminescent blue lights radiating out as they hit a shield over and over and she growled out her frustration. Mabon stood his ground but was wide-eyed. After a particularly hard strike he released a hiss and there was an almost imperceptible change in the shape of his pupils. In his fear they had morphed to vertical splits. Now Mehkar smiled. Serpent. How long had the Vitar tried to hide that secret? And the irony was lost on all of them. They didn't know the human story, of the snake in the garden that led the human children to ruin.

'I think I speak for us all when I ask you to control yourself, Peeva. Mabon does not know what has happened to your kin. Without proof of his people hunting yours, you are only a feather's breadth away from breaking ancient treaties and inciting war. I may be Pes, but we are all Fae. Your loss is my loss. I do not want war for your people.' The source of the gentle voice was walking into the room, another beautiful dark-haired woman. Her skin was a soft golden brown, unusual for her often milky-pale kind, and her dark hair reflected the dark blues of the ocean just miles away. Against her dark hair, her pale turquoise eyes shown with power, a legacy of her Pes heritage.

Ursuna was the source of the shield currently separating Mabon and Peeva. Only Fae that were aligned with water could produce a resistant shield. The only evidence of her exertion was the fist tightly clenched at her side. She was one of the few Pes that had been invited to the Temple for an Awakening. The fact that she could use the water droplets in the air to form a shield, when she was miles from the coast, spoke to the depth of her power.

'Peeva, please.' The Djinn sitting next to Mabon implored, looking both bored and frustrated. She turned her vaporous form towards Ursuna as she took her seat. 'Your reflexes put us to shame.' Of all the members sitting on the council, the

Djinn were the most exclusionary, wanting to keep themselves as separate from the Fae as possible. But Mehkar had always found Nikka fair, even if she seemed as emotionless as a corpse. Nikka billowed in the room, and the misty outlines of her being appeared turbulent. She wore a deep purple dress of a pleated cloth, trimmed in a coppery metal that was favoured by her kind. Her skin was so dark it had an almost midnight blue tinge to it.

Peeva finally sat on the arena floor just feet from the huffing Mabon, who was trying to control his own response to the assault. While she appeared to be out of control, not even the smallest hint of electricity was trickling around the room. Peeva was one of the most gifted of her kind in making storms, particularly damaging lightning storms. Mabon sat back down, trying to appear unfazed, but his eyes remained serpentine. Wars had been started for less among Fae kind. He was displaying a deep sympathy for her position, allowing the breach in protocols in the face of her grief.

'Seven flocks have vanished.' Peeva gave the ragged admission. 'They have gone without a word, without any message to their loved ones. Food was on the tables, homes left untouched. So many are missing, and so many are without answers. We demand justice,' she intoned, 'My queen demands answers.'

The Djinn looked at Peeva, turning her head to the side and pinning her with a birdlike gaze. 'Peeva, you have made it clear that the losses are personal to you.' The Djinn always saw what you did not want them to.

Peeva flinched, closing her eyes in hopes that they wouldn't witness the truth, that her favourite cousin was among the missing. As she knelt on the ground, her dark hair fell across her face as her wings beat gently. She stood gracefully with a few strong wingbeats, stepping backwards towards her seat to leave the floor open for another speaker.

Pelidren was nervously tugging at his formal attire; the purple cloth around his neck was itchy and stiff. He felt covered from head to foot in material when he was accustomed to wearing the loose clothes of his work space. But today he was going to represent the Orchidru; he had a chance to build a bridge for his people.

'Are you ready? Now is the best time to speak. They will hear you out.'

'Mehkar, why do you always make it sound so easy?' Pelidren flashed a grin and his spring green eyes while getting the blue disc in his hand ready.

'Living is easy. Dying is the painful part.' Mehkar chuckled as he pulled the much taller man's hands from his picking at his clothes and held them still. He told Mehkar with a look to breathe, to be still.

'They need to hear what you have discovered. I am grateful that you trusted my house to bring you here. Why didn't you speak to Chandara? She would have been the ideal choice? Or the Evandrus?'

'You are quite famous for your … sympathies to those who do not belong.'

'Ah. My human life.' Mehkar stared up into the sun pouring through the skylight. He saw swirling glistening particles and thought briefly of a different sun.

'What I have to say shouldn't wait any longer. Announce me?'

With a curt nod Mehkar started to walk down the stairs

lining the walls, descending in line with the curve of the room. Everyone looked up, and a few gasped as they finally noticed the being that followed him from the observatory. The Orchidru were almost never seen on the ground, their people had long since decided to move their kingdoms into the skies. The floating cities were often seen in this part of Beluvial; the magnetic intercies helped keep them powered and floating. Many believed it was the same reason so many of the Air and winged Fae chose this corner of the world as home.

'Friends and esteemed nations, I present to you Pelidren Obarak, Prince of the Seventh house of Ordison, Noble among the Orchidru.'

'That title, while acknowledged, will grant him little power here,' came a voice from the lower door.

Mehkar cursed under his breath as he had hoped that Chandara would have been delayed. It was impossible to get good help these days. You used to be able to trust that when you paid off a messenger Spraxa, they would gorge themselves on pollen and not deliver important messages.

Chandara was physically a beautiful match for the Orchidru. They both had pale white hair down to the small of the back and a tall, slim build. Where she differed from the Orchidru was that for a reason Mehkar could not understand, that vapid and spiteful creature had been blessed by the gods and given impressive powers.

'We will discuss later why the Orchidru decided to approach you first.' As she addressed Mehkar, her purple eyes pinned Pelidren to the floor, and he clutched the blue disc more firmly. She was wearing a white suit, cut at sharp angles. She spun and looked out across the room to see who else was in attendance.

Then she sat down sharply. 'Speak, Prince. We have never banned your kind from joining us here in the dregs of the hallowed earth.'

Pelidren licked his lips. This was only the third time in a hundred years that he had set foot on the soil of Beluvial. He took a deep breath and walked straight into the centre of the arena and threw the disc into the air. The disc rotated several times and spun, floating just inches from his head. Instantly a topographical map of the Bhandi region of Beluvial appeared, covering the oceans to the south where the majority of the Pes thrived and the mountain region where the winged Folk live. The map extended up the coast of the continent to the plains inhabited by the Chivane and Henta beasts. They could even see the forests where the Vitar and Atriva lived. Bordering those forests was a deep canyon that ran hundreds of miles through the continent. It was here, at the border of these lands, that the Oahesa had gone missing. It was at the border on this map that Pelidren pointed.

'The Orchidru have for several decades made great strides in understanding the source of Fae power. The power granted to you in Awakening ceremonies.'

There was a silent begrudging acknowledgement from all of the beings seated in the room. While they were all aware of the Princes interests, the results of his investigations were only rumours. Many doubted that this young prince would unlock the inner workings of Awakening. There was a time when it would have been considered heresy, but now all the races were losing their hold on the precious commodity that was god-given power.

'I have been scanning the Fae life trying to detect what

we know now is a unique spectrum of light and energy that is emitted by all living things. The Orchidru call it Elsivir in the old tongue. I believe you call it Ka, Mehkar?'

Mehkar raised an eyebrow at the mention of a human belief system. What exactly did this prince know?

'As agreed in the Brightening treaty, the Orchidru routinely scan for this energy. It is how we identify which of your young are likely to be chosen by the gods for the awakening ceremony and allows us to … learn why none of my people are ever chosen.'

'Could we move on from the history lesson? We are all aware of what you do in that floating rock,' the Djinn said with unusual impatience. Pelidren turned to the Djinn speaker; he would have loved to test a sample of her vapourous form. The word *Daemon* now had negative connotations, but long ago they had been greatly respected by the Orchidru—or enslaved, depending on who told the stories. He wanted to know more about a creature made of gases that moved like smoke through this world. But the Djinn were difficult to catch.

'Days ago this section of the map was bright with Elsivir energy. We were tracking a young one that would have been put forward to you as a potential. That light, and a dozen others, vanished. I scanned three times thinking there was a fault in the machines. I reset the sensitivities; I changed countless crystals in an attempt to find those lights again. The more I scanned, the less I saw.'

'Do you mean … Do you know that they are dead?' Peeva asked with a shaking voice.

'When a Fae leaves this world, their Elsivir energy takes many long years to disseminate. We are all singular and unique events in the universe, held against the scale of time and matter. What you are will never be again, and that presence and existence lingers in this world. That is what we have seen on my floating rock in the sky,' Pelidren explained with some bite to his words.

'There is a pure absence. They didn't fade. They are gone. And not just the Oahesa villages. The Beherna in those woods are vanishing too. At the time of the scans there were no Vitar who had left their Densions. Now some of those Vitar can no longer be seen as of yesterday.'

At this the Vitar visibly took in a relieved breath. Mabon knew that the predatory streak of his people was strong. He turned quickly to Peeva, whose sharp dark eyes met his. Her hands came forward, clasped in front of her, and she bowed her head to him. Mabon looked at her and turned away, remembering her fury only inches from him. But now he knew that some of his people had vanished without a trace. The Vitar were not used to being hunted. He turned his yellow eyes to her and realized that they were joined in their grief. Dozens of lives that would not be replaced for hundreds of years. He nodded at her, accepting her wordless apology for now.

'And where have all of these Fae gone?' Chandara asked.

Pelidren looked up at the glowing map, orange, blue, violet, and white lights scattered across the many lands of the continent. And at the centre of the image was a dark empty section of map. 'I do not know.'

CHAPTER 3

RIBBEN IS HERE.

Amara shot up like a bolt in bed and looked out the window, again to the trees outside. What was that? She could have sworn that there was a voice in her head. She glanced at the clock next to her bed and saw that it was four in the morning. Then there was a shuffle and branches shaking followed by a cracking noise. She lay back down and convinced herself that she must have been dreaming. She didn't know whether to pretend she heard nothing or go back to lying down. Or she could accept that she was a lunatic. She looked again at the stone that shouldn't have been there. This time she heard a definite crash outside the window, followed by a yell. This could not be a dream.

Amara steeled herself and stalked towards the window, looking out to the grass to see a branch on the ground and something else. Definitely not nothing. *What the hell is that?* Her stomach dropped as she couldn't believe what she was seeing. Was that a blue person? A little blue person? What she saw was a small creature with grey-blue skin that was bumpy and marked like an exotic tree frog, with dots and stripes decorating out from its spine. It was turned away from her and started brushing leaves off itself, looking down at the ground and kicking at the branch making noises. Buzzing noises, the same buzzing noises that she had heard before.

She shoved herself from the window and almost flipped over the bed. *It's aliens. It's the invasion. Who do I call?* And then the buzzing seemed to ring through her ears. It went from a buzz to painful clarity as her ears popped.

'*Stupid force of wind. Can't believe he did that. He knows I has to be here. He knows it, and he's still an ass. Knocking Ribben down when he's working. Typical big Fae behaviour.*'

Amara's eyes were wide, and she was holding her breath with a death grip on the bed as she listened to the tantrum continue outside. She was going mad. She was officially bonkers. Lost the plot. What was she going to do now? Call the police? The hospital? The mental asylum? Her brows furrowed, and she got up again to look out the window and see if it happened again. She stood looking as the small blue creature that was only three feet tall picked up the solid tree branch as if it were a paper airplane and knocked it onto its shoulder. The blue creature was still muttering but now she couldn't hear what it was saying. It turned around and she could see that it had long pointed ears and a smooth face that tapered to a small pointy chin. A button nose poked out of the face, which had a slit for a mouth and large cobalt blue eyes. It was cute almost, if it wasn't so obviously not human.

For a moment it glanced up at the window and saw her and then kept walking toward the tree trunk. It looked up again and froze as she locked eyes with it. She knew that it knew that it was seen. *'Keirin. We has problem.'*

'You shouldn't even be there, Ribben. My father told you to find her, not stalk her. And really we just sort the tree out and get your pixie ass back to the Veil.'

Amara started screaming full out. Now she was hearing voices for real. She was hearing voices, and she started barrelling towards the living room to get as far away from the blue creature as she could. She ran straight into the living room heading for the car keys to escape when she smacked straight into a chest like a stone wall. Keirin stood in front of her. In her flat. His hands were up, and he was begging her to stop yelling. A calm quiet voice through tight lips.

'Please stop. Stop. It's OK. You just have to stop, and I will explain.'

'You get the hell out of my flat!' she screamed moving away from him and falling over right onto the ground and crawling backwards on her hands. He took a few steps towards her. 'I'm really sorry about this.' He said and put his right hand in the air palm up and whispered. Everything went black.

Amara woke up with a throbbing head. Had he knocked her out? And why couldn't she speak? Oh god, her leggings had been tied into her mouth. She was going to die at the hands of a sexual predator; with a blue alien.

'Keirin, you not supposed to harm her,' she heard the first creature keening.

'If you weren't such a clumsy creature, this wouldn't be happening, and her landlord lives ten metres away, I'm surprised they haven't called the human police already. She just needs to have things explained to her. And how did you get a stone in here? I took me forever to unweave the ward you placed.'

'Not long enough.' Ribben huffed and then turned to find Amara awake. She gripped the arms of her wooden kitchen chair and full on growled at them. That got them looking at each other, and Keirin actually smirked. 'Damn, I knew she was stubborn but now I can add scary to the list.'

'She's going to be mad. If you hadn't knocked me out of the tree this wouldn't be happening, and I'm going to sit outsides until I'm invited ins again.'

Then he was gone. One second there, the next second gone. Amara fought against her restraints anew, not sure if it was actually them she was fighting or her mounting panic.

Keirin walked towards her, and she peered up at him, staring into his eyes as he lowered himself in front of her so that he was squatting. With a steady stare she looked at chocolate eyes, and he said in a smooth, clear voice, 'Amara, you're safe and not going mad. You're safe, and Ribben is one of the small folk, a type of pixie. He was sent long ago to watch you from time to time and has never harmed you and never will. Blink twice if you're with me and not hysterical.'

Amara took a few ragged breaths and then blinked twice. His hands were still on her arms and they were warm and solid. 'OK, I know you have questions. Your head will feel better in a few minutes, and I'm going to remove the gag so that you can ask them. If you scream, I will knock you out again. Understand?'

Amara's eyebrows came together in anger again but she blinked twice. Keirin reached up and hesitated for a second before pulling the too tight leggings away from her growling mouth.

'How dare you!' she hissed.

'Ribben has said there was steam in you from time to time,' Keirin said, still looking at her with unwavering eye contact. 'We didn't want this. You shouldn't even have the sight. It's unusual. We had to watch you, have had to keep track of you because, well … you're a descendant.'

'Who the hell is *we*? And what do you mean that little blue thing has been here before? Are there more of them?'

Keirin ran his hand over his face looking tired and knowing he couldn't answer all her questions. 'I thought perhaps your father knew and had told you. I could tell today that you knew nothing, and I didn't want to—there's so much, Amara. What I have to admit to you is that there is a world within a world. One that runs parallel to this, one that exists in the same space. A Fae world. One from your myths and legends. I am one of those Fae.'

Now she was laughing. Laughing out loud. 'It's the truth. And despite what your stories say, I can lie, but in this I'm not.'

Amara's laughter started to faulter. Even if this man was crazy, she was still in danger. What was it about her that drew lunatics in her direction? Did she give off a pheromone? Why was this happening? She looked at him then, and her anger gave way to terror and fear. She looked at him, wondering what would happen to her now. Clearly one or both of them were mad. What would her parents do if she died? They'd be so broken.

She looked at him then, tears welling in her grey eyes, and implored him, 'Please. Please untie me. There's been a mistake. Untie me, please.' And he heard the panic in her voice mounting as she began to stretch the restraints that were holding her, and they cut into her skin. In a second the restraints were gone, and like a ghost Keirin was on the other side of the room. Amara shook and looked at him and then lifted her arms. She lifted herself up from the chair and stood wrapping the robe around her and became aware that she was naked under it and utterly vulnerable.

'I have to go, Amara. I won't stay in your house any longer. I'm sorry.' He almost whispered the last as he looked at her. She heaved a sob. She took one step towards him and squared herself in his direction, and he looked surprised. He stood silent and watching her movements. And through another sob she said, 'Get the hell out.' Her voice was defeated. It was a sound he had heard from her once before.

His eyes were wide for a moment, and his expression went from surprised to thoughtful and then they filled with understanding. He could have handled anger and swearing and insults, questions and accusations. 'I'm sorry, you were just screaming. I can show you it's safe; I can show you. Ribben, get in here.' He rasped out the order.

Amara found herself looking around for the blue creature. She stood clutching the bathrobe around her body, but was searching outward, craving seeing it, knowing for sure. From the corner of the room out of the shadows of her side table the little creature walked out again, arms posed in front of him clasped together. Ribben.

She sucked in a breath and raised one hand to signal the

creature to stop. She just stood there staring for a minute. 'So you're real?' A real pixie.

The corner of his mouth perked up; he had no lips, but she was sure he was trying to smile and gave a small wave and nodded his head yes. 'Has been watching Amara long times now. You is good girl. Kind girl. We sees it and have been glad to watch you. You has to excuse Keirin; he is a rude big Fae. Doesn't know how to be on this side because he no like it here. I'm sorry about the safe stone. They meant to helps. But I thinks, I thinks when I put the magics near you, it woke you up. Too soons. You is too youngs to be awake and to see.'

Amara backed up a bit and slid into the chair she had been tied to. She looked at the creature who kept making sidelong glances at Keirin. Keirin stood in the dark just watching her, and she finally looked at him. 'Turn on the lights. The switch is behind you. So I'm not in the dark talking to—' The lights were on in a second, and she could see Ribben even closer. He had dark soft blue-black curls on his head. He stayed in his spot but squirmed under her inspection. She must have sat for five minutes not saying anything and looking from one creature to the other.

Finally she turned to Keirin and looked at him again. 'Um, aren't you supposed to have pointy ears and unearthly beauty or something?'

There was a scoff, and then Ribben said, 'Yeah, she be OK, Keirin. That sound like an Amara comment for sure.'

She threw a glare at him then. What did that mean exactly? Keirin cleared his throat. 'Well, I haven't had any complaints about my looks before, but no, we don't have pointy ears and such. We look like you do. Most of the time.' And that's where he left it without explanation.

Amara started breathing a little more steadily. Then she got up and said, 'Wait here. I just need clothes. Just wait.' She scurried into her bedroom and pulled some slacks and an oversized T-shirt onto her and then cracked the door open to look through. Keirin and Ribben hadn't moved. She was half hoping she was mad and they would have disappeared. She walked out again onto the carpet, then from a safe distance she cleared her throat.

'OK. One. Why are you here? With me, why me? I heard you in my head,' she said, glaring at Keirin. 'You said that your father wanted me, what was it found, watched? Why did I hear that?'

Keirin sighed and looked at Ribben. The blue creature walked forward a few steps but stopped when he saw Amara stiffen. 'You are human mostly,' said Ribben. 'But way backs when, there was likely a Fae great great grandpappys, sort of. Only two ancestors of yours in 600 years was able to sees, has seen world within world. We watches them, to give guidance when this happens.'

Keirin finally seemed to relax and slipped his hands into his pockets, watching her every movement. Amara whipped her hands through her hair and looked at him. 'The sight? You mean seeing you,' she said almost to herself instead of them.

'We go now, Amara. We sorry. But we cants leave you just yet. Ribben has to watch, but won't intrudes anymore. Keirin is Lord of Air, so if you whispers into the wind, you can speak with us again. Be well.'

Amara could have sworn they were there, and then they

were gone. She was standing alone in her living room. The lights were on, and a chair was in the centre of the room, and nothing else was out of place. For a startling moment there was a vacuum of what had been, and she questioned it in an instant. A hallucination. She ran into her room and slammed the door shut and locked it. Looking out of the window a whimper escaped her when she saw the tree branch was gone from the ground, the tree intact and not a leaf out of place.

Amara turned turned to her bed, she saw the same pale blue stone sitting on her pillow with a handwritten note on it. 'Pixies don't give gifts often, and a safe stone is precious. Ribben thinks highly of you to protect you. Keep it. Stay safe.'

CHAPTER 4

T HE NIGHT HAD BEEN hard, spent tossing and awake, perched in the middle of her bed, clutching the blue stone and turning it over and over. A few times she laid her head down, but she kept staring out the window wondering if she was going mad. She cried twice; tears came and went, and once her sobbing stopped, she was exhausted and numb. She had to get her bathrobe because the flat was cold in the morning, but she didn't dare leave the room until daylight had come through the window. In November that took hours and hours in the United Kingdom and it wasn't till 9 in the morning that she felt like finally leaving the flat, whose oppressive silence seemed to be adding to her mental assault.

She grabbed a leather gym bag and shoved a few days' worth of clothes and underwear in it. She pulled on jeans and a cream turtleneck and threw her hair into a smooth bun. With her knee high boots on, she fled the bedroom, grabbed her keys from the kitchen counter and ran out the front door without even locking it. Her car was freezing, but she didn't care as she turned it on and drove straight into town and to the train station. She left her car in long-term parking and ran into the station. Only when she was surrounded by crowds did she feel OK, and she examined the screen to find the next train home.

Randall was going at 10:15 from platform 2. Once on the train, she sat at the window and stared at herself in the reflection as the countryside flew by. She looked exhausted, with dark circles under her almond shaped eyes. The grey of her eyes, which usually looked cool, was rimmed with red today. She sat with her hands clasped on the table in front of her. No one spoke to her.

About an hour into the train ride when she saw the familiar sight of green fields and Galloway cows sliding into view, she pulled out her phone and dialled her mum.

'Mum, I'm going to be at the station in an hour.'

'Amara, are you OK? You sound really shaken, hon.'

'It's, uh, been a bad night.'

'Like before, hon? Oh, sweety, I'm so sorry. You just make your way, and I will be there to get you. You're lucky as well; I was just making a batch of vadas for your dad to have when he's back in from lunch. The boiler at the Martins' farm blew up, and he's been trying to fix it for two days. Part after part. Well, it didn't really blow up; then they'd have to get a new one. But you know your dad. Always trying to fix it.'

'Yeah, he's good at that. Thanks, I know I sound bad, but it will be better once I'm home.' Amara smiled finally at the sound of her mother's constant chatter. She didn't know how to be silent. It was something so completely normal in a world that was unravelling.

'See you soon, sweetie. I love you.'

Amara hung up the phone and stared out the window with her elbows on the table and her head perched on her hands as she thought about last night again. That guy had been in her house. What was that little weird childlike creature? It had to have happened. She pulled the small blue stone out of a pocket in her bag. It felt good in her hands. The stone was cool, and the rough surface was soothing. She turned it over and over as if it would give her the answers. The train finally pulled into her station, and she jumped out. The station was so small she only had to walk ten feet from the train doors out to the parking lot where her mother was waiting for her.

Pinkie Clarence she was called. Her real name was Priyanka, but no one called her that. She was a tiny woman at only five feet tall, and in her later years she had gotten a little round and pudgy in her middle. More to love, her husband always said, as he planted a kiss on her cheek. She had the faintest crow's feet around bright brown eyes and large smile for her only daughter. She opened her arms as Amara, who was several inches taller, hunched down to bury her mother in hug.

'Amara, you're shaking,' Pinkie said with a worried tone.

'It's just love vibrating out of me, Mum,' Amara said, muffled in her mother's wiry curls. Salt-and-pepper grey made her look distinguished.

'Well, come on, dear, did you bring anything else with you? I know you feel the need to leave your room fully stocked with clothes. Maybe you should have brought a suitcase so you can take some of it back with you this time instead of cluttering up my house.'

Amara sighed with contentment. Yes, this was home for sure. They turned around the corner and started walking down the sidewalk; her family home was only fifteen minutes away on foot down a winding road. Stone walls flanked them, and you could look out over a river on the right and see small stone houses on the left. The town looked like something out of a postcard. Small gardens surrounded each house, with flowers speckled through the yards. They sauntered down the narrow path that took them to their own small stone cottage that was two storeys tall with ivy growing over most of the walls. It was a few hundred years old, but with all the love and care the family had put in, it only looked old on the outside.

Barking broke out as they opened and closed the spring green gate that led into their yard and Amara smiled at her dad's border collie, Grey, ready to play. He was posed at the French doors that led into the back entrance of the house once you walked past the vegetable patches and fish pond that were lined up outside. Stone slabs led the way to the doors. Grey's tail was high in the air and his head down on the ground jumping forwards and back. At one year old he still had puppy attitude, and Amara adored it. She readily jumped down on the ground to roll around with him.

'Do not encourage that behaviour. That dog has been so close to death this past month, I'm surprised the grim reaper himself hasn't already asked me to stop teasing. Dug up my dahlia bulbs from the back shed. My favourite Dahlias! He's lucky he's got such a cute face.'

Pinkie had never hurt anything in her life, so Grey had

likely gotten no more than a scolding. They walked straight to the kitchen once they entered the French doors, and Amara sat down at the table and waited for the expected cup of tea her mother was going to make. The table was a single large piece of wood with a clear coat on it, and she had often sat here circling her hands over all the lines in the wood. The whole kitchen was set within stone walls, but there was a modern oven and burner with an exhaust hood.

Then she spied the batter in a mixing bowl. Oh god, yes, the vadas. She glanced at her mother and grinned. There are those who would say that food is not love. Those people do not eat with Indian people. Food was the part of her heritage she would never want to be without. Amara rose and filled the red water kettle and set it on the stove top.

'Talk to me, Amah,' her mother ordered as she started heating up oil to fry the batter into donut-shaped fritters.

'It's not about Derek,' Amara said as she pulled down two mugs from the cupboard. 'I think it was just a panic attack. Like before, but it wasn't about Derek.' Amara's mother was silent as she listened to her daughter's words. She had always been able to tell when Amara wasn't being totally honest. She also wasn't going to let Amara get away with subversion.

'When you feel like telling me what really happened, then you can have a vada,' her mother said as her hands worked quickly to shape the thick batter into rounds and popped them into hot oil where they sizzled and floated to the surface. The smell of frying cumin and curry leaves wafted into the air.

'Oh, come on, Mum.' Her mother gave her a slanted look over her shoulder and continued to fry in silence. 'OK, I got scared. Something broke a tree branch and made weird animal noises outside. I got a massive scare and stayed up all night, and then I ran here.' Her mother looked over her shoulder and squinted at her. She turned back to the vadas and popped a few onto some tissue and worked on the second batch.

'You used to run around this house at night to jump out and scare me and your farther nearly to death when you were a kid. You ran out into thunderstorms. Since when did noises in the dark scare you?'

'Since Derek. Since he made me afraid. Since he threatened to kill me,' Amara snapped. 'How about then?' She shovelled sugar into the mugs and went to the fridge for milk, opening and slamming it a little too hard. She had come home for safety, not an interrogation.

'He can't hurt you anymore,' her mother whispered. 'He's in jail now, thank the gods.' She blew out a big breath. She sometimes couldn't reconcile that her daughter was changed, that the carefree girl she had raised in this house was not quite the same anymore. Part of it was just growing up. Part of it was the unfairness of life. 'I'm sorry. You know I don't like when you're not honest with me, and I just overreacted.'

Amara strained the teabags, placed the two mugs on the table, and curled up onto the wooden chair, legs underneath her, as her mother brought over the hot vadas and set them on the table. With impeccable timing as ever, her father walked into the kitchen. It was like some law of attraction that he found his way in when food was on the table. He hadn't grown up with Indian food, but since marrying, he had taken it all in stride. In fact, Eddie Clarence was open to all food and annoyingly somehow managed to stay tall and lanky.

'Bumble! You're home! This is a nice surprise,' he said as

he dropped the toolbox onto the floor. He was in overalls and covered in grease, but he stormed over to hug his daughter. He wearing square glasses that Amara could not make him part with and had deep-set blue eyes and a round and ever-smiling face. One that always looked like he was ready for a joke and a laugh.

'It's a surprise visit. Just 'cause she loves us,' her mother said with a wink as she started sipping her hot tea.

'Dad, Grey is getting fat.'

He gasped. 'You shut your mouth about your brother.'

They all laughed together, and Amara settled into the wooden kitchen chair and cherished this place. She watched her father coo over his dog and jokingly whisper sweet nothings to the animal as they stared lovingly into each other's eyes. Her childhood had been so good. For a few years as a teenager she had rebelled. She partied hard and slinked into London clubs. Her parents almost killed her when they found her cigarettes hidden under the bed. In the end she had found a calling in trying to study nature and the environment, and that had led her to college. Through it all they had supported her, showing her what love and acceptance was—especially when through the years more than a couple of people had judged her dad for having a mixed wife and daughter. He had never once made her feel anything but wanted.

After a few hours of banter and chatter, Amara told her parents she needed a nap, and she went up to her old bedroom, small and overlooking the woods in the distance. She looked out for a moment until she fell onto the pink comforter and old pink fleece and blissfully found sleep.

What she didn't know was that perched on a tree in those

woods sat Ribben. He knew her window, as he'd watched her for the past twenty years. He'd seen her unicorn figurines and obsession with baby pink decorations. He also saw the books that held Fae legends lining her bookshelf. She had been drawn to dozens of such books and never knew why. He saw her fall into bed, the blue safe stone placed on the bedside table.

'She finally sleeping, Keirin,' he whispered.

'We really must have scared the shit out of her.'

'I really likes her, Keirin. She no deserve fear.'

'No one ever does, buddy,' the wind whispered back.

CHAPTER 5

S HE LANDED ON THE ground with both feet and barely
made a sound. The earth was soft, and the air smelt of acid
and salt as she slipped into the deeper portions of the forest.
The moss-covered ground left a narrow path between fallen
trees. She tossed her silver white hair over her shoulder, the
thick braid still managing to reflect the light even under the
heavy cover of the trees. She was going to find out what the little
folk were so afraid of in these woods.

Two of the female Behrena had died already. They had said
the women came in from gathering and had fallen ill over days.
They didn't want to eat or drink and then slowly faded and
wasted away. Behrena should live for fifty years—some of the
shortest lives among the small ones, but Venti found them to
be the most beautiful. She had known the two girls personally,
as they had often come to the gardens of the one cottage she

frequented when she wasn't sleeping under the stars. They would always seed and tend to the new spring flowers.

Venti jumped over a fallen tree trunk again and adjusted the bow that was slung at her back. She was tall even among the high Fae, but instead of the lithe appearance of most of the woman in her family, she had a voluptuous quality. The curved bow arched above her head and tucked into the small of her back. She breathed in the damp moss scented air, grateful that she was alone.

She wore more traditional clothes than the rest of her kind—long tan suede pants that were laced at the side to allow as much stretch and movement as possible. Her hunter green tunic had slits over each thigh and hung to her knees to allow her cover and protection. The sleeves were long and tight to her wrists, and today she wore a grey and black feather-lined vest; the soft, warm material gently moved in the wind and wrapped around her soft pointed chin.

Although many of the ancient families no longer looked like the old world, the way they had been on earth beyond the time of remembering, Venti's family still had the strange, other-worldly tones. Like all of her family, within a gentle round face she had dark piercing green eyes that were large and youthful. She was deemed to be the most elegant and beautiful girl child born to the family in generations, the apple of her father's eye and his greatest pride.

That is, till she had aged without showing any signs of strong magical ability. It would have been tolerable to have been denied the chance to gain active powers. Awakening was rare among her kind, but Venti could not even access the most common of magics. Basic mirror spells were barely achievable; luck spells and growth spells all seemed to be out of her reach. Her father had spat on the floor when she was a young woman and called her something she had never heard before. 'No better than human.' In an attempt to gain political ground they had tried to marry her to a dozen suitors whose bloodlines still produced children of power.

Venti stole away in the night, forever leaving her home and name. She became part of a sisterhood called the Elai. It was a sacred path that women could take when they were lost. Many were women whose gifts made them suitable to work in the temples as acolytes, speaking with the gods as Oracles. Others would train to become warriors or forest wardens, wandering the lands. It was into this order that Venti had been taken in, even without god given power.

She was a force unto herself. Moving like a great liquid cat, she bounded onto the top of a fallen log that was as wide as she was tall. She tiptoed forward as she realized the area was becoming quieter, more chillingly still. There was no rustle of leaves, no stirring or chirping of birds. There was a stillness as she advanced, and she couldn't help feeling her skin crawl, her instincts shouting at her. She felt fear that she couldn't explain. Her fists clenched as she mastered herself to walk forward; she was no youngling to run from the dark forests. In one swift movement her bow was swung over her head and deftly held at the ready.

A small figure began to creep out of the bushes. He was only a foot tall and moved slowly enough that even though she had drawn her bow, made of redwood and blue metal filigree common to the north, she did not fire on him. Traveling in these woods she carried training arrows, non-lethal and meant to be a deterrent more than a weapon. She wore her Sehvat glove that would make the bow lethal. As she watched his every move, the hunched figure crawled out from under the bushes. He was weeping and sobbing and speaking the same phrase over and over again. He was a male Behrena. He was one that had been mated to Wenda, the second female to fade away. At his sounds, Venti reached behind her taking an arrow out of her quiver.

'You aren't supposed to be out here, Oron,' she said with a steady voice. Without lowering her bow, she edged to the far side of the clearing, the tip of her arrow firmly pointed on the small figure. Behrena were small, one-foot-tall Fae that generally had brown to black skin. What made them beautiful to Venti was that their skin looked like soft flower petals that had been artfully bound together over their bodies. She had held the small hands of many of them and felt the silken-soft skin. She had often been told that long ago they lived among the leaves and flowers and growing things and had been made to blend in and tend those spaces without being seen. Who or what had made the small race was a mystery. They were very slight in build and almost reminded Venti of deer in the way they moved and darted around. They had small faces, and their eyes were large and black, without centre or iris. The women had long sunflower yellow hair that often fell to their backs.

'She's gone, she's gone, and I can't find her,' he sobbed.

'Oron, I'm sorry but you need to go back to the village. It's not safe out here; this is where she got sick. Why are you here?'

'She's out here, I know it!' he howled before he fell to his knees and started pulling frantically at his hair. That's when she noticed the silver running up his neck. It looked like a toxin running through his veins into his skin. She had seen the same thing in the girls hours before they had lost all connection to this world and died—faded, as their kind did.

'Where have you been, Oron? What have you seen? You're not yourself.'

Oron started to strike the ground and wail and then he dragged himself up and looked at her with rage. With a bellow he started running towards her with lightning speed. Venti shot an arrow exactly where it would trip the small creature, and he went skidding face first into the dirt. Even before he hit the dirt, a snap of her fingers on the Sehvat glove drew forth a sparking blue rod of raw energy. The sharp ray cracked and sparked but came to a fine point, the blue light illuminating Venti's face and the static making her hair dance above her. If she let loose at her mark again she would aim to make a killing blow.

He scrambled up, screaming, 'You were supposed to protect her! You high Fae piece of shit, none of you care about us. You let her die!' He raised a small clenched fist; the normally soft and gentle nature of his race had been consumed by his rage. 'She's not here anymore. Aleved wasn't mated so no one knows that she is gone from this world. But I can't feel Wenda anymore. Don't your race know what happens when one of our bonded passes on? The other follows. We fade in kind because we can follow them. But I cannot feel her anymore!

'Why have you let this happen? You with all your power and your cities in the skies and high magic, you let her die. You let worse than death happen to her. She's gone! She's gone!' Again, he was on his knees, and now she felt an eruption coming from him. His rage seemed to spread through the silver veins, and they started to glow red as he screamed out in pain and grief and agony. Soon the glow from within seemed to consume every part of him, and he was a small figure frozen in his agony on the ground. Venti realized that he had turned into what looked like ash. She had never seen anything or anyone fade like this. Slowly ashen chunks of him started to slide off him even as his face was still frozen in rage and anger.

She started to back away from Oron, realizing that whatever was causing the Fae of all kinds to become ill was out here in the Foghorn woods—right where she was standing. She let loose the Sehvat arrow so that the electric blue blade landed into the dark shadows of the woods, the blue light flashing for only a second before snuffing out as it hit the ground. For the first time in many centuries she felt a chilling fear run through her veins.

CHAPTER **6**

A WEEK LATER AMARA SAT in the coffee shop typing the last of her report. She had been monitoring the heavy metals and pollutants coming out of the estuary for months now, and there was some compelling evidence that the levels were rising and that the government needed to come down hard on the industrial plants close by. Her fingers whizzed over the keyboard as a cold chai tea latte sat next to her. The small coffee shop had been a godsend when it opened up—right in the middle of town, and there was blessed Wi-Fi.

Jess had been messaging non-stop and so had the college wanting her findings. She had been hiding for a few days. Watching classic movies at home with her parents had worked for about three days, and then she had to go. The time to leave had been pointed out by the sudden questions about her dating life, her least favourite subject these days.

Sid the barista was tapping his foot behind the counter again. The man was short with a hilarious goatee that ended in a point. Amara was sure he was going to show up to work as a French musketeer one day. The image of him in a fluffy-necked blouse with a sword was all she could think of when she saw him. Especially when he made a point of leering at her for being in the café for three hours and still not ordering another drink. She hunched her shoulders and turned slightly away from him. Didn't he have a coffee machine to clean or something?

'Uh hum,' Sid grunted as he approached her from behind. 'I was just wondering if there was anything else that I could get for you,' he asked with all the concern of a cobra.

Amara aimed her best smile at him and said, 'No, thank you, dear. This chai tea was just so filling. May hold me out till teatime.' She levelled another smile at him as he harrumphed and walked back to the counter, saved by two old ladies walking in who looked to be dressed for church.

The man is a pain in the ass. Why can't he be stalked by blue creatures and hot men? She stopped herself because she hadn't spoken out loud about what had happened. She didn't know if she believed it. But the memory didn't fade. She remembered it in disturbing crystal clarity. *That doesn't happen if it's a dream, right?* The small pale blue stone had been on her person for days, she would run her fingers over it throughout the day. 'He really had the nicest eyes I've ever seen,' she whispered.

'Could I join you?'

Amara nearly jumped out of her skin as she turned around to see Keirin. *Where the hell does he come from?* She was so surprised she didn't say anything as he sauntered around the table and sat down. Today he had on a leather jacket and a black T-shirt and jeans. The red-toned leather seemed to make his skin glow a golden brown. Should she really be noticing that right now?

'I just wanted to check on how you are doing.'

Amara looked around and then at him. Mainly she wanted to know if other people could see this guy or if she was having a full-on Beautiful Mind moment. Sid seemed to be skipping over. Fantastic.

'Well, hello there. May I get you anything?'

'Sid, I said that I didn't need anything else.' Keirin leaned back in his chair.

Keirin smirked. 'I was asking the handsome gentleman with you.' The ass.

'Would you be so kind as to bring me some hot water with a slice of lemon in it, if you have lemons?' Keirin said, flashing Sid a golden smile and a wink. Amara glanced between him and Sid, incredulous. So this was why that little brat never warmed to her; he was totally gay. That, and her paltry tips, maybe.

Sid nodded and rushed off with a gusto that Amara had never seen from him. She turned her full gaze on the man sitting in front of her. Her eyes narrowed to slits and her lips tightened as she thought about what he had done to her.

Keirin watched the emotions play across her face, and before she exploded, he leaned in towards her. 'I'm sorry, Amara. You weren't ever supposed to be harmed. I wish it had been different. That you had seen us differently.'

'You tied me up with my freakin' pants,' she hissed. 'And how do you even know where that is kept? Are you some kind of perv stalker?'

Keirin flushed at that. 'They were what Ribben handed me.' Though he didn't deny that it had been a violation. Amara stared at him a moment longer and then glanced at the two elderly ladies now eyeing Keirin up with appreciative looks. Talk about robbing the cradle. Amara's face scrunched up as at last it hit her: He was real. If he was real then that meant the little blue guy, Ribben, was real too.

'Why were you trying to speak to me before? And … and he watches me?'

'Do you remember what Ribben said, about you having some Fae heritage?'

She scoffed. 'Yeah, though I don't know if I believe it.'

'A full-on Pixie Cobalt says you have Fae blood, and you don't believe it. So much for seeing is believing.' He sighed and smiled as Sid swanned in with the hot lemon water and set it before Keirin with more server skill than Amara had gotten in three years. Why didn't he just throw himself in Keirin's lap?

'It's on the house, love, can always spare a slice of lemon.' Amara's mouth dropped open in disbelief. The man would charge her for sugar packs if he could.

'Oh, thank you,' Keirin said with a roguish smile. 'At least someone is being nice to me on this side,' he muttered under his breath.

Amara sat watching him sip the hot water for a while. Still just trying to take him in. Still trying to convince her brain of things she had been sure were not real.

'So it's true. The Fae are real. Fairies and a Veil. There's another world that you're from?'

'Yes.' was all he said.

'The little blue guy?'

'Ribben.'

'Why is he watching me? *When* is he watching me? And who are you to him? What is a cobalt pixie?'

'Glad to see you're accepting this all in stride. No, really as a human you're doing well. It's a Pixie Cobalt. There are several dozen types of pixies. Ribben is one of the largest. They sometimes serve a family of their own will. Ribben has the rare ability to Nix between worlds at will. Even without a gate. He has served my family since I was a boy, which believe me was a while ago. We saved his mother for a time, and he's been grateful since. My family is the Femish line.

'Long ago one of your relatives was from the Baelin line. They say he fell in love with a human girl he met by chance. He gave up living in our lands in Beluvial to live out his life with her. We didn't know then that the rest of the Baelin line would die out. Their last request was that their human kin be looked after. My father was your ancestor's best friend. His name was Baeldor. Close as brothers, as my father tells it. So it was my father who had you watched. Several times we had to fend of Fae creatures that were drawn to your family's blood. There was one time your great grandfather ran like the wind without any pants on from this Pouka. I nearly wet myself—'

Amara stared at him. That was a story she knew. It was told at family gatherings about how her great grandfather had come home one day running out of the woods with no pants on straight into a dinner party swearing that a creature had tried to kill him in the woods. He was only seven at the time, so it was funny to everyone else and assumed to be a child's overactive imagination. But he maintained the story till his death, said over and over that it was Fairy monsters chasing him. What made this even more disturbing is that it had happened more than eighty years ago, and the man sitting in front of her didn't look older than twenty-five.

'Anyway, we slayed the Pouka. They usually don't get so rabid, but I think it was to do with coming onto this side of the Veil.' Keirin stopped talking to see that Amara's eyes had gone wide. 'So you're finally getting it. That's good. Because you have to come to Beluvial, soon. Ribben can't stay on this side forever, and I can't watch you.'

'I am not going anywhere with you,' Amara spat out.

'This thing that has happened … we call it an Awakening. Even in our kind, to access further powers, it doesn't happen till about age fifty. If you stay here in this state, you're going to call things to you, things that are not friendly. You have to complete transition. Your scent and your power are being cast out to all the world until you complete the Awakening.'

'Whoa, whoa—a transition into what? What have you done to me?'

'Nothing, I swear. Well, actually it might be the stone Ribben used, but I know he meant well. They are ward stones. Only pixies can make them, and it would pretty much buy you a house in Beluvial if you wanted to sell it. And I mean a big house. I don't know what you will be—it's only revealed at the end—but I know that it's been in your blood all this time. We aren't making you anything different; this has always been you.'

'Unbelievable.' She slammed down the top of her laptop and stormed to the counter with her teacup. 'Sid, another. Right now.' She stormed back to her chair and slumped into it with her arms crossed. She sat there in relative silence while Keirin stared at her.

'Um …' He started to look around.

'Nope, shut up. I'm thinking,' Amara said.

'Care to share those thoughts?' he said while leaning his elbows on the table and picking some fluff from the sleeve of his jacket. Did he make everything look good?

'So either I'm totally insane, or you're real and totally insane, but then there's a blue guy. So if you're not insane because there's a blue guy, then it means that what you are actually saying could in fact be true, and then I have to potentially go to some other alternate fairy dimension, which, frankly, is the craziest thing I have ever said out loud, and let me tell you, I have done a lot of pot brownies so I have said some crazy things. Go to another fairy dimension. Yeah, of course.'

'I shouldn't have asked,' he said with pity in his eyes as Amara started to chuckle. Tears formed in her eyes, and she kept repeating, 'Fairy dimension.' Then her slight chuckle turned into a slightly hysterical cackle. Keirin started to look around feeling the uncomfortable attention.

Amara finally slapped the table, taking a few gasping breaths as she stopped laughing. 'Yeah, no, No way,' she said, giving him a grim smile and a headshake. No, there was no way she was going anywhere with what she believed were creepy Fae beings from another dimension. In fact, wasn't this what the legends always warned lowly humans about? Don't follow the Fae; don't eat or drink at their tables or else be trapped with them forever; guard yourself with iron; make fairy paths through your land so they pass through without causing mischief.

A small part of her looked at him then. Keirin in turn cocked his head with a questioning look as he saw her shift in thinking all over her face. He was starting to like the way she was so transparent. Among his kind, especially the old ones, expressions and personality seemed to descend so far inward that even he had trouble interpreting them. On her, every smile and look was an animated life-filled story. Except that last rant about Fairy. That was just verging on crazy, and he wanted to back away slowly without making fast motions.

'What else is there?' Amara finally asked.

'Could you be a little more specific? You mean in Fairy or the universe or the coffee menu?'

'Stop being a smug ass,' she quipped and pinned him to the chair with a look.

'I can't really answer that. It would be like me asking you what else is there on earth. Where do I start?'

'Try, or I'm walking out of here and don't want to see you again.'

Keirin swallowed because he didn't think she was manoeuvring or joking. He'd heard Ribben say that she was stubborn and committed at times. Had heard that she had walked out of the lives of men who loved her and never looked back. It was a strength he had yet to find after four hundred years.

'Not all of your legends are true, and in Fairy there are things that Man has never seen or known. Long ago we left earth. It was our home too once, and we would walk between worlds the way you commute to work. We separated ourselves to save the rest of the life that lived here. The war couldn't continue, or the worlds couldn't have survived. So now we reside in Beluvial. Much is the same, but after ten thousand years things have evolved differently.'

'How many thousand?' Amara asked, open-mouthed.

'Oh, right ... uh, your scientists are a little off. They are coming around though. Can't be worse than when you thought the world was flat.'

This was heading beyond what she could cope with. Sid came over and slammed a chai tea latte on the table next to her, leading to another startled jump in her seat.

'OK, I'm gonna be honest. Part of me, a very small part of me, is fascinated by all of this. I used to love those myths and legends growing up.'

Keirin smiled at her. 'Most of your kind lose that as they grow up.'

'I think a lot of us want magic in the world.' *Our kind.* Humans, he meant. She didn't plan on staying much longer. She grabbed her tea and sipped it, holding it in both hands, and looked at the man—er, the *Fae* sitting across from her. He seemed more relaxed and real. He had the most chiselled jaw, and while everything else about him was sharp lines, his eyes were soft brown, hopeful and patient. He kept one hand around his mug and let the comfortable silence drag on. 'What about you. What's your story? The little guy—Ribben—he said that you were Lord of Air?'

He gave a half smile and studied the table for a minute before looking up and clearing his throat. 'It's a long story. That's a title I have, yes. I am a Scholar, in your terms. We call it a Clairver. Someone who passes through the veil to document changes in this world, and sometimes …they have magic.'

'So you're a wizard?'

His face fell into a glare, and through thin lips he said, 'No. Not a wizard. I hold a very respected and elite position within my culture.' Wow, the man was touchy. 'I haven't really liked the human monitoring part. We try not to involve ourselves in any of your history or development. The past century has been … disturbing.'

Amara couldn't disagree with him on that one. But still with the bad there had come the good.

He went on, 'I can move air at will—well, with a concerted effort.'

'So you can … make wind?' Amara said with a face that was about to break into a smirk, lips tight together and corners inching upwards.

The chair on the table next to them rattled over, bouncing off the ground several times before coming to a stop. And then a buzzing started. The next thing Amara heard was bellowing laughter as the ghostly outlines of her own personal pixie started to show through. Amara had to cover her mouth as she also started snickering. 'Aha, she got you good Lord hot air.' His laughter continued as he rolled on the floor, and Amara was practically shaking trying to restrain herself from spitting out some of her tea. For a moment the laughter stopped until the blue eyes of the pixie caught Amara's, and they descended into peals of uncontrollable laughter. Keirin took some slow breaths and got up, straightened his jacket, and mustered a haughty sniff.

'I will leave you two comedians … for the time being.' He dropped a five-pound note on the table. 'For your tea. Think on what I've said. You're not safe now. It will be just a few hours to get you to Rehna and back. Once you're Awakening is complete you can control what you give off.' With that he stepped over the pixie and headed for the coffee shop door.

The pixie was translucent, but she could make him out. Although it should have worried her, she actually found his presence a little comforting. 'How are you doing that, and aren't you worried that you will be seen?' she whispered.

'You should be more worried that people will see you talking to yourself,' he replied as he lay on his stomach with his head on his steepled hands. Amara did notice the old ladies giving her a few questioning looks, so she straightened up and looked straight ahead while saying, 'Thank you for the stone. I really like it.'

'You is most welcome' was all she heard before he was gone.

CHAPTER 7

KEIRIN GLIDED UP THE stone steps, shoved open the cathedral-style wood doors that were engraved with metal filled vines and Sapros star leaves, and entered the Citadel. The building was tucked on the furthest edge of Rehna where the city met the forest. Its high stone towers were some of the few that reached into the sky, a relic from an old time when they styled the buildings to look like an old human civilization whose name was forgotten.

He was glad to be back and inhaled deeply. He loved the smell of the books and scrolls that were stored in the temple. The high arched ceilings were lined with colourful images of his people's legends. Golds and dark purples, ocean blues, and deep reds were vivid among the faces of his ancestors looking down on him. The open oval windows that lined the uppermost portions of the walls allowed in beams of light, which fell on rows of wooden bookshelves.

They would always keep the paper records, a precious piece of their history. But what Keirin wanted was to get to Sehvaral room so he could search the digital records quickly. He walked down several decorated hallways to the back of the hall of records and approached a circular room that was humming gently. Passing through two swinging wooden doors, he entered the chamber, which was built of the same dark grey stone as the rest of the building. But this room had a cool blue glow. Inlaid into the stone walls were hundreds of tiny rivets, which anchored a network of pale blue lines that were pulsing back and forth. The lines were set in a pattern that stood at right angles to one another and were spread from the ceiling, which was their source. Down each of the seven walls and feeding across the floor, the pulsing lines converged on a centre table. On this wooden table was a clear glass circular screen tilted at an angle for easier viewing.

'Kenna, I need to look up the Baelin bloodline. Look up their powers.' In a flash a very petite blonde girl with green eyes stood next to the glass screen. She had on a pale green dress that was tied just below her small chest. Gold embroidery trimmed the bottom of the gown, and it featured large open sleeves. The colour matched her bright green eyes. Her sharp features looked up at the ceiling, and her heavy straight blonde hair fell away from her face.

Keirin waited patiently with his hands interlaced in front of him. He looked at her with such pride. He had not yet had a child, but Kenna was wholly his creation. She was an interactive construct that he had created when he converted the library into a non-tactile form of storage. He had initially tried to create a manual interface, but it took too long to sift through information. The old ones were throwing long and bitter tantrums trying to use the filing system he had created. So he had created Kenna, who could do it all for them, like a permanent live-in librarian.

'There are a few official documents about births and Awakenings, Keirin. The same that would be found for your family and the other three extinct lines.' She raised her hand, and on the glass screens beautifully calligraphed documents appeared on the screen. This was why the paper copies were retained, and he had taken such pains to keep them safe. They were beautiful. Once or twice Keirin had tried to learn the old art of writing, the beautiful art of letter making, but sadly that was not one of his gifts. Old Mason had told him he could leave the chickens to walk over paper with inked feet and get the same results. But what Keirin lacked in artistic talents he made up for in mastery of Sehvat technology.

He started to breeze through the lines and saw much of what he already knew. Baelin was one of the oldest of the twelve lines. They had often been called on to fight during wars, and the family generally tended towards powers that were elemental, water being the favoured expression of the line. It did say that a rare few of them tended towards fire, the rarest of elemental alignments. This made sense because the Fae would freely intermarry between lines. They were all Fae, though the families were maintained because like gravitated towards like. The gentleness of the Pa line would often suit the outgoing Brextin line but almost never the bull-headed (in Keirin's opinion) Onyx line. Though if Onyx were joined to Brextin, there would be no objection. As they were long-lived creatures, any unions that would lead to fertility and children were welcome. In fact, the mixing of lines was seen as a gift that led to unique and beautiful individuals.

Baelin line had died out for the same reason as the other three. The family lines had simply stopped producing children, and one by one the old ones had faded or died. Some family lines had fought extinction, using old and twisted magic, begging the gods for children. The Baelin line seemed to just fade without concern. They were gone before Keirin had been born. But they were the only line in this part of Beluvial that had produced human progeny, something that was looked down upon.

'Water, I knew it was water for her. I saw it.'

'There is an old legend, Keirin, a child's story,' Kenna said, 'but it references the beginning of the Baelin line.'

'Another time, Kenna. Thank you as always.'

'As always, Lord of Air, I do not need your thanks. I do have other reports to give you. Three of the ten scouts have returned to say that the infection is present in the areas of Beluvial that they were meant to scout. They travelled far; it would appear at the moment that 23 per cent of our sector is showing signs of disease.'

'That's double what it was two months ago,' Keirin said with a strained voice.

'Your father has already been in to review and correlate the results. He had much the same face that you have now.' Keirin did have to see his father. He had to ask, once again, why they had to maintain this constant watch over these cursed human offspring. Secondly, he had to tell him that Amara was

Awakening. OK, that second point might be the answer to his first question. This was rare.

What he looked for next in the records was the other two who were human but showed signs of Fae powers. How Ribben knew this was a mystery to him. Pixies didn't say how old they were, and it was rude to ask. According to the records taken, one had shown powers, and it was Baeldor's daughter; there were three brothers who showed no signs. Four children from one Fae? That was totally unheard of. It must be human fertility. There was obviously a reason there were now eight billion of them on Earth. He flicked his hands over the glass screen and the images flashed away and forward till he found the second on an age yellowed paper. Two generations after Baeldor's daughter, her granddaughter had shown signs of power as well, but much weaker powers. He read an entry discussing the human life of Baeldor.

Baeldor's daughter had his gift with water. It would bend and sway like a living creature for her as it did for him. But what he admitted was that her connection was closer; the water seemed to need her like a lover yearns. Being in the human lands she kept her powers hidden, even from her own brothers, for fear she would be accused of being a witch. She would not even enter Beluvial to finish the Awakening ceremony and only survived to an old age because of her father's presence and protection. Together, there was no enemy that they could not vanquish. Baeldor passed 120 years after he left Beluvial to live on earth; he survived his wife for so many years because of the many grandchildren and great-grandchildren he had; that gave him joy beyond measure. His granddaughter did finish the Awakening, if only to bind her weaker powers. At the final moments she rejected the gifts that had been given to her, so that she could live a safe human life. That was the last day that Baeldor walked the earth, for once he knew she was safe, he passed away. He confided in me that not for a moment did he regret giving up the millennia that the Fae might have. The love of his family was worth so much more; what was time if you had nothing and no one to share it with? My friend through many ages, I will miss him always. - Mehkar

Keirin looked at the log and saw that it was his father who had logged this entry. He knew his father had said they were close, that Baeldor had been kind in the early days of his transition. That piece of writing held more emotion than he had seen from his father in a long time. But Mehkar was past a millennium in age, an Old One.

'Kenna, make sure these files are kept available for the next two weeks. I don't have time for the reports. If they have already been viewed by my father, I'm sure he has informed the Mehsari so they may form a plan.' He looked her over. 'Do you need anything, Kenna?'

His construct didn't change a muscle of expression or move. 'Nothing, my lord, my systems are running at optimum levels. The reactor is running at 70 per cent production, and spare power is being sent to your mother's greenhouse.'

He wanted to ask her if she wanted different clothes. He wanted to ask if he should create a portable system so she could exist outside these walls. Wistful, he knew that he was not being rational. She was a program and didn't want anything. Not like Amara, whose wants were written all over her face. 'See you later, Kenna,' he said as he turned and left the room to head towards his family home.

What he hadn't told Amara was that he also had the rare

power to Nix. Only a handful of Fae did, and they believed it had to do with his elemental connection to Air. He stood outside the doors of the stone Temple and glanced up at the dozens of pointed towers that made up the roof of the building. Lichen covered the aged stones that were draped in moss and purple star shaped flowers. His mother had told him the name years ago, but he had forgotten, too many other worries occupying his mind.

He syphoned his will into the air around him, and a familiar whipping sensation started around his legs and ascended up his body, as if the air had congealed into something solid and caressed him till it was wrapped around him. His eyes closed for a moment as he thought of the front steps of the house, and when he suddenly felt bereft of the heavy weight around him, he stepped forward and knew he was home.

His mother's family line was known for being blessed with powers that had to do with air elementals. Their family home was outside of Rehna, the city that the high Fae occupied in this continent of Beluvial. His family and his father had wanted to be closer to the heavens than the city that sat by the sea. Rehna sat in a valley surrounded by mountains, the meeting point of five sacred rivers that were now pooled into the Bay of Astta. The great arena was the first of a system of locks that fed the lower levels of the city. Half a mile of these locks opened up into the shallow bay hugging the coastline in front of the city, protected by a chequered archipelago of coral heads and reefs.

His favourite place was to perch on the top of the high conifers surrounding the house and look down at the city when it was lit at night. The lights were all soft Turine lights of varying shades of yellow greens and blues. Houses were covered in all manner of plant life; roofs were encased in green moss, ferns, and grasses. Large ancient trees rose between houses and were many hundreds of years old; some of the oldest held houses in their branches. The Nyugen line had the largest of these houses, and the home filled the entire set of winding branches. Magic supported it of course, but the panels of wood and glass that was engraved with gold filigree was still a marvel.

He turned towards his home, which was unusual in that it was built with large quantities of dark steel. The Fae found metalwork to be especially sacred, and it was reserved for sacred objects and the few weapons that they carried. The house was etched into the side of the mountain, large glass square and rectangle chambers that were clear and in this weather open to the elements with balconies extended. His mother's influence was one single dome that was overflowing with flowers, plants, and vines that had started creeping out to all of the other thirty domes of varying sizes scattered across the face of the mountain; they looked like ancient temple stones that had fallen apart and landed on the mountain. Instead of standing out, they merged with all the sharp, straight edges of the stones around them.

His mother stepped out onto the balcony and gave him a broad smile. Most high Fae looked like humans. His mother looked like something humans had dreamed up in their legends. She appeared only about thirty years old, tall, and very blonde, with hair that was a warm butter yellow. Her warm pale yellow eyes were set wide apart. All of her features were soft and rounded. She darted from the balcony, and Keirin knew she was running for the stairs with a childlike enthusiasm. He heard a crash and someone yelling, and then she burst out on the grand hundred-metre-long steps that led to the house.

'Keirin, he's here. We have to go.' She smiled as she gave the firm order. Then she was off running like a deer fleeing across a field. For a second Keirin saw one of the maids gathering up bed linens strewn across the floor, and he looked an apology at her once he understood what the cry had been earlier. She smiled and shook her head in an exasperated way as she collected the cotton sheets off the floor.

They ran with his mother's dress flowing behind her, and she shifted left and then up the stairs to come to the verandah at highest point of the structure that stretched the length of all the houses. Long grasses and spindly maples and short spiky aloes were arrayed around small shallow pools made of the same dark stone as the mountain. They were so dark that all they did was reflect the blue skies above them.

Staring out across the expanse of their city was his father with his hands clasped behind his back, looking like a solemn figure. He wore a bright purple tunic and white cotton pants. It was about comfort when he was at home, and he still liked to wear the clothes he wore when he was human. Mehkar had black hair that fell straight down to the middle of his back. Long hair was a sign of power even now. He looked to be a man in his early forties; never really sure of his age, he only told them that he was lucky to have lived to that age. Where the rest of the high Fae seemed to be without a blemish or wrinkle, Mehkar had crow's feet and silver lining his temples.

'Keirin,' his father cooed as he hugged him, 'your mother has been waiting all day. Where have you been?'

'Watching her' was all he said. He gave his father a look to indicate they had things to discuss but not when his mother could hear.

While Kavira was beautiful and vivacious, she had a delicate nature. 'I will leave you to it then,' she said, knowing instantly that she was being left out. 'Dinner will be ready soon, though, and I want you both to be there on your best behaviour. I'm going to have them bring out your favourite wine, Mehkar.' She ran a hand down her husband's arm and squeezed it before she flitted off once again. Keirin watched her go, thinking that his mother always seemed to be perfectly still or in directed forceful motion; there was nothing in between.

His father brought himself up to full height after smiling at his departing wife. Then he looked up at his son, who was taller than him. The two of them could have been brothers because of how the Fae aged. For many years Keirin had been teased because no one really understood how someone of such a dark complexion had come from a woman as fair as his mother. Until they saw his father. But where his father was tall and thin, Keirin had come out broad-shouldered and imposing.

'She has started the Awakening process,' Keirin said flatly.

A small raise of an eyebrow. 'That is unexpected, but there were whisperings,' his father said. Whisperings from where, Keirin didn't know.

'She *saw* us. Saw Ribben. She heard when I broadcast my thoughts over common channels.' Keirin walked over to the railing and leaned his arms onto it. 'I don't know why you want her watched. If you knew something like this could happen, a warning would have been nice. It could have been done a better way. I could have spared her a lot.'

He turned to look at his father. 'I can confirm she has a gift. I saw it, just as Ribben had said. Water pulls towards her. I had to look, in our way, but it was there.'

'Baeldor's blood was strong,' his father said with a chuckle. 'Did you get a report from Kenna? I assumed you were there for a weekly check-in with your creation. You know your mother would be a lot happier if you gave her a grandchild in the old-fashioned way.'

'Could we focus, please?' Keirin hung his head low. What was this obsession with family lines? Could he not live first?

'She has to finish the process on this side of the Veil. A full offering. The old gods still speak to me sometimes. I would have kept an eye on her just to keep a promise to a friend. But they say she holds something that was lost with the Baelin line. Something we are going to need to end the desiccation that is spreading through Beluvial. It is happening in all other cities, the other continents.'

'No one will tell me what is happening. You and other Mehsari have to speak out. You can't keep this silent counsel amongst yourselves.' Keirin's hands gripped the railing a little tighter. It took them so long to make any decisions to share anything. Reflection upon reflection, to say or do anything. 'You know what is happening; you know why the land, the water and plants and trees are weak and dying. Why won't you tell us what is happening?'

His father turned around then and sighed deeply. 'We are not agreed. Unfortunately, given all that we know and the centuries between us, we do not know exactly what is causing this. All we can agree upon is that is has to do with our connection with Earth. Ties that we have forgotten.'

'So why Amara?' Keirin asked.

'I don't know yet. How did she react to your offer? To bring her to the land of milk and honey?' he asked with a sarcastic edge.

'As if I had offered to kill her cat.' Keirin laughed, remembering her refusal.

They both turned when they once again heard a crash and tinkling laughter. 'Was she always this much of a disaster? I think if weren't for her sweet disposition, the servants would have killed her by now.' His father got a proud smile on his face and said, 'She was tripping down the aisle for our wedding ceremony.' And they both laughed as they headed towards food and a night with each other.

CHAPTER 8

SHE **STARED DOWN AT** rose pink toenails that were peeping from under the bathrobe that she was snuggled into, while she lounged in the long cushioned chair that was set under a twinkling light display. It was supposed to mimic the night sky. It was quite relaxing actually, watching the lights fade and dim back and forth. Beyond that she could hear Jess rambling on about how much men sucked and that really women only needed each other and that if she was so inclined, really, they should get married so that they would never have to look at another man again.

'What do you think, Ams? Would you be my wife?' she asked with a coy smile. 'Hey are you even listening to me, or is the prosecco going straight to your head?'

'I could really use a man in my life,' Amara replied with a big sigh and a head tilt. She sipped from the tall fluted champagne glass in her hands. 'A hot man, with lots of stamina.'

'Traitor. But you're not taking about a man. You're talking about batteries. Big batteries to go in your big sex toy.'

Amara feigned horror. 'I will not be corrupted by your unladylike ideas.'

'Says the girl who had the stock items memorized the last time she took me shopping in a sex store.'

'Yeah those were the days. But sometimes you don't want to be alone.'

'Well ... You could always make the moves on Micheal.'

'He's pretty to look at, but there has to be a reason it's never happened. And I'm not inclined to fight that reason.' What had gone wrong there? She had certainly spent many a night lusting after him. She tried to shove away the lump it formed in her chest, while turning to Jess.

'So what's next? Seaweed wrap? Mud on my face?'

'Well, seeing as all the pampering staff are headed home,' Jess said with a smirk, 'the only thing left for us is dinner and more wine. Oh, right, and the hot tub outside.'

'No way. How did you get us into this place?'

Jess got up and slid on her soft slippers. She was taller than Amara and had soft round hazel eyes. Her brown hair had a natural curl and wave with blonde sun-kissed ends. She was British, but somewhere back in the family there had been a Mideastern relative, giving her skin golden quality. Amara had always thought her most alluring feature was her mouth, which was full and turned into an effortlessly sultry smile.

They both got up and sauntered at an easy pace down the halls of the spa, making each other laugh till they came to the locked automatic doors that would let them out the heated sunroom. It was evening, and through the glass roof they could see an impressive pink and purple winter sky. A large rectangular swimming pool had steam rising off it and raised up in the corner of the room was a hot tub. Jess and Amara slipped into it, both sighing with relief.

'This is the life,' Amara said. 'Why don't we live here all the time?'

'I know. I told you we needed a weekend away.'

'Thanks again for covering for me. Once my next pay cheque comes through, I will pay you back,' Amara said as she tied her hair up into a small bun and then leaned her head back onto the side of the tub. The bubbles were rolling around them, and the steady hum was hypnotic.

Amara was in a two-piece suit that was black with white polka dots and was cut in a style that was a throwback to 1940s pin-up girls. A broad belt at her waist helped to make the most of her wide hips. Jess with her slim figure was wearing a tasteful one-piece that was gold in colour but somehow appeared modest and elegant. As she turned around, it dipped suggestively low in the back. Amara looked out through the tall full-length glass panels at the sight of the woods behind a long stretch of green lawn, lit with bright yellow floodlights. The lawn stretched further and further back to a garden pond with a towering and imposing fountain that was also lit from underneath. The spa they were in had once been a country estate. The grounds were immense and still had the beautifully designed hedges and gardens that could just barely be seen past the fountains.

'Did you think it would be like this? Being a grown-up?' Jess asked quietly over the sound of the water.

'No. I thought I'd have things figured out. I thought being adult meant knowing things. I feel like I know even less now than I did when I was a teenager. At least back then I thought there was some huge master plan, a purpose to the universe.' Amara finished the last by flicking the water in front of her, which seemed to spray more than she intended.

'Hey, no need to drown me. I just asked a question,' Jess said holding her hands up in defence. 'I know you talked a lot with that therapist about Derek, but I'm here if you need me. Sometimes I feel like I can't help. I've never … I've never been in that position. I will always be here to listen. And even though I know I make suggestions about dating, you should take the time you need. God knows I'd be done with men if Alex had ended up that way with me.'

'You know what's the worst part, Jess? He's not even in jail because of me. He's in jail because he slammed into a light pole drink.' Jess rolled her eyes and muttered about what an idiot he was.

Amara could see it so clearly. She was back in her last flat on the ground floor of her building. She knew something was wrong when she walked in through the door and saw the kitchen window above the sink smashed in. She turned her head and looked down the living room to see her door ajar and hear rustling and things breaking. A crash and then a curse. Her memory was all so clear—the TV remote turned at an angle, the large fern on the windowsill, and the mahogany dining set of table and chairs that she had picked out with him.

'It doesn't mean that what he did wasn't wrong. He should have been prosecuted for what he did.'

'Part of me wishes that I had come forward. Part of me just

wanted him out of my life as quickly as possible. I'm just lucky that he was too drunk to aim straight.'

'Pig,' Jess said, almost spitting it.

His screams echoed through Amara's head again. She turned around to fold her arms on the edge of the tub and looked out into the dark forest. It was beautiful now that the sky was a dark blue-black. From the corner of her eye, she saw a skittering movement in the woods enclosing the big stone estate house. She started and pushed away from the edge of the tub.

'What's happened?' Jess asked. 'Sorry to be talking about Derek.' She reached out and put a hand on Amara's shoulder, squeezing gently, eyebrows pinched in concern. 'I'm sorry, I know it's hard to talk about.'

Amara hadn't seen or heard from Ribben and Keirin in a week. And before them she would have told herself that she was seeing things, but this time she was humming with adrenaline. She continued to look but didn't see anything.

Jess took a few strokes forward and peered into the darkness as well. Then she looked a question at Amara. 'Are you OK? You're acting a little spooked.'

Amara, after staring too long out the windows, questioned her own sanity for the millionth time. She then turned to Jess and plastered a smile on her face. 'Thought I saw an animal, like a fox or something,' she lied. Then she started chewing her lip, hauled herself out of the hot tub, and reached for the plush bathrobes hanging on the side pool chairs. 'How about we start getting ready for this dinner then? Time to wash my hair and fix myself up for you,' she said to Jess with a huge smile and a wink.

Jess wasn't buying it, she was a barrister, so seeing through bullshit was something she did on the daily. However, this time she decided to go along with it. She got out of the hot tub and then gave her friend a hug, crushing her in and sighing. 'Don't worry, if you're losing it, I will make sure the men taking you to your padded room are really hot.' That got a muffled laugh from Amara as she was crushed into Jess's chest.

They headed to the room they were sharing for the night. The room looked out over the front of the estate house and the curved gravel drive that wound between many large and twisted trees and ended at stone framed wooden doors. After a game of rock paper scissors, Amara got the bathroom first and turned on the shower. With the steam building in the air, she stood in front of the long mirror, dropped her robe to the floor, and looked at herself. She placed her hands on the cream marble surface of the basin and stared at herself. 'You are not going crazy. You are not, I repeat, not going crazy.' She let her hair out of the bun and ruffled it loose, it was spiked and rough looking, and she blew up to get it out of her face and chuckled at herself. 'Take a shower, chill out, get it together. Keep calm and forget the Fae people.'

'About time.' Jess said with sarcasm in her voice. Amara jumped into bed and leaned back on the white pillows. She reached into her leather purse sitting on the bedside table, and pulled out her phone. No messages and no calls. Exactly what she wanted to see on a Saturday night.

She stared out the window again at the night outside and thought again of Keirin—well, the Fae—and the little blue pixie. She hadn't had the courage to tell Jess any of what had happened. She still had to convince herself of it. After she had tipped Sid, for the first time, with the money that Keirin had left on the table, she had spent fifteen minutes rolling her eyes at the million and two nice things that were said about her dark, handsome stranger. So she couldn't be making him up.

She wondered too about the pixie. How many were there? If there were pixies like that, were there real-life fairies—the kind with flower wreaths on their heads and dragonfly wings? While she wistfully thought about what else there could be in the world, she knew that she was nothing but terrified about any suggestions of leaving her world to enter another one.

After several minutes of primping and blow-dryers and continued banter and laughter, Jess and Amara were ready. Both dressed in jeans and fancy tops. Amara's was a dark grey silk halter that brought out her eyes, and Jess was wearing a pale pink billowy top that pooled at the bottom and was snug around her hips; the sleeves were loose, and the shoulders were cut out. They took the stairs down to the dining area, both already complaining about the heels they were wearing.

The dining area was a beautiful example of restored Georgian homes. The walls were lined with blue and gold wallpaper, and the square tables were each decorated with acorns and berries surrounding tall white candles; a fireplace was roaring in the back ground. Amara was laughing at another quip from Jess when out of the corner of her eye she saw a man stand up, and she stopped abruptly causing Jess to bump into her.

Keirin had looked rugged and unkempt before. Now he stood straightening his vest as he reached his full height. He was wearing a dark grey suit, almost black in the dim light, over a white dress shirt that was casually unbuttoned to reveal a glimpse of golden chest. His pants were perfectly fitted to his slim waist. The jacket with a single button seemed to emphasize the broadness of his shoulders. He had a five o'clock shadow, and long sections of his hair were smoothed back. The hair above his ears was trimmed very short, a style that only seemed to bring out his angular facial features. Amara swallowed a few times and then locked her eyes with his warm brown ones. Keirin smoothed a hand down the front of his stomach again and then stepped from his table and started walking towards them.

'Holy shit, that man is fit!' Jess whispered between her teeth. Keirin strolled up to them both, and it became clear again that he towered over Amara. He had a radiant smile for both of them and extended his hand to Jess.

'Amara, fancy seeing you here. It's been ages,' he said as Jess took his hand. 'And who is your friend?'

'Uh ….'

'Jess, the name is Jess. Amara's oldest friend, basically since we were in nappies.'

'Jess, nice to meet you.'

Amara finally pulled herself together, crossed her arms over her chest, and narrowed her eyes. So they were friends? So he must have a story. Interesting. Part of her had to admit she was intrigued.

'Yes, Jess, this is Keirin. He's an old friend from college,' she said wondering what he was doing here.

'I was taking a history degree; turned out the damned thing was useless. But at least I got to meet some lovely people, Amara included.' One of Amara's eyebrows shot up. Someone was definitely trying to get on her good side.

'What are you doing here, Keirin?' Amara asked with a flat voice that didn't hide her annoyance.

Jess looked from one of them to the other, clearly confused

but beaming a smile at Keirin whenever he was looking at her. 'Oh god yes, I'm just here with my partner. Having a hidden weekend away, you know? He is always complaining that we don't have enough quality time together. He's a little high-maintenance if you ask me.'

Keirin, you are one hilarious piece of shit. You wish that I would let you near this body. A voice rippled through Amara's head. Her eyes went wide, and she looked to Keirin for answers. He continued to smile while Jess tried to hide her utter deflation at Keirin's admission that he wasn't at the spa alone. Amara saw Keirin look over her head and behind her. She turned to see another tall red-haired man enter the dining room.

Where Keirin was handsome, this man seemed to fill the room to the brim with charm and charisma. He was extremely fair with red-gold hair that was tied back in a small ponytail, one or two locks falling onto his face. He had a long face with a cleft chin and a long, sharp nose. His eyes were a shade of green that narrowed to an almost orange centre, and they practically glowed with mirth looking at Keirin. He came towards them, unbuttoning the suit jacket over his light tan vest, and strolled up to Keirin, leaning in to plant a kiss on his cheek. 'Hey, sweetie, where are we sitting?' he asked with a slicing grin.

Keirin grabbed the man's arm. 'All right, honeykins,' he said with a clipped tone. 'We don't want to make these ladies uncomfortable with PDA, do we?'

Amara got a pinch on the arm from Jess and looked at her. Amara wasn't hiding a wide-eyed expression that said she was equally smitten with this red-haired god. 'This is Theylin, my partner for too many years.' They stood together in what was now a square, and finally one of the servers approached them.

'Will you all be dining together?' asked a short gentleman with dark hair and a moustache, ready to set up a table for four.

'Oh no, we wouldn't want to impose on your intimate weekend,' Amara said as quickly as possible, shaking her head no at Keirin.

'Oh, don't worry,' Theylin said. 'There's more than enough of me to go around. And besides, K and I have all night to do the dirty.' He grasped Keirin's chin and shook his head gently from side to side.

Keirin smacked his hand away. 'Such a sweet creature,' he grumbled while smiling.

Look, I needed a believable cover story for us both being in this ridiculous place. No need to milk it by groping me. That time Keirin's voice was flitting through her head.

But you're so gorgeous, baby, Theylin purred in her head.

'Well, there really isn't anyone here this weekend. If you guys really want to join us, I don't think Amara and I would mind,' Jess said, looking at Amara with a shrug.

I wouldn't mind wine with this one, Keirin. How can you call someone so adorable an annoying human chore?' Theylin asked while he nodded to the server to prepare a table for all of them.

'He called me a *what?*' Amara snapped.

Theylin looked at Keirin, his lips pursing together, looking ready to burst out laughing. Keirin looked up at the ceiling and took in a deep breath.

'Amara, I don't think he called you anything,' Jess said, looking slightly confused. Amara continued to glare at Keirin with her arms crossed and was seething as she shimmied herself into a chair around a square table. She sat with Keirin to her left and Jess to her right. She couldn't think of a way to get out of this. Jess and Theylin started chatting like old friends, starting with where he got his clothes because he looked so amazingly good in them.

Amara leaned into Keirin, getting within inches of his face. 'This human chore does not need you stalking her,' she murmured through a forced smile.

'It's dangerous for you now. You need to be watched. Theylin is one of our best warriors.'

'So it was you earlier, in the woods?' Amara asked with exasperation.

'What woods? When?' Keirin asked, his interest piqued. He looked at Theylin, and immediately gold-green eyes were turned and focused on them. While he laughed and sipped wine like a playboy businessman, Amara saw a flash of something predatory flicker through his eyes.

'As the sun was setting. Wasn't it you?' she asked again feeling a little unsure.

'We were in one of the rooms while Ribben was watching, but … I don't know where he was, so it may have been him.'

At that Theylin leaned both elbows onto the table, holding the wine glass in front of him with one finger swirling around the rim of the glass. Jess was glowing with his attentions and had a glass of some fancy red; she prided herself on knowing wines. Amara had often joked that if someone put car oil in front of her, she'd probably drink it.

Keirin and Amara still sat in tense silence when the server came over with the menus for the night. They started to pass the time hearing the story of how Keirin and Theylin started dating, which was expectedly flamboyant and ridiculous. She thought childhood friendship that had blossomed into a secret romance, resulting in a bathtub full of rose petals and declaration of undying love, was a bit much. Jess was doe-eyed and sighing, buying every bit of this bizarre story. The girl was so sweet.

The meals came out steaming in front of them. Both men had opted for vegetarian pasta dishes. Amara and Jess got the creole fish and a pepper steak, respectively. Amara couldn't help but wonder how these men sustained themselves on vegetarian diets. Theylin in particular was muscled under his vest and shirt.

'The high Fae tend not to eat meat. It's a practice of not taking life once we are older and more aware of our place in the world. Still, I can't speak for all of us, for some practice cannibalism. And there are a lot of muscles under here, if you'd ever like to look.'

Amara spit out some fish and choked as she reached for some water and maintained eye contact with Theylin. He was smiling and looked pleased with himself as he leaned back in his chair and crossed his legs, wine glass in hand. Jess laughed at a joke that Keirin was telling her as he glanced from one of them to the other. While Amara was at first shocked, she slowly started to smile back at Theylin.

More of the evening passed with them talking about life goals, how different things were now that they were on the heavy side of their twenties. Jess talked about the time she wanted to be a classical musician and realized that she couldn't play an instrument to save her life. Despite herself, Amara began to relax. Hearing the men talk, their voices so animated and smooth, so sure of their views and what they wanted, she got a sense that they were not so different from humans. If it was an act, she was falling for it.

'Keirin was always a bookworm. When we were young, we were training together, and I found him studying sword techniques from a book.' Keirin squirmed but didn't deny it. 'I of course made fun of him and took it double hard on him the next time we were facing each other. For most of the round I was hammering him back with brute force. Then at the last minute he does a move with his feet and sets me off balance and throws my feet out from under me, and I end up on my back with the blade at my throat. Two days later when I saw him sitting with the training manuals, I sat down with him.' He turned to Keirin with a warm smile.

'I had to do something with you being half a foot taller than me back then.'

'That must have been some fancy school,' said Jess. 'All we got was field trips to some Viking hills that are empty now. So did you guys always know that you were swinging for the other side? Seems like you've known each other a long time; it's so romantic that you finally got together the way you did.'

Keirin for a moment had to reset himself as he remembered that the man across from him was supposed to be his lover. It wasn't hard to believe; they clearly respected each other.

'On that note, ladies, I'm going to take my special man away from you,' Theylin said.

'Oh my god, of course. Well, thank you so much for joining us. We're taking off tomorrow morning. When do you guys leave?'

'We will be here till tomorrow night, I believe,' Theylin said, standing up. He leaned over to kiss Jess on the cheek. He circled the table, and Amara felt herself tense as he approached her to do the same. He pointedly caught her eye and slowed down as he brushed a kiss along her cheek, and to Amara's surprise, she leaned into him, turning her head so they were cheek to cheek, and placed her hand on his shoulder. He straightened, not taking his eyes away from her, and slid his hands into his pants pockets.

Keirin cleared his throat. 'Have a wonderful evening, ladies. Amara, we should keep in touch. Whenever you want to speak to me, you know how.'

'Room 8 Amara, I have questions about what you saw,' Theylin whispered the order into her head.

Amara remained seated at the table, the candles lower after their hours-long dinner. They had dessert, which was chocolate mousse covered in berries. Jess was still sipping red wine. 'How did you never tell me about that guy? You went to university with that and never told me? I mean, I guess since there was no hope of getting into bed with him, but still. Why are all the hot ones gay? And his partner, what a dreamboat. I'm so jealous over what they have. I thought we needed a girls' weekend, but clearly, we need a hot gay man weekend. That thoroughly cheered me up.'

Amara smiled, pretty sure that they were putting on a show, but a small part of her had to agree: those two made a cute couple. She wasn't sure how she was expected to get to room 8. She was feeling languid and tired, and that thought of fresh clean sheets and a bed was really appealing. 'Another glass of wine, Jess?'

Jess smiled and winked as she gave a nod to the server to beg for another glass of wine. She leaned back in her chair and smiled wistfully. 'This was one of the best things I've done in a while. Life has been so ridiculous lately. I'm always sitting under this feeling that I'm an adult, and I'm supposed to have things figured out. I have this sense that I'm supposed to … I don't know—make some huge discovery. I'm supposed to affect the world in some way.'

'That's deep. This is always what happens when I get a little red wine into you.'

Jess replied with a knowing grin, 'You're not alone, though. I feel that way too. I make a lot of money pushing papers and getting legal crap done. Of course, I dreamed of defending the innocent, putting criminals away. Life didn't turn out the way I wanted it to. Doesn't mean it's not a life well spent. Or so I think, anyway.' She pursed her lips as she slipped her hands across the table to gently grasp Amara's. 'I know I can't have wasted my life if I have someone like you who loves me, who still sees greatness in me.'

'That will never change,' Amara said as she squeezed her hand. 'In this whole world, I know that at least we have each other.'

CHAPTER

9

THEYLIN STOOD AT THE windows of the room they were sharing. His vest and jacket had been thrown on the back of the wooden chair, and he was staring out at the night sky through the window. His hair was now undone, and the loose waves of it fell to his shoulders. He'd undone his shirt and stood with his hands in his pockets. Since coming to the room, he hadn't said a word as they waited in hopes that Amara would make her way to them and accept the offer they had given her. It wasn't normal for him to be on this side of the Veil. He was usually carrying out sentinel duties in their world. He was constantly moving back and forth from the Westlands to his estate and rarely the centre of Rehna.

Keirin had specifically asked for Theylin to join this mission because of their old friendship, a deep trust earned over decades together. He had also seen Theylin fight, and there were only a few who were faster or more gifted in battle.

Tonight Theylin was on edge. This was unknown territory; even the stars seemed to burn differently. Only a few of his people were allowed to visit this world to know it or even interact with it.

He had initially been excited to see this mythical sister world. He had spoken many times with Keirin about it on drunken nights in the tavern. It wasn't nearly as devoid of beauty as Keirin had stated. In fact, the countryside and the hills were lush with woods and greenery. All around him he could see signs of life; he'd even played with a fox earlier today in the woods. It had initially been afraid, a trained reaction to humans, but after a few thoughtful Fae intonements, the creature had chattered towards him. Sharp nose and bright yellow eyes full of curiosity. No, it was nothing like what he expected. Amara was certainly the most surprising thing of this adventure. She had that same quality; a brightness and curiosity that shone out through her eyes.

Keirin was leaning against the headboard on the huge king-sized bed that they were sharing, but he was still dressed, and his knee was pulled up towards his chest. They hadn't spoken—not one word since coming back up to the room—and it had been over two hours. His leaned his head back with a soft bump onto the headboard and stared at the moulding on the ceiling, which circled out from the hanging lights.

Amara wasn't going to come. His father had all but demanded that she make the journey, but he couldn't kidnap her. Well, with Theylin he probably could. If he thought about it, he certainly would not be the first Fae to steal a human.

Finally they heard a soft tap at the door. Theylin and Keirin looked at each other with raised eyebrows, both surprised. It was Theylin who moved towards the door and opened it and stepped aside as Amara slipped into the room past him. She was wearing white slacks now but still had on the same silk grey top as earlier. She moved quickly into the centre of the room to stand near the end of the bed and looked nervously at them both.

'Sorry it took me so long; Jess usually passes out with that amount of wine, but tonight we were really enjoying each other, and she wanted to talk. It's been a while since we were together.' She stood wringing her hands and looked towards the two men who were now focused on her. 'So I still really haven't come to terms with everything that's happened. Could I talk to Ribben?'

There was a knock on the other side of the bathroom door. Then it shifted open, and Ribben bounced out and waved at Amara. He swayed back and forth and smiled at her. 'I hasn't left you. Been right with you. Have to keeps extra close watches now, since you smells different.'

Amara smiled at the blue creature; his good spirits and large eyes seemed sincere and childlike. She hadn't told him that the stone he had given her was something she'd started carrying around all the time—in her pocket or bag, but it was always near her. She had started to think of him more as a small guardian angel, except very blue. 'Was it you in the woods this evening, as the sun was setting?' she asked.

Ribben squinted and got wrinkles on his smooth forehead. He looked to Keirin and shook his head no. 'I was with you when you were in the hots smelly water. Why you peoples make water stink so much.' Keirin gave him a look that said *stay on topic*, and

Ribben shuffled his feet slightly. 'No, was watching you from inside the building.'

Theylin asked her, 'Can you describe what it was that you saw, in as much detail as possible?'

Amara turned to him and took a moment, trying to remember. 'I thought it was strange because it moved like a ripple. The trees stayed in place, and birds weren't moving through them. It was almost like that swirling ripple you see with a mirage, and it shifted from left to right and lasted a few seconds and moved quickly. When it was gone, I questioned if I had even seen anything. Everything remained the same.' She turned back to Ribben. 'What do you mean I smell different?'

Ribben snickered and looked again to Keirin, who with his face communicated some kind of reprimand. 'You have always carried Fae blood. What is happening now is that the power in that blood is turning on. Awakening, we call it. When it was dormant you were essentially just human. Now the wilding creatures that make up fairy will know that you are at least partly one of them, they can smell the difference; they can smell what Theylin and I are. It's because of that change in your physiology that you are now attractive to other things. Dark things. The Veil prevents most large and dangerous Fae from passing into your world and the high Fae like Theylin and myself have restrictions. We have to travel through a gate to pass through the Veil. Other Fae kind can easily pass through the Veil themselves, evade humans, and alter your world. Most of those creatures are harmless. Humans used to know what it was to be hunted by a big cat, sometimes the predator they ran from wasn't just a cat from this world.' Amara took a big swallow at the prospect of being hunted.

Keirin went on, 'High Fae tend to also smell particularly delicious, apparently when they first come to their powers. I once had a kelpie describe it to me like a starving man smelling his favourite meal. Something irresistible.'

Amara looked at Ribben and felt a little self-conscious. The last thing anyone wants to hear is that they smell like food. Did she smell like good food or weird food? 'So that's why Ribben is watching me now. What about before?'

'It was a promise my father made long ago' was all Keirin offered.

'It sounds like a Misgrive,' Theylin said as he walked to the window and peered into the night.

'A what?' Amara asked more than a little concerned. 'Is that dangerous?'

'Yes,' Theylin answered. 'I'm going to walk you back to your room.'

'Amara, will you come with us? It's not so different there, it will be like visiting another country. And it's beautiful, our world is beautiful.'

Amara had been thinking about it back and forth. That nagging feeling that something was unfinished in her life came again and again. She looked at the two men, and then Ribben slowly walked in front of her and extended a small blue hand. It was the size of a small child's hand, but there were four fingers instead of five and no fingernails. Maybe humans thought they were aliens. She knelt down in front of the small blue creature and slowly reached out to grip the hand extended to her. He placed his other hand on top of hers and tapped their hands in approval.

'I saw you once, long ago when you were a child. You ran and ran through the woods. A wild creature. Do you remembers a day when your father lefts out chicken wire? It was rolled, and leaning. In the wires I saw a raven had tangled, wings ruffled in holes. He saw you and accepted death.'

Amara did remember the raven. It must have gotten caught looking for food, and she couldn't understand how wings and feet were meshed in between the layers of metal wire. She'd wondered how the creature could have done that to itself and how long it had been there. There was no forgetting the utter stillness in its dark black eyes when she had approached the roll of wire leaning against the garden shed.

'It thought you would kill it. But I saw you save it. Gentle, gentle. Fingers teased it out. And looked and checked, you makes sure it well before you let it go. I watched. You did it and never tolds anyone.'

'There was nothing to tell, Ribben. Lots of people would have helped that bird,' Amara said.

'You not like other humans. You not see yourself as other. You see yourself as part,' he said squeezing her hands.

'I don't understand.'

'Humans see themselves as other. Always has, always different. But you see yourself as one of the earthborn.'

'Ribben, that's enough,' Keirin said.

Ribben looked uncomfortable and then dropped Amara's hand. 'You deserves to be with the high Fae, you deserves it. To know. You care about the small ones too. You sees them as part.'

Amara still didn't really know what Ribben meant. He was so small. She wished she had gotten to know this little creature the way he seemed to know her. Theylin at this point had turned around from the window and was watching Amara and the pixie. 'You has to go to Rehna. Please. So you stays safe. Theylin good warrior but not allowed to stay with you for lifes.'

'Thanks for including me as a protector,' Keirin muttered under his breath.

'I just don't think I can, Ribben,' Amara said. She was disappointing him, and she knew it. But surely traveling to another world was not a good idea. She gave his hand a squeeze, stood up, and looked at Keirin. 'I'm sorry, but no. I just can't do any better than this right now—talking to you and being OK with you here. That's as much as I can do.'

Theylin let out a breath that he didn't know he had been holding. He looked to Keirin for confirmation that what Amara was saying would stand, that there wasn't some other plan they could pursue to induce her to join them. From the look on Keirin's face, which was also frustrated, he knew that they would have to accept her answer for now.

Ribben looked the most disappointed of all of them as he threw his hands in the air, muttering, 'Foolish big Fae,' and stormed off to the bathroom, which he had used to enter the room. Theylin could see how torn Amara was at upsetting the little pixie; her brows were furrowed, and her mouth and soft pink lips were working in the effort to form words of explanation.

How could she come with them? Till days ago, all of this was fantasy to her. She was young by any standards, and they were asking her to believe the impossible. And here she was, worried about the feelings of a pixie. Theylin smiled, knowing that she couldn't have cared less what either he or Keirin thought of the scenario. *The small ones.* She cared about the small ones; that's what the pixie had said. Even his mother, who had been able to access common magic, had seen herself as above the wilding fey that wandered the worlds.

'Let me walk you back, then, for the night,' Theylin said. He grabbed his jacket off the back of its chair and drew it on in one smooth motion. Keirin stood and seemed to be trying to find something to say at the last minute to convince her to come with them. He ran his hands through the thick strands of his dark hair and came up with nothing.

'Amara. I will hear you when you call for me. Just think of me, direct it to me. Anywhere. It's not like the common paths that allow you to hear our thoughts. I can hear you anywhere, even between worlds.'

Shock went through Theylin at that admission. 'You kept that secret well for all these centuries, brother,' he said with an almost cold accusation.

'I had to. The Mehsari would think me … too powerful,' Keirin said with a steady stare at Theylin.

Theylin didn't say anything as he placed a hand on the small of Amara's back and started leading her towards the door.

'Um, that mind thing. Can I do that?'

'Why don't you try it?' Theylin said stopping before the door.

'Goodnight. Thank you for trying to protect me. Even if it's a chore.'

'You're welcome,' Keirin said out loud, looking a bit embarrassed.

Amara smiled and then stepped into the hallway as Theylin joined her and shut the door quietly, still utterly in control. The hallway was lined with fancy red and yellow carpet with forest designs. There were only two floors, and fortunately they were on the same one, so it was a slow, quiet walk between rooms. For several metres Amara didn't say anything with the tall red-headed warrior walking slowly next to her, towering over her. He didn't seem mad at her, as Keirin had been. She couldn't really tell what he was thinking.

'There are private paths as well, you know,' Theylin said.

'Private, for talking? How much more private can mind to mind be?' Amara asked.

'For close friends and lovers, a new path forms—one that is just between them and that other person. No one else can hear it.'

'Guess you and Keirin have that?' Amara asked.

'It took two hundred years, but yes,' he said again with a smile playing on his lips.

'I've only known Jess for decades, and I would die for her. I can't imagine what is between you guys.'

'He isn't lying to you or trying to trick you. We are in new territory as well. Not many offspring with Fae heritage develop powers. Most just have an appeal; they're charismatic or gifted. Things will find you. Normally they wouldn't be able to reach you, but now that you're Fae, they will be driven to you and you to them.'

'You have to know this all sounds crazy.'

As Amara turned the corner to get to her room, she started to hear a whirring sound and a rhythmic *click click click*. She looked a question at Theylin, who raised a finger to his lips to signal her to be quiet. She realized the closer they got to her room, the louder the clicking got. Theylin moved against the wall as Amara ran for the door. Before she could open it, she felt Theylin's hands grab her from behind and pull her against him.

'It can't get to her. She's not Fae, and she's not tangible to it. It will reach for her and pass through her like a mirage.'

The whole length of her was pressed against him, and he was whispering into her ear. For a second she was struck by his strength and his clean, masculine forest scent. She turned in his arms and growled.

'If something is in there with my friend, I'm going in there,' she said as she threw his arms off and struggled to get her key card into the door. The light on the reader finally flashed green, and she opened the door and started screaming.

Jess was still in bed. Above her, curling along the corner of the ceiling, was the most horrible creature Amara had ever seen. It was several feet long, a mustard yellow colour and covered in scales like a snake or a fish. It was about the size of a large python, the body thicker than her thigh. Four feet were placed near the end of its body, which tapered into a thin, whiplike tail. What horrified her was the head of this creature, as eight glassy black eyes and pincers stared back at her. *Click click click* again scraped through her brain, as large dark pincers erupted out of what looked like a giant spider's head.

Through all of this, she noticed that Jess was still asleep as she stared at the creature that had placed itself above her. But something was wrong. Jess was pale, and her breathing was shallow. She wasn't asleep; she was unconscious.

'No,' Theylin whispered in disbelief.

Then from his hands erupted a massive blade that was on fire. It was three feet long, and while the flames started off blue at the hilt, they whipped and curled to a bright yellow tip that looked like a sharp and unmoving point. It was an extension of his arm, and he moved in front of Amara just as the beady eyes found her. For a moment she saw them both reflected in the black eyes, saw herself become the centre of its attention, and heard a hiss escape it as it launched off the wall and right towards her. It managed to get within a foot of her, moved just past Theylin's shoulders to the spot that Amara was occupying behind him.

But Theylin had been waiting, with his arms raised for the moment when it was right in front of his ready blade. In a single strike, Theylin impaled the creature and drove blade and creature into the wall next to Amara. She screamed, fell to the floor, and scurried backwards on her hands as the body of the creature thrashed and a high squealing noise came from it as it gave its last thrashes of life. Theylin had both hands on the hilt of his blade and then he seemed to press further into the creature. The flames from the blade spread out and across the length of the creature. It spread in seconds from head to tip of tail in seconds and went from yellow to the deep indigo blue of the hilt and the next thing Amara saw was an ash copy of the creature falling apart and away from his blade.

Keirin Nixed and appeared right between the two of them and looked from Amara on the floor to Theylin. 'What happened?'

'Misgrive,' Theylin answered.

Amara finally pulled herself together, dragged herself up off the ground, and shoved past both men to get to Jess. Her arm was hanging off the side of the bed, and she was blanched on the pillow, still having made no response. Amara was frantic and started yelling her name. She grabbed her hand and clutched it while she held Jess's face with her other hand. She found that Jess was still breathing but wouldn't respond.

'What's wrong with her?' she asked the men now standing behind her. Keirin went to the end of the bed and started moving the sheets and running his hands over Jess's legs. He got to her left knee and he threw back the sheets and stared in shock. Just below her knee were two blue-green circular marks that looked like bruises.

'This isn't possible,' he whispered.

'What is that, what did it do to her?' Amara asked, furious and going stiff with anger. 'Is she going to be all right?'

Theylin's blade was gone now, vanished as instantly as it came. He had a hand on Amara's shoulder, and Keirin was on the other side of the bed looking at Jess. He placed his hand on her head, studied her skin, and felt her pulse.

'She's going to be OK but will feel terrible in the morning.' He knelt by the bed and let out a breath in relief. 'This isn't supposed to be possible. They can't touch this side. How are they doing this?'

'What do you mean? You still haven't told me what it did. Theylin, you said they couldn't touch her!'

'They shouldn't be able to,' he said softly, in apology.

'It's fed from her, her life force, but not enough to kill her. It might have if you hadn't gotten here when you did. They are usually so far out in the wilds we almost never see them. It's come here because of you, Amara. And it's just the start. The longer you stay here without completing the Awakening ceremony, the more will come.

'I was always taught this could never happen. We aren't allowed to affect the human world. I don't even know what the Mehsari will do if they hear of this, Amara. Our laws are strict. If they find out your presence here is endangering lives, they may take you by force,' Keirin finished as he tucked the sheets around Jess and she moaned and rolled her head to the side.

'They won't have to,' Amara said. 'Take me now.'

'What?' Theylin said.

'If this is going to happen to anyone I love because of me, I have to fix it. So we are going to go now. Well, in the morning, once I know Jess is all right. But I have a bag of clothes. I will go with you,' Amara said as she smoothed Jess's hair from her face and held her hand to her chest.

Suddenly Ribben appeared at the door, and he ran towards Amara where she knelt by the bed. He crawled under her arm and onto her lap to get to Jess so that he could check on her. Amara helped the small blue pixie stay on her lap and stabilized him. He looked intensely at Jess for several seconds and then nodded his head. 'She will lives. Hangover of a lifetimes though.'

'Are you sure?' Amara asked as her arm came around the blue pixie and she held him to her. She was surprised by how warm he was, how his skin felt rubbery and smooth.

'I would never lie to you,' he said without looking at her.

'Uh, Theylin?' Amara asked.

'Yes, what can I do?' he said, still standing behind her.

'How are you going to explain that burnt hole in the wall?'

CHAPTER 10

'I DON'T KNOW WHY YOU enjoy it in this place. Every inch of it is filthy,' Maedaria spat out as she pulled her long skirts up her legs to keep them from touching the ground. Her nose wrinkled as she took in the dank smell of moss and vegetation. This was the only room in the Retorandun that held this much of the Below World's vegetation. She gave a cursory glance around the space, circular with a cathedral-like ceiling, arching and full to the brim with large-leafed plants, cascading vines and flowers, tendrils inching into every available nook and cranny. In the centre of this heaving mass of green was a large moss-covered fountain. It was lost to memory what the fountain had once looked like; now it was just curves of moss with one central flat platform, covered in delicate white flowers in dense balls, like little bouquets bursting from the green. 'Haven't you seen enough of the Below World? You only just arrived back from it. What did they want? Why did you go in such a hurry?'

Her cousin sat playing with a flower, delicately stroking it with a single finger. He had a perverse attraction to this place. It was something he had gained from his mother, who was no longer among the court. Pelidren, as one of the princes in line to inherit a great seat and obtain the title of head of his house, should have gone with her into exile.

She had to admit that he was the most beautiful example of her kind that she had ever seen. The Orchidru had at all times tried to preserve the beauty of their race. He had a long sharp nose and spring green eyes. His hair was thick and shining, and following custom, it was grown out to middle of his back. It was also starkly white, which pointed him out to be of the purest blood. It was known that if the Fae of the Below World tainted the blood, the first feature to change was their beautiful white hair.

He sat with his long limbs stretched in front of him, leaning back on one elbow while playing with the flower. 'The fact that you do not enjoy this place gives me all the more reason to come,' he whispered in his deep, raspy silken voice. She hated that he could affect her so. When she was around Pelidren she felt repulsive. No matter how she prepared herself, she only seemed to be able to pour bile and vitriol at him once she was in his presence. Inconvenient, since she was meant to convince him to marry her. She dropped the dress material of soft pink that she was wearing, thin material that was tied around her neck and then barely covered or hid the lithe curves of her Fae form. She was the ethereal, delicate creature sought after in her people's legends. At least that's how she appeared on the outside.

Her own pair of stark indigo eyes locked with Pelidren's, and she held his gaze until it was uncomfortable. The Orchidru came in shades of black or white; no other colour was allowed. They had long ago tinkered so much with their own genetics that children were born only expressing either a skin so dark and rich that they were almost blue or else a pale, crisp white. Maedaria's position was comprised by this monotonal view of what an Orchidru should be. Her hair grew thick and black at the roots fading into grey and then white tips—an escaped genetic fluke that many saw as impurity. Pelidren knew this wasn't the case

The Orchidru had tried for so long to control what they were; genetic manipulation and strict breeding programmes to control family blood lines had many millennia ago cost them dearly. They had stopped hearing or seeing from the gods; they had stopped being worthy of Awakening. But to Pelidren, Maedaria was proof that what had been done could be reversed. He had educated himself in all of their science in the hopes of understanding what made power manifest. Sitting up he made and exasperated sound and gave a great sigh. Understanding the elements of the Fae body, the channels of energy that gave them power, was a quest he had started decades earlier.

He was barefoot in cotton pants and loved the feel of the wet moss under his feet. The courts would laugh about it, the barefoot heir dancing through the weeds of an old world. Pelidren looked out to his left, to the open veranda that gazed out on the world below, the one that Orchidru had left—or been cast out of depending on what history you read. Small streams and rivers drained into a pool close to the edge, and droplets and mist poured out of the opening.

From the outside there was just the smooth silver-blue surface of the Retorandun. There were open-air gardens on the higher levels, open to the public and the courts. But this particular room, a private sanctum for his mother, had been forgotten; she had collected countless items from the Below World and set them up here. That was the irony of her punishment, that they sent her to the Below World, which she had spent a lifetime dreaming about.

'What have you come to beg for this time?' he asked. 'There has to be a good reason for you to interrupt me in this place. You know I don't like to be disturbed when I come here to think.'

'What could you have to think about? Are they still upset that you haven't found a single suitable candidate for their precious Awakening ceremony in over two decades?' Maedaria, curling her nose, stared at the ceiling, taking in the mossy drip and dodging drops that were falling to the floor. She shuffled on her feet and pursed her lips in a way that she knew was inviting. She glanced at a large string of bulbous flowers hanging on a vine from the ceiling, magenta petals the size of her face giving her a few moments of amusement.

'I did find one. And then they vanished.'

'It died?'

'No. Them, they, our fellow Fae, they vanished.'

'If this is some riddle that you want me to figure out, I am not in the mood.'

'Mae, do you really not care that living, breathing Fae like you and I, with dreams and hopes and loved ones and joy and laughter, are just gone without a trace? No bodies. No trace of even their very souls.'

Maedaria turned to him then. 'You said souls don't vanish. You said you could see their mark for years or decades.'

'That I did. It makes my skin crawl, Mae.'

His tone stung. She knew that he saw her as shallow. She wanted everything in her life to stay the same. Looking at Pelidren, she knew that with equal will and desire he wanted everything in his life to change. It had all changed as soon as he had met the Evandrus Fae.

'Adreaus is pushing for a marriage to me, he's close. A few more meetings about a dowery and he will have me, once he finds the right price for my father.'

Pelidren barked out laughing and almost fell sideways. He looked at the shock on her face, which only instigated more laughter. He was bellowing almost to the point of tears.

'What exactly is so funny about this, Pelidren?' she shouted between his pants for breath.

'You nosy cow. You think all those meetings were about you? They have been meeting because your father plans to purchase the 17th Retorandun. Adreaus is going in as a business partner because while he has the money to fund the purchase, he doesn't have the bloodlines to obtain a title. Only you, cousin, will be able to claim that because you have sweet blood of Persephor house. He has been granted marriage to one of your cousins from the Third Circle. Your father is keeping you as a prize for another day.'

If not for her deep blue-black skin, Maedaria would have flushed pink. She had only learnt the barest level of reading because she had decided that women in her society did not need it, but now she realised that she had misread the meeting notes that had been brought to her. Marriage was part of the bargain, but not to her. And here she was about to beg Pelidren to marry her instead, to save her from marriage to that obese, unpure Fae. He might be of the Above World, but he was beneath her. At the thought that she wouldn't have to marry him, she sighed a deep sigh of relief. She had been scared of that fate.

'I would have found a way to keep you from a marriage that you did not want, cousin. But I would not have married you for anything.'

'You know, if we were married, not only would the strength and purity of our children, our bloodline, guarantee their place among the Houses, but they could be put forward to be First Circle. Why is that so abhorrent to you? You have spent a lifetime scolding my nature and chiding my every action, but you stand by me, always. Why won't you consent to this? Why won't you have me?' She screamed the last question so that it reverberated in the room.

Pelidren flinched. He didn't want her to see that she had wounded him. For decades they had played out this dance. There had been times when he had played along, flirted and touched, implying he wanted things. Now he was exhausted at playing the same role. He had toyed with her, and she with him, on so many occasions that he no longer knew what he wanted from Maedaria—except that he never really intended to hurt her. Up till the last decade, he had not thought that she had heart enough to be hurt. He unclenched his fists and sat up, crossing his legs while stretching out his hand to her, beckoning her to join him. She took his hand and gracefully moved closer and sat next to him, crushing the white flowers that he had previously played with.

'I don't want to be Royal, Maedaria,' he whispered.

She started and turned to him wide-eyed, her round face conveying pure shock and her pink mouth shaping a silent circle. She reached over and held his hand. 'You cannot mean that.'

'You will be safe, child. Stop being dramatic. Both of us are good reservoirs of Persephor blood, and they will not expunge us from the registers. Your pretend fiancé has more of a chance of that happening to him than to any of us.'

'Pelidren, it is easy for you. You are not marked. You can stroll here and there and frolic in the Below World with those … those mixed creatures. If I wear the wrong set of earrings, then I bring shame to our house. What happens to me if I am wed to one of the other princes? I could marry any of them, but they would also see me as an adversary, a womb not needed beyond what my blood and body can provide for them. If we married, I would be secure. They would have to give us Royal holdings and resources and the security that Royalty receives. I would be safe.'

The Orchidru had long been in the Above World; whole generations had not touched the solid ground of Beluvial beneath them. There were hundreds of Retoranduns that sailed through the upper atmosphere of the Fae world that they had once inhabited. When the barriers had been put in place between Earth and Beluvial, some among the high Fae wanted to leave Earth but not abandon the knowledge that the Starborn had given them. They kept the fusion reactors that powered their massive ships, giving unlimited energy.

When the Below Fae still required fuel, they could combine the very building blocks of matter and gain energy that could be converted without end. For several centuries they had built and spread across the skies, and the Retoranduns became floating cities that would be visited and moved across the nations.

And then war had occurred, a war between the Fae of Beluvial, and from that war came a separation of the high Fae from one nation into dozens. The Orchidru had survived through two millenia.

'You know, I saw one of the Djinn today,' Pelidren said with a smile.

Maedaria whipped her head to him, and he saw a flash of curiosity before she schooled her face. She wrapped her arms around her knees and rested her chin on them. 'I don't care,' she declared with an expert pout.

Liar. 'She had skin like yours, Mae. That beautiful black tone. I've never seen one before. And then there was a Pes as well. I … I think they are beautiful.'

Maedaria wouldn't look at him but kept looking straight ahead, not wanting to fight with him. It was now his role to be an ambassador to those people, not a title to be disregarded. But she couldn't understand what anyone could want down there. She loved living on the Retorandun. She loved looking over the hundreds of homes made of glass, the metal towers that compromised the homes and temples of her people. She loved the great ballrooms and council chambers. She loved the open-air viewing galleries where the clouds drifted overhead and there was no end to the horizon.

Only in the last hundred years had Pelidren taken part in the exchanges and meetings with the Mehsari. No one was surprised when he volunteered for the position, given his mother's obsession with the Below World. It had been sixty-six years ago that he had met a high Fae who came from the only family to routinely travel between both worlds. Erid Fae Evandrus had been one of the few men in the worlds who he considered a friend.

Pelidren's thoughts drifted to Erid with a gentle smile on his face. Maedaria was looking at him intently and swept her hair out of the intricate headpiece and let it fall to one side of her face. This was a quiet moment between them, and for once they seemed to keep the animosity at bay, remembering they were family. Pelidren looked at her and decided in that moment to speak a truth he had been harbouring for centuries.

'I love males, Maedaria,' he whispered into the silent echoing chamber.

Her eyes widened for a second, and then in an instant she was withdrawn and silent. Shock and fear coursed through her. This was not the Below World. This was a terrible secret, a dangerous one. She wished she could twist back the clock and unhear him. She was swelling with rage, but only Pelidren knew, because she put on her most beautiful courtly mask. She gathered her skirts and started walking slowly and ever so calmly towards the door. Anyone watching her leave wouldn't think she had a care in the world.

She floated, graceful and beautiful, but Pelidren saw the seething rage in her. He caught his breath and wondered if he had made a terrible mistake. For years he had feared her, but he thought for a moment, just one moment, that she was on his side.

He watched her walk away. 'This is why I never agreed to the marriage, to any marriage. It would be a lie, and you would be desperately unhappy. I would never be the husband you want, and I don't even know … I don't even know if I could give you children.'

At this she swung around, the whites of her eyes bright and panic strung across her doll-like face. 'Stop. Stop speaking of this. There are ears everywhere here. It is death for you—and death for me, for harbouring this secret. You have cursed me, cousin.'

'If we are cousins, how could I keep lying to you? How could I see you in pain and rejection for decades more? I do love you, despite it all. You have always been there, even with the venom and the political games. You are always there.'

Tears welled in Maedaria's eyes. She had in all her long life never heard those words spoken to her with sincerity. She was a body to be bargained with, a vessel for procreation, a beautiful commodity. She used what she could to hold her place in life. She breathed in deeply and held still, to let her eyes calm and the tears dissipate, a skill learned over the centuries. Never let them see you cry, or you are sure to die.

CHAPTER **11**

AMARA SHIFTED HER DUFFEL bag on her shoulder awkwardly as she watched Jess board her train back home. She waved at her pale friend as she lurched into motion, giving her a grim, stiff smile.

Jess had woken feeling like she was dying. Fortunately, she blamed wine for her state and said she was just getting old and having the hangover of a lifetime. They had a late checkout, so Jess managed to slowly make her way downstairs with big Chanel shades. They hid the dark circles under her eyes. Instead of being completely put off by food, she said she had never been more ravenous in her life.

Amara had wondered if Keirin and Theylin would make an appearance in the morning, but they were missing. Overnight she had refused to leave until she knew Jess was OK, insisting that she would at least take her to the train. Ribben had been her last source of comfort when he offered to watch Jess over the next couple of days if she would agree to stay with the men. The burnt hole in the wall had vanished, though Theylin wouldn't let her touch the wall. He wasn't sure his glamour would be the same in this world and wanted to be cautious. Amara hadn't slept all night as she watched Jess sleep, tossing and turning and groaning uncomfortably. They had assured her that Jess would be OK, worn out for a couple weeks as her energy levels returned; but nothing else would happen to her. Keirin had promised.

Amara stood in the sun at the station, slipped on some shades, and looked up at the clear blue sky. It was a rarity in the winter in England, so she took a few moments to bask in it before she went back out the gates to the front of the station. She wasn't even sure when she would see the men or how they were going to make the journey to this supposed fairy land. She had the unnerving feeling that she had been watched ever since leaving her room this morning, so she figured they would find her. She was wearing a robin blue suede jacket that had been a guilty splurge. The black thick belt sat right beneath her chest and the jacket flared out to accommodate her hips. She slipped her hands into the side pockets and walked in her blue jeans and ankle boots to the front of the station and waited there for a few minutes wondering what to do.

'Keirin, are you coming for me?' she whispered into the damp, cold air wondering if she looked like a crazy person. She wrung her hand on the cloth handle of her duffel and wondered if she should just head back in and catch the next train home. Or maybe get a train and stay with Jess for a few days, to make sure she was OK. As she was about to turn around, a large black

SUV with tinted windows pulled to the curb next to her. It was atrociously big and looked like a monster compared to the other cars that were normally found in the UK. The window lowered to show Keirin behind the wheel.

'Get in, it's a thirty-minute drive from here.' Amara stared at him for a split second, making a final decision. Was she really going to do this? She thought about what she had seen circling her friend last night, and a shiver went up her spine. She grabbed the door, opened it, and got in, dumping her duffel on the floor. That was never going to happen to anyone she loved, ever again. She was going to make sure of it. 'Where is this place that we are going?'

'One of the gates,' Theylin said. 'One of the remaining gates. Keirin is one of the few beings in existence who can Nix, but not even he can go between worlds. The rest of us mere Fae creatures have to travel through gates.'

'So you can't all pop in wherever you want?'

'No,' Keirin answered looking at his friend in the rear-view mirror. Theylin was slouched in the back of the SUV with ample leg room. He was wearing a tan wool turtleneck sweater and stylish jeans with his hair in a ponytail while he looked grimly out the window. Keirin had hidden from almost everyone the true extent of his power. His admission last night that he could hear Amara in either world if she called for him was something that would be terrifying for most Fae. He especially had to hide his powers from the Mehsari, who were already suspicious of his abilities and strength, cautious of his heritage. He would have to speak with Theylin soon. Even a small slight for the Fae could turn into a chasm.

'Well, thank god for that at least. People popping in wherever they want—ridiculous,' Amara muttered next to Keirin. She gave a side glance at him. 'You can drive?'

He reached across her, his arm brushing her leg, which caused her to shimmy back. He caught her eye for a second but didn't give away his thoughts. He pressed the button to glove box and flipped a wad of papers and a driver's license onto her lap.

'Since I'm here from time to time, the UK, that is, I have an identity. I noticed over the last few decades it's become necessary to prove who you are and that anyone without a bank account or credit card is a suspicious person.' They turned onto a dual carriageway, and Keirin settled in for a long drive.

'This, this house address—it's in the village next to mine!' Amara yelled as she held up his driver's license.

'After everything you've seen and witnessed this weekend, you're going to get mad about where I own a house?' Keirin said with more than a little exasperation. Theylin snorted in the back seat. This was going to be a fun drive. A car full of cheer.

Amara stuffed the paper sheets and license back in the glovebox, slammed it shut, and stared out the side window. 'Well, how would you feel if you found out you had been stalked your whole life? I'm not even who I thought I was. But you know what? To both of you, I'm still human. I don't feel any different.' She reached over and fussed with the heaters in the car and turned them towards her so she was blasted with warm air. After a few minutes of uncomfortable silence she flipped through the radio stations until she found one she liked, hoping music in the background would help her calm down.

Keirin had never expected to speak to Amara. What she didn't know was that he had watched her father and her grandfather grow up. He had been elevated to his position only 150 years ago and given permission to cross the Veil for research. He didn't know what to tell her, had never prepared for this conversation.

It had been many generations since any of her ancestors had shown even a hint of Fae Power. He had often complained to Theylin that he had to carry out his father's request. It was babysitting to watch people who, as far as he was concerned, were just human. They had been good people though. He had seen a family history of kindness. They had always made the world a brighter place when he watched them from afar. She looked very much like them but with a touch of the something different from her mother's side. Her skin matched his in a pale golden brown, and her short, straight hair suited her small sharp chin.

'Well, I'm glad to be going home, and I was never here to stalk you, Amara, if that helps,' Theylin said, trying to sound a little more cheerful.

After more silence, Amara turned around in her seat and looked at him. 'What's it like? Where am I going?' she asked softly.

Theylin leaned forward and placed his hand over hers, gripping the back of the chair to keep her turned and facing him. 'Don't be afraid. For you it will be an old world. Much of it looks and appears like the British Isles. But we have left it unchanged and untouched for millennia. It is beautiful and peaceful, war is a distant memory even for the old ones. And Rehna is a beautiful city, even if I don't prefer to live there myself.'

'Will there be more things like that Misgrive?'

'There are many creatures roaming around Fairy. Not many look like us; in fact, the high Fae are considered odd-looking, according to a wood sprite I know. As long as we are in the city or close to it, you shouldn't encounter any of the wilding creatures. Even the strongest and oldest of us avoid the ancient parts of our world.'

'What does a wood sprite look like? What about other magical things? Are there witches and unicorns?' Amara asked with a playful glimmer.

'There is a lot in Beluvial, but I don't know what a Unicorn is, and thankfully all witches have died out, hunted to extinction by both of our kinds.

'As for wood sprites,' Theylin smiled, finding her bright, childlike interest endearing, 'they have wood brown hair with long thin red and yellow leaves growing throughout it, but when I have touched the hair, it feels like silk. They have violet eyes that are almond-shaped like a cat's and young faces. I don't know if they ever age or even how they are born. My mother's grandmother was a wood sprite. I meet her from time to time in the woods around my house. She looks younger than me, if you would believe.'

Amara wondered how much there was in this sister world that she had never known about. Or had she? Surely when she was a child this had all seemed possible. She remembered seeing magic everywhere, that it was a real and playful thing. She used to play with unicorns in her back garden, and she laughed and giggled with fairies and spoke to wizards. She was sure of it—that it had been real once. She looked at these men who appeared all too human, but there was something about them that seemed to draw you in. The edges of these men where sharper, like there was an extra layer of detail to them. She couldn't get enough of watching them move; it was so liquid, as if it was tied into everything around them. Amara caught herself staring at the way Keirin's hands were turning the wheel back and forth. He was driving comfortably, like it was something he did every day. When she thought about it, he had probably been driving for longer than she had been alive. He had probably witnessed the invention of the automobile.

They were driving further and further into the countryside, away from London and up the coast. Trees curved over the road. Because it was winter, many of the branches were bare, and the grey dark sky shone between the brownish black limbs. Empty fields of crops were on either side of the roads, with patches of brown where the land had been left fallow over winter. They passed the occasional group of cows grazing lazily in the fields as a misty rain started to pour over the countryside. The air became cold, wet, and sharply penetrating. Amara noticed that they were following signs to Elveden Forest. That was a sweet piece of irony.

Behind her, she could hear Theylin yawning and stretching out his legs. Keirin was paying attention to taking the next exit. They had fallen into a comfortable silence on the drive up. Amara had a lot of questions and still wondered why she wasn't terrified of being in a car with virtual strangers. She reached into her jacket pocket to feel the blue stone that Ribben had given her, rubbing at it with her thumb. The rough surface of the stone was comforting, and she thought of Jess and keeping her safe.

'Keirin?'

He looked at her, surprised to hear her speak.

'Yes?'

'I had Ribben's stone with me. The one he left at my flat. You said that it was for protection. Why didn't it protect Jess from that thing last night?'

Keirin looked out onto the road with a few creases between his eyebrows. He had to think about it himself. Those stones were rare. He had heard of maybe a few dozen over the centuries. They had been more common when the small folk were not so separate from the high Fae—when the high Fae hadn't changed so much. It took him a while to think of the story that his grandmother had told him.

'It's only meant for you, I think,' he said, grasping at pieces from a memory. 'Ribben knew my grandmother. She was about my age when they met near the river's edge. Those are meant to be special places. Where water meets earth. We call it the betwixt place. It's a similar concept to the gates, really. The worlds pool on either side of a barrier.'

Amara looked at him confused at his description.

'Anyway, Ribben was a lot younger then too, though I don't know how old he is really. Aevena was bathing in the water when she realized that an entire family of Selfries was being hunted. She saw them running full speed through the forest, flashes of white and gossamer wings. And she knew the hunter who was leading a party on horseback after them.

'Their pelts were prized. They would grant the wearer a form of invisibility. You are only seen as you want to be seen, or not seen at all. Even the best Fae glamour can't accomplish an illusion of that skill. Theylin's illusion on the wall of your hotel room is only possible because he is aligned to fire, and naturally good at glamour spells. The power of Selfrie pelts could change the entire layout of the room; you would pick up cups that didn't exist and have your senses fooled.

'It was an old lover of Aevena's who was hunting them. She started screaming at the top of her lungs in the lake, yelling his name and begging for help. Of course, the party started straight for the edge of the river and came to a halt. She dragged herself up out of the water and … probably wasn't modest. The lover sent away his hunting party and spent the afternoon in the grassy banks of the river with her. She'd done it just to distract him from his prey. Or I suppose to give him something else to hunt.'

'Days later Ribben appeared and left a white stone like yours on her pillow. As a child I never saw it. It had vanished long ago shortly after she left this world. But she told me that the pixie magic had woven itself with her. The stone offered an immense protection to the one it was intended for alone. That's why she said she never had to worry about anyone stealing it, because it would only work for her.'

'So you've never seen what it does. It might not do anything?' Amara said as she pulled the stone out to peer at it.

'I highly doubt that. Ribben has scared the shit out of me with what he can do. And if he's only made two of those stones in a couple thousand years then it can't be nothing.'

Amara turned to Keirin. 'Wait, how old was your grandmother?'

'I don't know, it's sort of impolite to ask the old ones. I guessed over three thousand.'

Amara grunted as the air left her lungs. 'And how old are you guys?' she asked through slightly gritted teeth.

Keirin looked in the rear-view mirror and smiled at Theylin. 'The old man over there has two hundred years on me.'

'Baby Fae,' Theylin replied with a smile.

'I have around five hundred years. That's fairly young by our standards.'

'Obviously.' Amara said with a squeak to her voice.

They had been walking for twenty minutes into the woods. Her shoes were covered in mud and her feet were frozen. She couldn't have been more miserable; that is until the skies opened up above her. Cold sleeting rain started to fall on them, and Amara realized she had just been asking for it. She ran her hand over her face to get the water off of her and her sodden hair. The men didn't seem to be fazed by any of this. She wondered if it was some kind of Fae magic that was keeping them warm despite being as soaking wet as she was.

'How much farther is this gate?' Amara asked, not bothering to hide her annoyance.

'Not far now. We just need to take the next left and follow the woods down by the pond.'

They weren't quite in Elveden Forest. In fact they had gone down so many side roads Amara couldn't keep track of where they were. The country roads had merged together. Bushes and stone walls gave way to tall dense trees. Now they were in woods that she couldn't see through.

The trees loomed overhead and arched over them, blocking out what little light there was on this grey December day. Dark black branches snaked out like spiky arms; even in the winter the trees that did have leaves were a sharp yellow green. The grasses were yellow and collapsing all over the ground, and the well-worn path they were on was covered in mud and stones, becoming slick with the water. Amara had lived here her whole life; she still found these woods beautiful and lush. They must have been traveling along an animal path because it was getting narrower until the dense trees suddenly gave way to open grassy fields. There were still patches of trees, but they looked like islands in an ocean of grass.

Keirin and Theylin started making a beeline to a towering tiny grove of trees that actually reminded Amara of a small hut. The shape of the trees made a rounded roof.

'This is it.' Keirin said.

'What's it? This is a small patch of trees no bigger than my bathroom,' Amara said, able to circle around the trees and examine them. She gave them a questioning look and muttered, 'I'm going to be murdered in the woods. I knew it.'

'It's one of the oldest gates this world has ever known. I suggest you pay it some respect,' Theylin whispered back.

In unison Theylin and Keirin stood next to each other and dropped all the duffels and backpacks that they had been carrying. Then with perfect timing they each bowed at the waist. Each had his open left hand wrapped behind and resting in the middle of his back. Their right hands were outstretched and open before them.

Amara was surprised by the display and started to shuffle and face the direction of their attention wondering if she was supposed to follow their lead and do the same thing. She looked at them, pausing incredulously. With a characteristic eye-roll she eventually stepped in line with them next to Theylin and followed suit. Peering at Theylin, she could see he was smiling in approval at her.

'The earthborn request passage, Father of the Green. With the hand that takes withdrawn, we seek only to give to the worlds that sustain us.'

Amara stood still waiting for something to happen. The moments passed and the rain kept falling. The leaves and grass swayed in a gust of wind but nothing in the green fields seemed to change. Amara gave a questioning look to the men, and they had their heads stoically down. Keirin closed his eyes and breathed out a large sigh, almost of contentment; the sound she would expect to hear if he was getting into warm clean bed sheets at the end of a long day.

Then she felt something in her chest. It was a vibration, a deep rumble that seemed to be hitting her just below the heart. Her eyes went wide, and she glanced again at Theylin and Keirin, who had now raised their eyes in unison to stare at the small patch of trees. She followed their gaze, and for a split second she saw something, a smiling old man.

His face was ancient, with wrinkles upon wrinkles, and the skin was a leather brown with what appeared to be whorls in it, like wood. But his eyes—he had bright spring green eyes that seemed as fresh and new as a child's but held the weight of untold time. He looked straight at her, yellow circling the irises that seemed to leak out into the green, and he leaned one arm above his head resting against the larger tree branches above him. She tried to look at his body, his clothes, but wherever she looked, the image began to blur into trees and leaves and twigs.

He looked at all three of them and then settled on Amara and smiled, the warmest, most welcoming smile she had ever seen. More than her own father, more welcoming than anyone had ever given her in one moment. She smiled back at him letting her own warmth shine through, wanting instantly to reciprocate the intensity of the acceptance being offered. Then something sucked at her stomach, a giant tug as if a thick rope had been attached to her organs. She started to yell, and suddenly she was off her feet and screaming at the world around her disappearing.

In a second she was sucked through darkness. She reached and gripped at nothing as blackness consumed everything around her. Then from a distance she heard Keirin: 'One second, it will be done in one second.' Her scream got louder as her legs tumbled up and over her and she lost all sense of up and down. And then she hit green grass with a thud and rolled to a stop on her stomach with mud on her face and jacket. She was gasping for breath and didn't move for a second while she tried to orient herself.

'Guess the whole not-telling-her-what-passing-through-a-gate-is-like plan worked,' Theylin said.

Amara looked up from the ground to see the two of them standing without even a hair out of place, as if they had been dropped onto the grass like delicate flowers. Their bags were tucked together in a neat pile between them. 'What just happened to me?'

'You passed between worlds. Well, some would say dimensions. It's disorienting if you fight it. But don't worry; everyone does the first time. Once you know what to expect and you don't fight, somehow you end up placed in the world. I was on my ass too the first time,' Keirin offered as he reached out a hand to help her up.

Smart-arses. Stay calm while experiencing inter-dimensional travel?

Amara was sure she would have listened to that advice if it had been offered. OK, probably not.

She was unimpressed but took his hand anyway and got herself up, blowing the hair off her face, and started to wipe her jacket and jeans. Brown leaves had stained her clothes with dirt and damp stains were all over her. She finally had the time to look around, and she stopped as she realized something. It was quiet. She knew it had been quiet before in the woods but this was different. It was quiet, but she felt as if everything around her was listening.

'Well, there is no doubt that you're Fae at least,' Theylin offered. 'The green man wouldn't have let you through. In fact, he seemed to take quite a shine to you.'

'Who was that?' Amara asked, spinning to find another small grove that looked just like the one they had left behind. It once again looked like a hut but this time there was a path that divided to encircle it, paved with white stones that were all kinds of rough shapes and with sharp edges that had been fitted together.

'That was the gate. It's ... well, alive. He shows himself to us now as a green man. He used to be something different. All the gates around the worlds are extensions of him—a network or interface between this sister world and earth. Humans are no longer allowed to cross the threshold. He used to take pity on some a long time ago. Some humans made it across, deemed worthy by him. Even then the Mehsari didn't question the right of any human found in Beluvial. They always had a purpose here.'

Amara was half listening and half taking in a crystal blue sky with clouds wisping by. While it had been a grey day on earth;

here it was a bright winter afternoon; the sun shone brightly and reflected off the leaves and trees. She looked up and realized that though she had been walking through woods, she was in something much denser and taller. The tree trunks were the width of small cars, and they stood at least thirty metres tall. The leaves were deep shades of maroon, red, and orange. If it weren't for the branches being sparse in winter, she didn't think the sun would be reaching them. The land around them consisted of beautiful sloping hills and wooded inclines.

Along the ground were small patches of crisp, clean white snow. It snowed so infrequently at home that snow was something left to her childhood memories. She saw her breath in front of her and liked the cold here. It wasn't damp and penetrating; it was crisp and felt full of frost and something playful in the air. Beyond the ancient trees she couldn't see much else, and she was craning her head to see down one of the paths.

'So this is it? This is Rehna?'

'Gods, no. This is out in the middle of nowhere,' Keirin responded.

'So where are we? Sorry I left my traveller's guide to fairy dimensions in my other jacket,' Amara said with more than a little bite.

'We are in the Adriat sprawl. The city lies to the south and it's several hours from here. I was hoping we could stop at your home, Theylin, so that we could change and get Amara into some less out-of-place clothes.'

Theylin nodded, picked up some of the bags, and started walking towards the right-hand path. Keirin looked at Amara, handed over her duffel, and waited for her to fall into step behind Theylin. She looked down the path to the left, wondering where that went. She had a moment of thinking this must be how had Alice felt when she ended up in Wonderland. Not even sure if anything was real.

'This place, it feels different,' she said, finally starting to follow Theylin. The road was smooth and well worn. It had been made wide enough that the three of them could walk shoulder to shoulder with several feet still available on either side of them. Theylin was already strides ahead of them with a spring in his step. He seemed right at home in the woods that felt so ancient it was almost oppressive to her senses. The trees looked the same, with leaves of varying shapes, and in the distance she saw rising cliffs lined with conifers.

She remembered what one of her professors had said once about the English countryside, that it had forever been changed by farming. The grazing of sheep and cattle kept it as open grassy fields, but they believed that left to its own devices, it would have reverted to huge expanses of forest.

'Is that a hummingbird?' Amara saw something glittering and hovering in the air; it had the magenta and indigo metallic tones that she had always imagined. She saw it momentarily as a flash, and then it was there again. She smiled up at it and stared it as it came closer but stayed high over their heads. The sparks were opalescent in the sunshine, and she could see that it was indeed a hummingbird. 'They don't live in England. What is it doing here?'

Theylin smiled back at her and then started explaining while he faced ahead at the path in front of them. 'They aren't the same as the ones you have. From what I'm told, they started off the same thing. Over time, everything changes and adapts.

But yours still have Fae magic in them, I'm told. That's why they can move the way they do.'

'Who told you?' Amara asked.

'I did,' Keirin answered. Amara forgot how he was the connection between all of them. Keirin reached over and took her backpack from her and threw it over his shoulder. She started to protest, but he gave her a look that said there was no point. 'It's going to be a good walk till we get to Theylin's. He insists on living outside of Rehna, says that it helps him stay focused, grounded to who he is. It's his grandmother's old cottage. Not really what one of our best warriors should be living in, but I will admit that he has made it homey.'

Amara saw the tall, striking figure of Theylin now even further ahead of them. The red of his hair seemed brighter; orange and dark red bands showed up in the sunlight. He seemed to be blending into the woods around them, as if he was stretching out and shrinking all at the same time. She glanced at Keirin, who appeared exactly the same and she wondered if seeing Theylin change was all in her head.

'It's not in your head. The woods do change him. He's part wilding. That's why he seems so much more here. I can tell he's glad to be back. He heard me talk about the human realm for so many centuries that to be permitted to go and see it was the adventure of a lifetime for him. But I did warn him, that it makes home all that much sweeter.

'Theylin Fae Marcus is actually from one of the old families as well. He could be head of the Onyx family if he wanted to be. He has the skills and the respect of the Fae.' Keirin looked at his friend and knew why he had turned down the title. The Fae thought they were so without prejudice. They were better than the humans, but there was still a class system and expectations to be met.

'Gods grant me blessed wind!' came a bellowing voice from the tall grasses in the ground above them. Amara looked to the men and when she saw they weren't worried in the slightest by the outcry, she let her curiosity guide her to walk towards it. From among the grasses, she started to see movement.

'Ribben?' she asked trying to peer through the grass.

Muttering was followed by sprays of black dirt being thrown into the air. The grasses rustled and Amara was sure that she was seeing the edges of wings. White elegant flight feathers were sitting over the grasses and pushing between clumps of grasses. The dirt continued to be flung into the air with no response. As the dirt started to fly towards them, Keirin finally had enough, and with a confident gesture of his hand, a stiff wind pushed past them. Within seconds the wind picked up enough strength and speed that it whistled as it pushed the grasses down. As it pushed further into the grassy field, they heard a shriek, and wings were rolling and protesting.

The small mass finally stopped rolling as the wind died down, and Amara saw wings delicately flapping. The owner of the wings was an ancient male Oahesa. Having the usual size of his kind, he wasn't more than a few feet tall and had a large rounded belly covered by one long smock. His face was wrinkled, but his purple eyes were clear and bright.

'Morisma,' Theylin said with a bland recognition.

'Lord of Fire! How wonderful to encounter you on this wonderful day.' The small being, who looked like a man with delicate speckled wings, started to dust himself off. 'I see you brought Keirin with you, expressing the usual lack of manners.'

'You were the one covering us with dirt!' Keirin snapped while he got his backpack off the ground.

Morisma enjoyed ribbing what he deemed to be an inflated air Fae. His purple eyes quickly moved to Amara, becoming sharp and penetrating. 'But who is this lovely lady?' Morisma asked as he stretched one of his wings behind him and quickly bowed. 'It's not often I see these boys entertaining one of the other genders? Please, please, come closer.' He walked towards Amara holding out two small human hands. Amara was entranced by his delicate wings, the soft and smooth feathers feeling so at odds with his round wrinkled face.

'She is visiting, Morisma. No need to slather on the charm,' Keirin chided; 'there's no money for you to extort from her.'

With squinted eyes, Morisma glared at Keirin for a second before beaming a smile to Amara. 'Let me introduce myself, lady, and I do apologise for the dirt. It is so close to Ehve that I am looking for Sarandu grubs. Such a delicacy.' He closed his eyes gleefully.

'Gods, we forgot it was Ehve. That's good news for you Amara.' Theylin beamed.

Amara was still busy staring wide-eyed at Morisma and after a moment of hesitation, put her hands out to gently touch the hands extended to her

In a second the jovial elderly creature stilled and tilted his head with the sharp accuracy of a bird. 'What are you?' he whispered.

'Um, Amara … I'm not like these guys.' Amara took back her hands and stood up. 'I hope that's OK.'

'Not like them, indeed. Humility, kindness, and certainly more beauty.'

Keirin made a stuttering noise before Theylin gave him a wan grin to tell him to accept the truth.

'Don't let him fool you, Amara,' Theylin cautioned. 'He's older and more arrogant than either of us. Morisma is one of the winged folk who grace these woods. While most of them bow down to Keirin, as he's Lord of Air and all, Morisma has been particularly immune, and Keirin hasn't ever forgiven him.'

'I don't care what that pigeon thinks of me,' Keirin snapped, feeling all eyes on him as his tone implied otherwise.

'Your wings ... they are beautiful.'

At her comment there was a rumble in the air, and the eastern sky started turning to grey. Morisma was smiling at Amara. 'I am part of the land here. As long as an Oahesa resides here, the rains are gentle and the spring will follow the dark times. That's what Ehve is dear, since you are unfamiliar with our ways. You are not my first human.'

Amara wasn't sure what to say. Was it supposed to be a secret?

'Welcome. Be welcome.' He warmly intoned. With one sweep of his wings Morisma launched into the air as a storm continued to rumble in the distance. He floated in the air at eye level with Amara, purple eyes starting to shine. 'Take care of this one, Keirin. I know I don't often give you the acknowledgement that you deserve, but what you have here is rather precious, though I don't know fully why.' With a smile he rocketed into the sky, taking only seconds to be out of sight heading towards the grey storm.

'He was, he was amazing! Wait, how many are there? What else is out there?'

'He is one of the storm folk. They can stop a storm, or start one if they so choose,' Theylin explained while grinning at

Amara's enthusiasm. 'You should see it one day. Their wings beat forward, and in a second a ball of light energy flies from them into storm clouds. Depending on what they want, the storm dissipates or grows.' Amara's mouth dropped open, and her gaze followed the sky to where Morisma had flown.

'Listen, you have had a hard few days. There are literally hundreds of Fae folk that we could tell you about. They call this the Land of Wings with good reason. But let's make our way back home. Rest. Plus, I have an idea once we are in my house. It's tradition that on the night before a Fae's Awakening, their family throw a private celebration, before it all gets lost in the city's festivities.'

'The city? Why would the city be celebrating?'

'Amara, you are the first Awakening in twenty years. People are going to want to celebrate. The day after the ceremony, people are usually some combination of hungover and exhausted. Do you know what this means to us? That the gods haven't forgotten us! So here is the great idea. Keirin and I will throw you a party!'

'When did you start throwing parties?' Keirin asked.

Amara looked at Theylin and beamed. 'I get a party?'

Keirin knew to be quiet. She loved a party. Loved planning them, loved crafting to make decorations for them, loved making the food for them. The horrible balloons that he had witnessed over the years. The confetti. Keirin shuddered at the memories.

'Ehve is a very sacred omen. Theylin is right, we should make an effort. But if this is our party for you, then you have to agree to stand back and let us do all the planning.'

'I'm OK with that! I still can't believe I saw an angel. Sort of … more wrinkly than I was expecting—but I will take it!'

'They are air elemental Fae, not angels as your myths describe them. Full of storm magic. A lot of them almost worship Keirin as a god,' Theylin said with a wink.

They started on the path sloping upwards and Amara began to love the woods even more. The reds became more vibrant and the trees even denser on either side of the path. The air became cooler and crisper, and the smell of damp leaves was sweet in the air. She felt like every breath taken into her lungs was soothing. She was almost vibrating with energy.

But still not as much as Theylin, who was almost bounding ahead of them. He jumped upwards from the path like it was effortless, He landed lightly on a stone wall curving around one side of the path and started running. Keirin and Amara kept a steady pace and turned the corner to find him sitting cross legged and smiling at them. Amara realized that his green eyes were blazing in the woods. They were sharp and crystalline and clear. He loved it here.

From a hundred feet away, they heard a crash and movement through the trees. They could see the trees shaking as something tore a path towards them, and then Amara was sure that she heard a nickering noise. From the bushes further down the path burst a huge white horse. It came barrelling onto the path and in a rolling burst of muscles and hooves was heading straight towards them.

Amara let out a shout and put her hands in front of her face, sure the creature was going to run her over. She had her eyes squeezed closed, and everything was silent and still around her except she could feel hot breath on the top of her head. Next she heard laughing from both Keirin and Theylin. She got up the nerve to crack her eyes open, and she saw the huge beast was right in front of her and was actually leaning down to inspect her. It was much bigger than any horse she had ever seen. At the withers it was seven feet tall and its arching thick white neck easily cleared another three. Amara peered along the side of the creature and could see the white coat was shimmering. Its legs stretched on forever till they reached the ground, but even with obvious muscle they seemed slim and elegant.

'This is Seraf,' Theylin said with unhidden warmth. He stood up on the stone wall and started walking along it. Keirin began moving around the horse as well. Neither of them seemed surprised by the creature's appearance.

'Uh, guys … am I allowed to move?' Amara asked, still glued to the ground as the massive horse started snuffling its muzzle towards her.

'If she didn't like you, you would be dead by now,' Theylin said casually.

'What?' Amara quipped. 'And you let it … *charge me*?'

'No one lets Seraf do anything. She protects my home, and it's her home too.' Amara squared herself in front of the horse and saw the other men walking around the bend in the road.

'Look, Seraf, I'm exhausted, and I just have to keep going or I'm gonna fall asleep on the ground here. So don't stomp me to death. I'm gonna walk around you.' For a moment the horse raised her head and seemed to turn one large eye towards her.

That was when Amara realized the horse's eyes were the exact same colours as Theylin's. The large horse seemed to shimmy on all four limbs and danced till she was standing next to Amara, put her large head down, and shook it towards the path ahead. Amara finally laughed at the joy coming from the horse, and they started to walk together. Once they were around the bend, the canopy of trees gave way, and she saw an open field full of tall, beautiful grasses. Beyond that she could see the roof of a large house peeking above the treeline.

The roof was a darker green than the leaves that it was nestled into. The walls were made of large grey stones. Amara thought she was going to have to talk to Keirin about the definition of a cottage. Clearly, Theylin owned a mansion in the woods. Amara had to admit she thought it was rustic and beautiful.

Seraf started to nudge her through the grass fields and towards a large stone arch in the side of the building that led into an inner courtyard. The horse had to dip and lower her head to get underneath. She seemed to have a skip in her step, and her long white tail was held high. Her pale grey hooves were the size of salad plates, and Amara felt like a small toy standing next to her. In a moment of courage, she reached out and placed her hand on the muscled shoulder. Without instruction Seraf seemed to slow her pace, staying in step with Amara as she walked her into an open stone courtyard.

The large courtyard was clearly the back of the large building. There were two storeys and large glass windows lined every wall. It looked like a hunting lodge. The rich dark stones and dark hunter green trim suited Theylin. She walked further into the square and towards a group of individuals that were speaking feverishly to Theylin and Keirin. Keirin turned around and glanced at Amara and then went perfectly still. His eyes resting on Amara and Seraf, he reached out with one hand for his friend's elbow. Theylin looked down at the hand on his elbow, visibly annoyed, and was about to give Keirin some choice words until he saw the astonished look on his friend's face. He followed his line of sight. Theylin saw Amara laughing. The large horse dwarfed her, and she was skipping to keep up with it. He turned around, his mouth slowly dropping open.

Then the other Fae who were lined up in leather pants and in tunics of varying rich colours, tans, maroons, and forest greens. All had bows strung onto their backs. They consisted of wood and metal, but none of them had arrows, just special gloves on their dominant hand. When the archer initiated with personal hand gestures, the glove would produce an unstable shard of Sehveral energy. The shard, called a Trill, was as likely to burn the archer as the target, so only elite and skilled Fae would carry them. The men saw Amara too and started to question each other in whispered tones. Six of them of varying heights, all with brown or black hair, were looking past Theylin.

Seraf's hooves clicked on the stone tiles of the courtyard, and Amara beamed a smile at all of them as she walked towards them with her hair blowing into her face.

'Are all horses here this big? She's so beautiful,' she said giving the coat a gentle pat and then stood next to the horse, putting her hands into her coat pockets. She looked dishevelled, with her hair flying in the wind and mud covering one side of her blue coat. But she was grinning from ear to ear. She was glowing with blushed cheeks.

Then she noticed that everyone was staring. Theylin took a few steps forward and reached one hand towards the soft grey muzzle of the horse. She eagerly moved her head forward to meet his hand. Her head still only brushed the top of his, but he stared down at Amara.

'What's going on?' Amara asked.

'You touched her,' Theylin whispered his response.

'Was I not supposed to?' Amara asked, instantly worried.

'She never lets anyone but me touch her,' Theylin replied in the same soft quiet voice.

'Really? She seems so lovely. I mean … it just seemed like … I'm sorry,' Amara whispered back.

Keirin was also glued to the ground. He should have been worried about the reports. The other wardens had come back from their territories to report to Theylin. There had been such odd behaviour from the wilding Fae. But all he could do was watch his friend look entranced by Amara. He stood inches away from the Demestra, the Soul Spirit that was Theylin's most precious friend in the world.

Very few Fae ever receive a Demestra. High Fae like Theylin saw it as a sign of huge power, an outward sign of their true nature. At Theylin's Awakening there had been many quiet hours, with no response from god or goddess, and the ceremony had almost been ended. Then mirror messages came in from the country about a horse of fire thundering towards Rehna. All who saw her knew that she was of the oldest powers. She ran through the streets of Rehna, thundering around every turn, knowing every street that would lead her to the central Temple where all Awakenings for the high Fae took place. On arriving she nearly tore the doors down; the acolytes barely opened them in time.

The look on Theylin's face when the horse flowed into the circular arena, was a mixture of terror and awe. As she walked steady steps towards him and almost floated till she was inches from Theylin. For a moment everyone held their breath as the great creature bowed her head to Theylin. He had found a missing piece of himself that day. But today he had a glimmer of that look as he grinned at the small dark-haired woman who was touching his horse. Touching Seraf, that was so wild and untamed that in hundreds of years he had not seen a single other Fae come closer than a few feet to her. Even Keirin had only ever been allowed to stand within inches of her.

He saw Amara still smiling at the horse and looking even smaller. How could someone so small cause so much trouble? He glanced at the wardens, who were now staring with smiles and whispering to each other. He had always watched her, but when he saw the look on their faces; he wondered if he had been blind to the pull of her all these years. Or perhaps coming back to his lands was drawing out something in her, something that couldn't fully live in the human world. She cried out in laughter as Seraf flicked her tail playfully. Theylin started grinning from ear to ear at both of them.

'Lord, what would you have us do with the findings? We were on our way to report to your father and the rest of the Mehsari. Some of the wilding folk have requested help—food and supplies—as they have lost so much land.'

Keirin was struggling to pay attention. The afternoon sun was streaming over the roof, and large bright beams caressed one side of the building. Theylin was staring down at Amara. 'Make sure a message is sent to them. My family can send supplies. We have stores in the cliffs around Rehna. Send all the dried supplies that you can, peas, mushrooms, and potatoes. I know the wildings will want meat, but we don't have any.'

Theylin stepped in closer to Amara and spoke close to her ear. 'Everyone is staring because you're doing the impossible.'

'What's that?'

'Seraf isn't just any horse. And no, there isn't any other horse in this world that I know of that's like her. She's my Demestra.'

'A what?'

'Maybe it would be better if I explained this later. It's been a long day, and I'm glad to be home. Welcome, by the way. This was my grandmother's home—well, it was a little smaller when she built it. She was part wilding, you see. When I inherited it, I made some expansions. Let's get changed and settle in for a meal. I think we would be pushing it, trying to make it to Rehna tonight.'

Amara was still looking at Seraf, who seemed to toss her head in what looked like agreement, and the great horse began to trot towards the stone archway that led out of the inner courtyard. Once she was free of it, she started to gallop, kicking large clumps of grass and dirt into the air. She was so large you could feel the force of her footfalls, and in seconds she was gone into the woods surrounding the house. How could a white horse vanish altogether?

'Get out of the way!' yelled a shrill high-pitched voice. Immediately after this Amara saw three young teenagers stumbling out of the door. One with beautiful blue-black skin, one girl with pale pastel green hair, and a white haired boy with green eyes and tanned skin came stumbling out of the side door. They all bumped into on another, stopping in shock at the sight of Amara. 'She looks like any old normal Fae,' the girl said, almost rolling her eyes up into the air and crossing her long, thin limbs.

'Xianfe, your opinion, as always, was unsolicited,' Theylin grumbled.

'Who is she calling old?' Amara asked under her breath.

'Well, that is ironic since she just turned fifty last year,' Keirin said with a grin.

Amara shuffled closer to Keirin and under her breath whispered, 'Are those your kids? Or Theylin's kids?'

'You know we aren't a couple, right? That show was just for your friend,' Keirin said in earnest. 'And I am too young to have children.'

'You are as good as an ancient relic,' Theylin chuckled through their head.

'Well, for once you three will serve a purpose beyond driving me to frustration,' Theylin said, motioning to what must have a been a well-dressed servant in the house.

'Actually, if everyone would gather around, this is going to be an announcement for the house.'

The three young Fae all started to look at each other with sparkling eyes. The darkest Fae had violet eyes and stood taller than even Theylin, but there was a gentleness to his movements. He caught eyes with Amara, and they shared a hopeful smile. Amara wouldn't call herself great with kids, but she was sure she could find something to talk about with fifty-year-olds.

Berut decided to approach her. He walked forward and then bowed slightly from the waist. He was wearing what looked like an orange and red sarong and a tailored red shirt, with fine buttons running all the way to the collar. The colours flashed beautifully against his dark skin. He had a broad smile that reached his eyes. 'Welcome. My name is Berut Fae Astora. My colleagues and I have been eager to meet you.'

'Speak for yourself,' the green-haired girl sneered while picking at her nails. Amara couldn't help but look over her coal grey dress, made of a heavy cloth. The dress had slits to the thighs and underneath it was pale green pants that hugged shapely legs. Along the trim were white leafy vines and crescent moons in silver.

'Don't mind them; you are going to be their first human.'

'Does everyone know what I am and why I'm here?'

'Well, I can't speak for Xianfe, but I'm really glad to meet you,' said a crisp voice from behind her. 'My name is Astian Fae Astrellix.' He put out his hand, and Amara took it tentatively. He might look like a teenager, but there was nothing young about his demeanour. He was the most simply dressed in white loose cotton long sleaved tunic and dark leather pants. His eyes were a piercing ice blue, sombre and penetrating. 'Keirin told me once this is how humans greet each other. Is it OK?'

Amara grinned. 'It is, but if you don't shake hands, then what do you normally do?'

'Depends on the Fae really. In the land of wings, the wildings and faefolk tend to great each other with wing movements. But the high Fae tend to bow to each other.'

'How many winged Fae are out there?' Amara asked, falling into step with the handsome young Fae. Xianfe was huffing and giving Berut a shove as he shrugged and started to follow them towards the main house entrance.

'Oh, maybe fifty or so. Sprites, Pixies, Dragonfly paeries, Krevins, Orets … the list goes on. They say that a great winged god gave up his life in this part of the world. But his magic wasn't something that could be destroyed, so it moved and spirited into different Fae creatures, mixing with their own magic and giving them wings.'

'If I hadn't seen it …' Amara's gaze drifted to Keirin, who was still speaking with the scouts. They looked nervous and tense. She pulled her jacket a little closer around her and wondered if everyone in this world was so welcoming of a human.

'All right, enough chatter, though I know Amara wants to

learn about her Fae heritage. *I have a task for the three of you.*' Theylin thought the last into all their heads.

'What?' a defiant Xianfe asked.

'Plan a suitable Ehve celebration. Also, a suitable party for a Fae who is going to be Awakening.' The last was said with a wink at Amara.

Xianfe stared into space with her mouth dropping open. Her eyes welled up, and without making a sound she brushed past Amara and Astian, pushing them out of the way as she barged into the house and was swallowed up by the darkness inside.

'Uh, did I do something?' Amara asked, looking at the two young Fae.

'She was supposed to be the next to Awaken. But it hasn't happened yet.'

'Oh.' Amara wasn't sure what she could do and looked at Theylin for help.

'It will come in time,' Theylin said, exasperated. 'She's just impatient. It's been five years, and I haven't taught that girl an ounce of patience.' He beckoned someone from inside the doorway to make their way forward.

Finally a small woman came towards Amara, and with her head respectfully bowed, she said hello to Theylin, offered to take their luggage, and whisked them all into the house. The six wardens made their way out of the manor; Amara was told they were heading home to the villages that they lived in.

Berut and Astian were eager to help with the party preparations, while they enjoyed living with Theylin, the years away from their families were not without struggle. They stayed with Theylin, as did Xianfe, to be protected until the time they reached Awakening. As well as protection, living with a gifted Fae served the purpose of education. There was tutelage in weapons and combat, theory on the use of magic and mental preparation for managing their power when they received it. However, learning about Fae magic when you couldn't practice it became exceedingly boring. The prospect of a party, a change from the daily routine produced and electric excitement. 'We are going to send an invite, for other Fae? You don't mind if wildings and forest folk join too, do you? Some high Fae … don't like socializing outside of their kind.'

'No, please. I want to meet them all,' Amara said, finally giddy and excited about some part of this mad trip. 'As long as they are all friendly. I go home once this is all done, so I'd love to meet as many as I can.'

Astian and Berut grinned at Amara and then looked at each other and grinned even more. 'First one to the mirror gets to do the wine run, and loser is on lantern duty,' Berut said, shooting towards the stone arch Seraf had left through.

'You are seven feet tall!' Astian moaned as he chased after him.

She was going to ask how they would make it home before dark but was distracted as she walked into Theylin's house. She was struck by how very much it did not look like a British hunting lodge. The walls of every room were painted with dark purples and golds and beautiful scenes of Fae men and woman. There was visual story displayed in elegant pictures. Within the images was magic—magical objects and animals at every turn. Animals she didn't recognise, and beautiful Fae intertwined in their stories.

She walked into what she thought was Theylin's living room, furnished with bright white lounge chairs. The ceiling was eggshell blue, and along the walls were images of Seraf in different states of movement. Somehow they had managed to capture her arched neck and strength. The chairs looked like they were roman, short off the ground with rounded arms and backs. Their gold feet looked like feline paws. The room was clean and centred around a large, roaring fireplace. Theylin spread out on the largest chair, and Keirin stood at the window on the ground floor that looked out into the woods. With a sigh Theylin stretched, hooking one leg over the arm of the couch with the other one on the floor.

'This place is beautiful,' Amara said as she gingerly sat down on one of the benches. She undid her jacket and set it next to her, not sure what to do with it. The same girl from before came in. Now that she wasn't wearing a jacket, Amara could see she was wearing a beautiful full-length dress. The material was wrinkled and looked like rough cotton cloth. It was a pale cream colour with yellow flowers trimming it and was tied tightly just beneath her chest. The neck was rounded, and the shoulders of her dress moulded beautifully to her shoulders. Her mouse brown hair was in a loose bun.

'I can take that for you, Miss. My name's Jennas. Please let me know if you need anything. Any friend of Seraf's is a friend of this house,' she said with a warm smile.

'You guys have to tell me about this horse,' Amara said chuckling.

'Let's eat first. I'm dying for stew,' Theylin said, looking more comfortable by the minute.

'Why don't we change into normal clothes and make ourselves comfortable?' Keirin said, heading through the doorway without a glance back at either of them.

'Come with me,' said Theylin. 'There's plenty of clothes here. Keirin's sister is often spiriting herself around here every couple months, so you can borrow something of hers. She's shorter than you, but I think there will be something that will fit.'

'I've got my own clothes,' Amara said.

'No, we are having a gathering in your honour. You need to wear normal clothes. Fae clothes. And really, I want to see you in a beautiful dress tonight.'

'Oh. Well, if you put it that way,' Amara said smugly.

He walked her up a flight of beautiful spiralling mahogany stairs into a paneled hallway. They walked past several doors of what appeared to be bedrooms. Each one that she glimpsed looked luxurious, with four-poster beds and rich dark wooden furniture. The floors were covered in soft, thick carpets in colours that were dark grey or cream white. Finally Theylin opened a heavy door and walked into a bedroom. There was a large wooden-framed bed that was soft warm-toned wood with a canopy of white chiffon material. He threw open a large cupboard and started flipping through the garments hanging there. He stopped for a second, glanced at Amara, and then pulled out a dark purple dress. It was simple and elegant. But the material hung almost as if it was made of something liquid; it was a purple so dark and rich it was only shades lighter than black her hair.

'Is this how people usually dress for Parties here?' Amara reached out and touched the dress, thinking that she had never owned anything so wonderful in her life.

'This will be your room for the night. I assume Risa's taste is to your approval. She's a bit dramatic in her displays sometimes, but generally she has good taste. She's off at one of the other cities. Part of the job, being a Famish and all.'

'Where is dinner?' Amara asked, thinking she had only seen one of the four wings of the manor. How big was this place really?

'Dinner will be one room over from the room with the fireplace. Just follow your nose,' he replied ignoring her question as he slid his hands into his trouser pockets.

'Your home is really beautiful,' she said warmly.

'I'm glad you like it. This is my favourite place,' he said, leaning against the door frame. 'I'm glad you're here, finding this part of yourself. Get cleaned up, and when you are ready, come downstairs. I will send a message out, invite some of the Fae to join us to celebrate. I have some negotiations with the Amphera clan; I can ask for a reprieve for tonight.'

'What are Amphera?'

'A predator type of Fae. There aren't many of them, but a clan lives near here with an understanding. They protect me and mine at night; we protect them during the day. The clause is, if they catch anything out at night, it's fair game. That's why people line the villages with a particular flower. It lets them know they are part of the agreement.'

'I want to know more, but I'm exhausted. I think I've only found how much I need to work out. The walk here nearly killed me. And I still don't understand what happened coming through that so-called gate.'

'Believe me, if you touched Seraf, then you're Fae.'

'You keep saying this like it means something.'

'It does,' he said, exiting the room and closing the door behind him.

CHAPTER 12

THE SUN POURED OVER his back and her face in broad yellow bands that illuminated their skin. His was almost milky pale; hers was a golden yellow tone that was common to her people. Through the night they had been ebbing and flowing together. Silk sheets were pooled on them and over them, and the large bed they were in was canopied. The small, warm room had large windows facing the rising sun. She had nudged him awake with a long naked leg, and he had eagerly risen, devouring her from the moment he opened his eyes till these moments when she was gripping her legs around his waist and pushing him deeper into her. She arched her back as he rocked gently, keeping a steady rhythm, she made a keening moan that he had already become familiar with, a sound that let him know she was asking for more. They had spent so long being gentle with each other, but now she wanted something more urgent and demanding. To think that weeks ago she had been new to all that her body could offer. Now, as she lay in his arms, it was as if she was made for this kind of expression.

He managed to lift himself off of her, propped on his elbows, and sank his hips, groaning as his satisfaction peaked. His broad, muscled back was warm under the sun, and he had spent the final hours of the early morning lazily enjoying Maiura.

She had snuck into his room in the middle of the night, as she had done for the last two weeks. If her family knew what they were doing, what their heir had invited, she would be exiled from her clan. The Chianve were much more rigid than the rest of their Fae cousins when it came to moments of intimacy. Erid had been here for three months trying to establish trade with them and was so homesick he was counting down the days tills till he was back in the mountains around Rehna.

But now Maiura had made the weeks pass by in seconds. He looked again at her delicate face. Small bright eyes that were feathered with pale lashes around stark bright yellow irises, as if she were a cat or an owl. The first time those eyes had struck him from across the room, he had thought they were the most alluring things that he had ever seen. That is, until the first night when he had emerged from the bathroom and found her standing in his bedroom slowly undoing the ties of a silk bathrobe. He thought back to the night when he first saw the curves and contours of her body. The material had slipped to the floor with no resistance, rippling and pooling gently onto the ground.

Erid began to increase in pace eagerly. He brought his arms around her, under her back, so that he could wrap his hands onto her shoulders. One arm reached higher and snaked around the back of her neck while he pulled himself over her so that he was keeping her in place while he ground himself into the most delicate parts of her. Her response was to become even more liquid in his grip, giving in to everything that he wanted, loosening her grip on his hips, and anchoring her legs on either side of him.

Thank the gods for this ancient heavy bed, Erid thought as he gave up all sense of gentleness and started to grunt as he lost himself thrusting into her. They had already tested the limits of what was pleasurable and what was too much for her body to bear. He thought that perhaps one day someone would even have to take her towards the edge of pain. He had never enjoyed any level of violence in the bedroom. This was as far as he went, and he was going to be spent within minutes listening to her now panting beneath him, her grip on him getting tighter and tighter as they both rushed towards release.

'Erid, please' was all that she could whisper as her body curled, ready to explode with just a little more, just to hit that point a little harder. He knew it, and a guttural cry left him as his hand fisted into her chocolate hair at the back of her neck and hips pounded into her, the sound of flesh smacking into flesh. One of her hands finally seared him, nails running down his back and finally gripping his ass, dipping the sharp points of her nails into him, and that was the final moment for the lovers. Her grip made him cry out as he thrust as hard as he could into her, revelling in his loss of control, and she muffled her cries into the pillow next to her with her hips rising to accept his every thrust.

After they had caught their breath and spent a few minutes in a languid daze, Erid pulled himself into a sitting position on the end of the bed. His hair was so dark it was almost blue and was cut short and close to his head to keep it under control. He turned to the woman lying in his bed and smiled, shaking his head and laughing at how relaxed she was. 'You should be getting back to your quarters, shouldn't you?'

'I have my own ways; you don't have to worry about me.' She pulled herself into a seated position, wrapping her legs around him, perched her chin on his shoulder, and stroked his back lightly. 'It's a shame that no children of mine will ever have your eyes. I know that they always say your kind are odd-looking, but ... it's a shame.'

Erid turned his sapphire blue eyes towards her and smiled warmly. Even in the short time that they had been together, he had grown truly fond of her. He was sure that with time she would outgrow him and want different bedroom games, but he couldn't deny how glad he was to have shared this with her. 'I never assumed children between us would be an option. But I have to say, your hair and my eyes would make a charming combination,' he said as he ran his fingers through her silken chocolate locks.

'It was a good last night, wasn't it?' she asked, a little unsure.

'Perfect. Your mother will be pleased to know it's over, I assume.'

At the mention of her mother, Maiura's eyes shifted to surprise, and she quickly composed herself. 'You knew that it was her, that she arranged for you to be here?'

'She's been giving me this look, as if I was an unwanted servant whose presence she had to bear. The look became a little lethal after the first night that you were here. My cousin made a comment on my commission here, that I would find the

Chianve to be a most hospitable people. I didn't think a lot of it, but … was it the same for him?'

'It was never with me,' she said in earnest and held onto his wrist.

'It wasn't an accusation ….' He turned from her, wondering why he had brought up the passing conversation. Maybe he was a little jealous.

'No, it's not as you think.' She moved onto her knees so that she was kneeling next to him. 'Promise what I say will stay between us?'

Erid turned to her and nodded his agreement.

'Four generations of my family, of the women in my family, have used the high Fae as—I suppose as a way to rebel against our position in society. Nobles are invited to the feudal households, and for once we get to choose who it is we lie with first. Because you are high Fae, we know that you will not betray us because it will be a death order for you as well. For a few nights we get to choose what our bodies do before we are subjected to politics and family expectation.'

Erid had suspected as much. There weren't many marriages between the Chianve and the high Fae; those that did happen were controversial and the Chianve member of the coupling left their society completely. Maiura was the daughter of one of the royal family lines that ran their small nation. She likely had been betrothed to someone carefully selected from infancy. He hadn't expected to have more than this, these nights together. He was touched that she was admitting this much to him. He leaned his head against hers, so they were touching nose to nose, and breathed in the scent of her.

'Thank you for the gift of your body, and it was you that

schooled me, little one, not the other way around.' She laughed softly and laid a gentle kiss on his lips. Then she got up and wrapped herself in her robes. As he looked at her back, he couldn't help admiring the iridescent purple streak that ran from the base of her neck down her spine. The colour faded appealingly into a sharp point just above her buttocks. This was a mark that all of her people had, and it glittered and shimmered like precious stones, but Erid knew from his weeks-long experience that it only felt like smooth soft skin. 'It's a little disconcerting that your mother gave her consent to this.'

'She had her time. I can't say more than that; it's something that's spoken of only in our bloodline. I can't speak for the other families, so don't expect it there. I think it's our secret. Something we gift to ourselves.'

'Maybe it's wrong to ask, but do you seek freedom from this life? Are you unhappy here?'

'No, Erid, this was enough. To know you was enough. I'm so proud of who I am and what I am to become. When the time comes, I will give myself willingly to the task of ruling my people.' In a few moments the wanton and decadent creature that had been in his bed gave way to someone powerful and capable, full of dignity and force of will. She was a stunning creature.

'Then you had better go. Be safe. We have one final meeting with your mother, and then we leave today.' He stood up and hugged her as she smiled up at him, bright yellow eyes shining at him, both of them knowing that they would likely never touch each other again.

'You will always be welcome here, in my home. Always,' she said with tears brimming in her eyes.

'Go,' he said quietly as she slipped away. For two weeks he had never managed to see how she had entered or left his room. He would turn away and then she was gone; it must be some trick of her blood, and he had stopped trying to find her secrets.

There were four others with him, two other men from his family and two guides to help him travel into Chianve land. Erid was a little pleased with himself that he had been the one Maiura had picked when Mesvana and Ruat were both attractive high Fae. Maiura had spoken to all of them on the night of their arrival, and there had been no indication that she had favoured him. Her mother was the head of this family and the leader of the Shivaran clan, probably the wealthiest of all the clans but one of the smallest. It was a society maintained by matriarchs, with strict cultural rules. Someday soon it would be Maiura who ruled in her mother's place. They didn't live as long as the rest of the high Fae. Maiura was only forty years old, and her mother would live to be just over a hundred, as was common for her kind.

Erid dressed slowly in pale cream slacks and a loose white knitted sweater. As it was cold at this time of year in the arid hills, he wrapped a deep blue cotton scarf around his neck and began to gather his few belongings. He had to go to the throne room to formally leave. For his family's part and the families around Rehna he had succeeded in his task. They needed to maintain a source of Spruvat.

Spruvat grew in warmer climates and needed large amounts of sun, acidic soil, and dry conditions over the summer months. It was a grass that had many uses to the Fae. The seeds were ground into meal that was used in many foods, and the husks and stocks fuelled most of the energy stores in the outlying towns and villages that didn't receive energy from the city's engine. The Chianve were able to grow vast amounts of Spruvat, and in the past centuries trading between the two nations had been mutually beneficial. What they needed from the high Fae was magic. While they were still blessed by the gods, they never Awakened like the high Fae did. Some of them showed gifts and tendencies towards the elements, but there had never been a connection to gods that manifested in the same depth of power.

According to their own legends they came from the waters of the Purge Sea to the east. A sea god came out of the water in the form of a great dragon. He was large and long, covered in fine silken purple scales like skin. The god, Larius found himself cursed into this form under a large full moon. The story went that a young fae girl came upon a beached god writhing on the sand. Instead of running in fear, she gently approached the serpent to offer him comfort. His large head swung around, lips curled to show his daggerlike teeth, large purple whiskers poking from his snout, and large yellow eyes upon her. The story claims that she was the last of a dying line, tide creatures that were always between the shore and the sea and never had a place.

She came to the great sea serpent and with a kind hand raised up a small offering of fish. The god was so humbled by her offer that he accepted the fish and spoke plainly with her, asking her what she would want once he was free of his curse and could attend the sea again. He claimed that he would give her anything her heart desired. The young girl, whose name was Dio, turned to the god and said, 'I wish only to travel up the river with my family, leave this harsh shore, and provide for us all the days of our lives.'

For many years after that encounter Dio did not see the god again, after she slid his body back into the gentle waters of the sea. For years the god endured the length of his curse to remain in his dragon form. Once the curse had run its course, the sea god returned to the shore with the intention of leaving the sea altogether, for he no longer had any love for the mistress of the seas who had cursed him. He sought out Dio. Where Dio had been a young girl when she encountered the god, he found her to be a beautiful woman now. She was just as the Chianve were seen now, small and lithe. Longer in the limb and face than the high Fae, with shapely eyes that were stark yellow, with smooth faces and butter yellow skin, and all of them with dark chocolate brown hair.

Larius fashioned himself to look as Dio did and married her, taking her and her family to the centre lands away from the sea. They moved up the rivers and onto the steppe plains where there were only oceans of grass and land. Along the few flat plains with rivers, they established the clans of the Chianve, who claim to be all offspring of the seven daughters that were born to Dio and Larius. All of them bore the purple mark of their father along their spines, in varying shades of iridescent shimmer, a trait they now held sacred as a mark of the sea god that abandoned his home to give them a new one. From that time to this time, families were passed down from mother to daughter in honour of Dio, who was the mother of their people.

Erid had heard the story many times and admitted that there was something about the way the Chianve moved that did appear serpentine. He was finally entering the throne room. The room was covered in red panelling with red pillars flanking the room, and the low ceiling was covered in yellow and gold flames. The matriarch sat on the throne, and the court was moving fluidly around her. The men of the court all wore their hair in long braids that reached well past their backs. They were much shorter than himself or any of his comrades, but their build and colouring mirrored those of their female counterparts.

The ocean of people parted for Erid as he and his companions slowly walked towards the throne and knelt to show their respect. He was flanked by his tall blonde cousins. Mesvana Fae Toren wore bright blue silk robes with sliver sparrows woven into them and solid silver trim. His long hair was pin-straight and fashioned up onto his head in a bun with silver bells on strings throughout his hair, which beautifully brought out the silver grey in his hair.

'Erid Fae Evandrus, you have pleased this house with your fair negotiations. They did not lie to me, when they said that you were skilled.' Erid looked up at the ancient woman who still appeared regal despite her wrinkles. Mina Che Ru was the matriarch of this house. The birth of Maiura had been considered miraculous given her age. He struggled not to search the room for Maiura now, wanting to see her one last time. From his side, his cousins who had come to learn diplomacy from him were giving their thanks for being allowed to visit the Chianve lands.

There was a surplus of Spruvat this year. They had grown more than they could even store, and makeshift large barns had to be constructed. They had more than enough to share, but they needed help to sustain the irrigation of their land. Explosives were outlawed because of the damage to their land, and underneath the rich soil was a two-mile-deep granite basin the stretched the length of the steppe plains. Manual construction would take years.

This was where Erid and his family came into play. The Evandrus line had always had a connection to the earth. For five thousand years at least one in their family line had always been blessed with the gift to manipulate the earth and its constituents. Erid had been born three hundred years ago—young by Fae standards—and when he had gone to the Temple in Rehna for his Awakening, they said that mountains surrounding the valley city shifted and groaned, and the sound had echoed through the city. Erid had never revealed to anyone what had happened on that day. There had been silence for several minutes, onlookers watched as he stared at nothing. He began to shake, terrified at an unseen horror. A landslide had occurred in the cliffs surrounding Rehna that day and people from miles around had felt a tremor in the earth underneath them. Plates had fallen off of tables and water had rippled in their glasses from the vibrations coursing out from the temple arena. When he finally seemed to recover himself, and he walked out of the arena and vomited several times on his knees with his mother sobbing over him asking him what was wrong. He had refused then, or ever since, to speak of what occurred. For five years he kept his powers hidden till he felt he could control them. No one was prepared for the extent of them. No one in his family had ever been this strong.

'There are channels now that go from the main delta and extend into the heart of the Chianve Territories. I've fashioned them just as you have requested. The aqueducts are all based with granite floors that should last centuries. Some areas are deep and should be guarded. Bridges have been made for the wildings to cross at their leisure, and these are not to be removed or disturbed under any circumstances as per our request. You know the rules of our gifts: we cannot disrupt the natural course of the rivers without ensuring the life that they sustain is not harmed.'

'I'm well aware of all your gifts, Fae. Still, it would have taken us fifty years to do what you have done in three months, it's to be commended. Now we have a contract between us for the next hundred years, the longest yet acquired by your family. They should be proud. Well, Fae Evandrus, you have obtained all you wanted in these lands. I wish you luck and that your gods continue to bless you.'

At that moment Maiura slipped next to her grandmother and stood on the bottom steps of the dais next to the throne. Erid glanced at her bright silk tunic, which was the same iridescent purple as seen on her back. Her hair was pulled up in an intricate silver net, and she wore white pants that pooled gently around her ankles. She stood peering at all of them, not a flicker of emotion on her face. Only Erid saw Mina's right hand slightly grip the side of the throne, irritation about something he didn't know.

He bowed his head slowly in Maiura's direction. 'Then it is time for us to part ways as friends, my lady.' He stood, ready to leave, not looking directly at Maiura.

'Will you be back in time to see this new Awakening?' Mina asked, reaching for the small blue and white porcelin teacup next to her. 'The rumour is that the Fae Boron line has brought back a human; can you imagine? I would be interested to know if a human is granted blessings from the gods, even when they deny my people.'

Maiura looked nervously at her mother and shifted her stance, looking ready to intercede.

'I've not been in Rehna for a long time, High Lady. Your information will be much better than mine.'

'How do you always sound so polite when you look down your nose at us, your poor powerless cousins?' she spat from her seat.

'Mother,' Maiura said, in a reprimanding tone.

'Oh, please, he's known how I felt about him from the moment they set foot in this clan house. And how are you all right with this? They never invite any of our gifted to the Temple to undergo their precious Awakening ceremony, but you will stand by and watch a human step into their precious arena.

'Tell us, Erid Fae Evandrus, what was your ceremony like? Did the gods themselves come down and tell you that you were better than the rest of us, that they remain silent to?'

Erid turned his body away from the old woman, now leaning forward on her throne. The billowing layers of silk were stiff and layered around her so that she looked to be in the centre of a wilting flower. He was not about to tell this story to someone who so completely envied what he was.

'Each ceremony is unique to the individual presented to the gods. Even our own are sometimes not given what would be considered grand gifts; sometimes it is enough to be seen by the gods.'

He cleared his throat and closed his eyes trying desperately not to look at Maiura one last time, the curve of her neck or her soft mouth. 'Sometimes I have felt that the gifts they give us are attempts to complete us in some way. Maybe those who do not receive them are already all that the gods intended them to be—beautiful and unrivalled in their splendour.'

He whispered the last phrase, and by this time so many of the people in the room were intent on his words that it was almost silent. He knew that he was dancing along a dangerous edge. As soon as the words left his lips he desperately hoped that no one could see the pull and connection that he felt was almost burning between himself and Maiura. He stood still for several moments and didn't look, waiting for this final moment to pass. To know his heart's message had reached her.

'Wise words, Fae Evandrus.' Maiura spoke clearly and for the whole of the throne room to hear. 'It is good you remind the Chianve that they have much to be proud of. How we would have been lacking, if you had not been here.'

With that Erid was close to choking on his emotions. He turned his deep blue eyes, which had become even darker with emotion, to the ruling matriarch and gave a deep bow. Then, turning on his heel, he headed straight for the door with his cousins barely able to keep up after giving their own bows.

Erid nearly ripped the door off of the wooden clan house, shoving himself through the towering arched doors that were barely opened in time for him by guards. Finally, the fresh clean air hit him, dry and smelling of grass. Outside where they were heading was a Besmot. While most of the high Fae denied themselves the benefits of Sehvat technology, the Evandrus line did not. They were often the emissaries to other nations because of their diplomacy and ability to be seen as a neutral party, trusted and respected. For them, the royal lines of the Orchidru had gifted Besmots. The ship appeared as a huge silver disc, like a drop of liquid mercury that flew and floated without making a single sound. He walked towards the ship and watched as seamless doors opened, and he slipped into the rounded tubelike corridors.

'Gods above, Erid, could you have run out of their any faster?' Ruat said planting himself in one of the chairs of the semicircular cabin, which housed the control panel. He touched the smooth glass surface with pale blue pulsing lines running back and forth. After several touches on the surface, the coordinates to home were entered, and Erid threw his bag into the corner of the small cabin and slumped in a chair.

'I am definitely missing something here,' Mesvana said. 'Ru, tell me you feel the same way. But whatever is happening to our grumpy cousin, I am damn happy to be going home. If I had to eat any more of that liquid they call soup, I was going to fade away like my ancestors. I can't believe they don't have any options except boiled vegetables. Meat eaters. I'm going to eat myself silly when I get home.' He glanced back at his quiet cousin.

'Definitely missing something.' Ruat whispered as the final two Fae guides got into chairs and strapped themselves in. It was unusual to be surrounded by this much metal in their world, but then the Orchidru had learnt long ago how to obtain it from the Starborn children. Erid still felt slightly nauseated in the Besmots, but he had to admit it was the best way to travel. They would be home within hours.

There was the sinking-stomach feeling that lasted a few seconds as the Besmot pulled into the air, rising hundreds of feet into the air in seconds without making a sound. Outside, a crowd of observers gathered, coming out of the surrounding clan villages, gathering to watch them go. Erid didn't look back or speak. He simply sat staring at the floor.

'So is there a human going to the Temple in Rehna?' Ruat asked of the whole group now sitting in paired rows, all facing the circular windows. For miles they could only see clouds and layered grass plains. That was all they would see for several hours as they moved in the direction of Rehna.

'Don't be ridiculous. Humans never come here anymore. For all we know, that world has died,' Mesvana said, pooling his blonde silver hair into a bun on his head.

'It would be something to see, though,' Ruat said. 'Been a few decades since we had an Awakening in the city. There are normally some celebrations afterwards, right? What do you say, Erid? You have worked hard enough, shifting all that rubble to bring the grass people some water.' He was grinning from ear to ear. He had a broad mouth and a huge smile that lit up his tanned face.

'Yeah, I mean if we take a couple days before reporting back to old fuddy Evandrus, no one will know.' Mesvana finished with an elated shout and nudged Ruat.

At that comment, they did manage to get a snort out of Erid. He finally lifted his gaze from the floor, and Ruat caught his eye. Both of his cousins were from his mother's side, and they were golden skinned with blonde hair and blue eyes. They could have been twins instead of cousins. A hundred years younger than Erid, they still had a lot of rebellion to work out. Erid took a deep breath and sighed. 'All right, let's avoid the old fuddy for a few days.'

A triumphant cry went up from Mesvana and Ruat, and they started adjusting the settings on the panel in front of them. 'But let's be clear, my father will really kill you if he finds out you call him Ol' Fuddy behind his back.'

13

AMARA LOOKED AROUND HER. This was definitely a girl's room. She saw her things were tucked at the end of the large bed but also looked at the dress that was now lying across the bed. She started to get undressed and was amazed at how warm the house was. It was the middle of winter, and she usually expected there to still be a chill in the air. But she felt like she was wrapped in a blanket.

She put on the dress, sliding it up over her hips. It was heavy and cool against her skin. The dress had a large oval neck, and two thin straps of material held the dress up on her shoulders. It was actually held up by corset style ties on the back that made the dress fit snuggly over her torso. Even with her moderate chest she felt it flattered her without making her feel exposed. She could easily pull the ties that ended just above her lower back, the criss-crossed strings looked lovely cascading down her back. The rest of the dress was simple and free-flowing smooth heavy material that was somewhere between velvet and heavy cotton but was delicately soft.

She was wondering what shoes she should wear, as her knee-high boots were now off, and she noticed a pair of soft black slippers at the end of her bed. They must be bedroom slippers, but they looked comfortable, so she slipped them on. She loved moving in the dress. She felt so feminine and free. A final glance in a full-length mirror on the wall made her raise an eyebrow.

Whoever this Risa was, she had amazing taste. While the dress was simple in design, the material, with shimmers of purple and dark colour, was beautiful. She started down the hallway stairs, hearing Keirin and Theylin chattering. She could also smell something amazing. She saw the room painted with images of Seraf and turned to the next room, painted in deep terracotta red. The walls were covered in gold vines bearing grapes and berries along the ceiling. Even in here there seemed to be a story along the wall of a man holding a horn and food pouring out of it.

As Amara moved through the house towards the dining room, she could see that the last rays of light were giving way. The sky had a pink and orange glow, fading upward into a midnight blue sky spangled with stars. She glanced out one of the windows, thinking how odd it was to see different stars. It was so beautiful here, she hadn't thought she would be so entranced by this world. The houses and clothing all seemed to be a blend of ancient worlds, Greece and Rome, and the colours made her think of India.

Magentas, yellows, dark blues, and ocean green lights lit up the walls in the open air above the courtyard. Just as she thought she hadn't seen enough colours, she peered out of a window into the courtyard, shock and pleasure coursed through her. Strung up along heavy red strings were vibrant glowing paper lanterns. The shapes were orbs and circles, paper flowers and bells, birds and diamonds. Some were inches in size, and others were several feet high. They were all suspended between the walls and windows of the courtyard. She could see the three young Fae still working to put up the last ones, Astian hefting them up as Xianfe stood at the top of a ladder, looking even leaner and almost treelike in her stature. She then heard bells chiming as the wind rushed past them, and Berut was pulling a large tub of what looked like red wine towards the centre of the yard.

Amara finally walked away from the window and followed the smell of delicious food. Near a long table with high-backed chairs stood Theylin and Keirin, both chuckling. Keirin was now wearing a dark blue tunic with a gold pattern of flying birds, made of rough material with gold thread ties hanging from the neck and dark loose trousers that fell smoothly to the floor. Theylin wore a white rough cotton tunic with a leather vest inlaid with copper orange string in curved patterns, this was paired with tan cotton trousers that looked snug and comfortable. Amara suddenly felt overdressed and cleared her throat, folding one arm across her body while gripping the skirts of the dress with the other. Both men turned and stopped speaking simultaneously.

'I could have worn my own clothes.'

'And denied us the sight of you in that dress? I wouldn't allow it in my house,' Theylin said, grinning from ear to ear.

Keirin moved quickly around the table and pulled out a

chair for Amara so they were seated around the end of a table big enough to seat eight easily. Theylin was at the head of the table, and Keirin sat opposite Amara still not having said a word, barely even glancing at her. Jennas whisked out glass goblets and started pouring what looked like wine. Amara picked up the glass and had a sniff of the liquid and was surprised that it smelt like … chocolate and cinnamon?

She looked at the men, who had again started chatting between themselves about something growing in the woods and wondered what was going on. She took a sip of the liquid; it was cool and smooth but tasted like sweet wine and there was a strong burn as the alcohol hit the back of her throat. It wasn't too sweet and was refreshing. Suddenly the exhaustion of the day, the weekend, and everything that had happened with Jess swamped her. She held the glass in both hands and stared down at it.

'My father has to see Amara first. Before the rest of the Mehsari meet her.'

'K, the sun's down now, and there's no traveling at night through the forest. We can make these arrangements in the morning, can't we? Just eat and drink a little, let her catch her breath.'

'Can I find out how Jess is?' Amara asked quietly.

They both looked at her and saw the tiredness that seemed to have engulfed her.

Keirin made a move to reach for her hand but pulled back quickly. 'I checked with Ribben; she's sleeping it off. Called in sick to work and is safe in bed. I asked him to stay with her for longer, till she's back to herself.'

Amara nodded, still looking at the dark red liquid in her glass. It started to look like blood.

Jennas came out with three earthen bowls filled to the brim with what looked like a thick lentil stew. It smelt heavenly. Amara could see leafy vegetables and potatoes mixed in with the lentils and dark brown colour of the stew made it look like a rich gravy. She eagerly picked up the spoon and blew on it and started to eat. The rich flavours burst into her mouth, and she ate slowly.

'We didn't think we could ask you to wait before you joined the others to see what they have accomplished. It's quite a good job, given such short warning. Though I hope those silly Dragonfly Paeries don't fly into the lanterns, they do love a glow.

'So you performed a bit of a miracle today when you touched Seraf. She likes you too. We talked a little once I got you settled in the room. She said something strange. That you smelled like something … old. I tried to get her to explain, but she doesn't say more than a few sentences.'

Amara was about to express shock that Theylin had spoken to a horse, but then she had gone through a fairy gate today, so she thought she had better just start accepting that things were going to be weird from this point on. She rubbed her eyes, and Theylin and Keirin caught each other's gaze realizing that she was exhausted but unwilling to give in to it.

'It looks beautiful! I really hope they weren't too put out doing all of the decorations. Do you think I can go help?'

'What did I say the rules were about this party? You don't help. At all.' Keirin said. 'Just finish your meal first, drink. It's almost dark, and soon the forests will empty of the likely visitors. It's not often they get a night to themselves out of their respective nests and villages.'

'So how do you invite them? How do you communicate with each other?' Amara asked looking at bright yellow gold utensils on the table, touching the unpolished rough surfaces.

'Mirrors and magic,' Theylin answered.

Amara laughed and kept looking at them. 'Wait—what? How?'

'This is a land of magic. You use radio signals and satellites; we use magic and mirrors. It's a part of what we call common magics.' Keirin slid a small oval mirror from his pocket. The back of the mirror was lined with soft velvet and a metal cover was hinged over it, inside it was a simple mirror with a blue tint.

'How about we try you, actually? Most Fae can access forms of common magic. Easy things, mirror messages, mirror speak, luck spells, anti-theft spells, et cetera.'

'Oh, so like that glamour thing Theylin did on the wall?'

'Ah, no, glamour is a pretty unique form of magic. Fae like Theylin are good at it because their magic quite often comes from their own life force. I manipulate the air, but it already exists. So Theylin can actually manifest the glamour, which actually has a similar energy pattern to fire but, amazingly, without the heat produced by normal combustion. The excess energy is actually cannibalized by the spell, which is why the glamour is self-perpetuating. The research is pretty amazing.' Amara would normally find a scientific discussion riveting, but tonight in her exhaustion she gave him a blank stare. 'OK, you are right; magic theory on day one is a bit much.'

'No kidding,' she said, turning back to her steaming bowl, along with what looked liked fried flatbreads. Amara gave Jennas a thankful smile. With her next bite, she felt instantly ravenous and realized that she hadn't eaten properly since her dinner with Jess.

'So is this vegetarian?' she asked already shovelling in spoonfuls of the rich liquid into her mouth. She tore the flatbread; it was buttery and soft in texture, and she almost groaned as she dipped it into the rich herby stew.

'So that's just a snack, you realise.' Theylin grinned. 'The house cook was not pleased with me when I told her I wanted a party for the surrounding woodlands. She almost threw a pot at me.' He loved that he had already learned the accuracy of her aim from his childhood.

'We just don't harbour meat in this household, but there will be some amazing things from villages. So I did send messages, to everyone. Sweet breads, dipped flowers, nectar macaroons from the pixies, and my favourite is sugar silk from the Maradas. You have to try it all.'

The three ate slowly, easing into conversation about each other and the differences between their worlds. As a yellow sweet liquor was poured, Amara's laugh tinkled through the room. She felt as if she were visiting with old friends, and Keirin's familiarity with her own life on earth made conversation easy, if not unsettling at times. As the evening progressed and the light faded outside, a white glow slowly filled them indoor metal lanterns, initially a small marble sized ball of white light. As it grew darker, the ball of light grew to about the size of an orange, swirling yellow and white, giving a warm glow to the room.

But what Amara could see was that, as it had gotten darker, the coloured lanterns outside were casting more and more light through the windows. She was starting to buzz with excitement. She wanted to see everything that was here, to know more about Beluvial and the Fae. In an instant she felt a pang of guilt, she should want to go home as soon as this was all over. But seeing a new world? How many people could do that?

Finally Theylin stood up, offering his hand to Amara. 'It's time to greet guests.' All of them walked through the door to the courtyard, which had been propped open with what looked like ice-boxes full of bottles of drink. Amara grabbed a bottle and handed one to Keirin. Grinning, she skipped out the door, swirling in the dress so that the material danced around her. As she came to a stop and looked around the courtyard, her mouth dropped open at how beautiful they had made it over several hours. After a meal and with the site of the festivities it she gained a second wind, she wanted to see what a Fae celebration entailed.

Hanging from all the walls were chopped dark foliage with white berries. The beautiful lounge chairs from inside the house had been brought out into the open to allow seats and were positioned along the walls. Along with the chairs were also piles of pillows on the floor, meant for the smaller guests who might not find the chairs comfortable. And then Amara could see several dozen Fae already in attendance with more walking through the courtyard archway. In the centre of the courtyard there was a warm, glowing fire, in a steel black firepit. Tables of food and fruit were set out. The glow of the fire combined with the lanterns rippled and danced, throwing beautiful shadows over the stone walls. There was chatter and laughter, and Amara heard buzzing. She saw several small Fae no bigger than her hand flitting through the air, bounding back and forth between lanterns before they flew to a complete stop right in front of her.

Only a foot in front of Amara were two beautiful green-skinned creatures. They had arms and legs like humans, but there the resemblance ended. They had sharp chins and razored cheekbones, and their faces were indistinguishable from each other. Both had solid deep black eyes, that made them look a bit like insects. They stopped in front of her holding onto each other's arms, looking worried.

As they came to a stop, Amara could see they both had what looked like dragonfly wings, a delicate clear double set of wings that flicked with a soft humming sound. As they floated in the air, their wings slowed till she could see the curved motion they used to stay in one place, the tips slowing etching out an invisible figure eight, and the translucent membranes were pigmented with dark greens and magentas. The small creatures themselves had rich green skin that had a rough prickly texture, in contrast to the perfect smooth sheen of their single-toned eyes. The faces could never be mistaken for human with those eyes.

What Amara thought most beautiful about them were the soft cotton candy strands of pastel pink and purple hair that one had in a loose bun and the other in a long intricate braid.

'These are the twin priestesses of the Gillesian clan, they are Dragonfly praeries.' Theylin said bowing his head slowly. 'We thank you for joining us. I did not think that the invitation would reach so far.'

'We did not want to miss out on what has become so rare an occasion. Our grandmother told stories of living in the human world. She had humans that she loved, lands she sorely missed. She spoke of them … fondly.'

Keirin was trying to pour himself more of the honeyed wine from one of the wooden barrels as he glanced up to see the two gowned small folk hovering with the soft flicker of their wings. Amara's face was almost luminous with the iridescent light from their wings. He smiled at the glimmer in her eye, her glee at seeing the creatures of his world.

Her hands were folded in the prayer position in front of her face; she half giggled and half sighed. 'You are so beautiful.' Her words were crystalline and bold.

The creatures zipped a few inches higher, looking at each other as they entwined in each other's arms, whispering to each other. Amara had to crane her neck backwards, neck arching beautifully and her dark heavy hair falling backwards. After initial introductions, Theylin was leaning against the stone walls of his courtyard watching the scene unfold from a distance. This was a night for entertainment, and Amara was doing just fine without him.

The two creatures shared a maniacal grin and turned to Amara. Instinct made her question what had just shifted in the air, making her go still for a second before a haze of purple and pink engulfed her hair. After a short shout of surprise and a hand fanning the smoke that was drifting around her hair, the sisters giggled up into the air, looking down from a height as they held each other close again, the soft materials of their skirts folding together.

'We are enchanted by you too,' they said in soft hissing voices. Amara started to touch her hair gingerly. She felt small soft leaves and what must have been flowers weaved into the side of her head. Before she could start pulling at the foliage now entwined in two intricate braids on the sides of her head, Keirin's hands were gripping her wrists from behind. As he stood behind her, she was suddenly aware of his height, how he towered over her. Her breathing became a little rapid as she turned around in his arms, her hands landing on his forearms.

Before she could form a sound, he was speaking to her. *'It's a blessing; they just blessed you with Drianvah flowers. Don't worry, it's harmless, though it means a great deal. Small folk don't usually bless high Fae.'* The words whispered through her mind as he pulled down a beautiful soft white flower for her to hold, dropping it into her palm. The white petals were touched with pink, curving into a pleasing bell shapes.

'How did they do that? I didn't even feel them touch my hair.'

'They are exquisite spell casters. Theylin can make a glamour, and he's an incredibly good caster, but Paeries make things grow, so quickly their appear to be magic. They help the forest grow, make new flowers, and shape the land. And you should be honoured. How are you coping so well in this other world? The Amara I know struggled to learn how to drive.'

'Stop that. It's so creepy when you remind me you were watching me.' Amara folded her arms and turned to scan the courtyard that was still filling with Fae. 'The instructor was a bell end.' Keirin snickered in response. Now there were other high Fae coming in through the doors, the sound of chatter and music becoming a soothing background hum. 'Was it like this for you? At your Awakening, I mean.' Amara moved in close to Keirin's side, huddling into him as she felt the chill of the night air. Keirin was surprised for a second and then obliged her, rubbing his hands up and down on her arms to warm her up.

'It was bigger, more formal, and less fun. My family was there but not a lot of friends. Theylin and I had barely met. At that time there had been another Youth Guard. He was a good man. That's why those young Fae are here. The Orchidru have told us that they are to Awaken and traditionally, a warrior is charged with protecting them close to the time they are Awakened. They will live here for a few years until their powers call them to the Temple.'

Amara saw the beautiful green-skinned Fae dancing in swaying motions to the steady drum beat. Her white dress was simple and folded in sharp pleats, falling to the ground beautifully. She wore heavy copper bracelets and a large beaded necklace of the same material. The three young Fae were laughing and bringing small clear glasses together, saluting a triumph. 'Is that what you were to me? A Guard?'

Keirin went still. A flash of memory crept into his mind, a broken window, sobbing in the distance.

'I mainly just keep a record. A historian, basically.' He turned to look across the room sipping his golden ale tinted drink.

'So why were you watching me?'

A direct question. If he lied now, the spell of intention could twist his words till she heard only his truest intentions. Did he even know what those were?

'Are you going to drink yourself into a strangers bed like you did when you were sneaking off with Jess to London? I'm so grateful I wasn't there to see you falling over all night.'

'*Excuse me?*' Amara balked.

'What did I just walk into?' Theylin approached them, grinning with his own drink spilling over his hand. 'Amara, you won't believe it, but an Amphera is at the door. Wanting to pay his people's respects to you. He said something about being kin to anyone from the Baelin line. Come with me.'

Amara glared at Keirin, disgusted with the comments about her sex life, which only made him a pervert and a stalker.

'You're a liar.'

Theylin was looking incredibly confused, but beginning to glare at Keirin. If he had to guess whom to blame for a foul mood at a party, it would be Keirin nine times out of ten.

'You are a liar. You weren't watching me out of some noble Fae mission. What, were you babysitting me while I was out drinking? Did that have to be noted in some Fae history ledger?'

Keirin swallowed hard. Why was he pretending she was some idiot girl who could be distracted by a weak insult? He kept on drinking and turned to walk away, when Theylin reached out to grab his arm.

'Answer her.'

'The Mehsari and my father just felt you were special somehow. I was never told. I had to watch all of your family, not just you.'

'Wait—you said I was here to denounce my powers. You said that this was easy and that I could go home. What do you mean, what makes me special to them?'

Now Theylin could feel the alcohol burning away from his blood and clarity reaching his brain. Keirin had spent a great deal of time in the other world but had often spoken of everything but the woman standing with them. It was duty and research that drove him there, or so he had led his friend to believe. What kind of person would watch another life so closely without ever questioning why they were doing it?

Amara was beginning to seethe with anger now. It was unsettling, thinking that strangers knew so much more about her than she knew about herself.

'I'm going to finish this, and then I'm going home. Now if you will excuse me, I'm going to say as many thank-yous as I can and drink as many shots as I want to and stumble around as much as I want to. You can keep watching if you like, Keirin. It seems to be something you are good at.'

Theylin watched Amara glide away, heading towards the dancing circle of Fae with every intention of joining them.

Hours later, Keirin sat at the cleared dinner table, staring at it as he twirled his almost empty glass. Amara had spent hours speaking to as many Fae as she could; they were as enamoured of her as she was of them. Even Xianfe had ended the night warming to her. They shared small glasses of hard liquor; the two had found their stride and stumbled into the house together. Xianfe was laughing almost hysterically at a story involving Amara, two American tourists, and a London cab driver. Once Xianfe understood what a cab was, the joke had become even funnier.

Theylin looked at Keirin with a raised eyebrow. 'You really could have managed that a bit better. Aren't you supposed to be some kind of diplomat to the Fae? I think my butler could have done a better job than you.'

Keirin put his head in his hands and leaned over the table. 'Lin, I really don't know what is happening. The Mehsari are lying, something terrible is going on with the wildings and the spread of this infection. This human girl is supposedly important. My father asked me to bring her back here, and I don't even know why. She's right, I don't have a reason for her coming here. She does need to go through the ceremony, but I don't think that's the plan my father has for her. I don't think this is about her at all.'

Theylin licked his lips and put down the goblet. He could see his friend was struggling, full of dejected woe. He pushed back his chair and stood up. His eyes glowed a shade of amber in the dimming lights of the courtyard as he looked down at Keirin. 'If any harm comes to her, I will never forgive you. I gave her my word that she would be safe, that she wouldn't be harmed here. If you think they need her so badly, then why serve her up to them? You're being an ass. Don't think that I haven't noticed you watching her every move. You care about her. You're going to protect her from everything under the god-blessed sun, and you will get her home.'

Theylin left Keirin at the table sitting with his two clenched fists in front of him and a look of fury. In a few bounding leaps he took the stairs and then walked slowly and quietly along the long hallway to knock on Amara's door. She swung the door open, hair in her face and fully dressed but barefoot and swaying gently against the heavy wooden door. Theylin took a deep breath and sighed, giving her a lopsided grin. He stretched both hands up the sides of the door frame, putting himself up as a barrier and leaned his head down.

'I want to go home,' she said in a sleepy drunken voice, pouting as she leaned her head against the door.

'We can't travel at night here; it's not safe.'

'I'm not a prisoner here, and I want to go,' she said swaying on her feet. 'Theylin, what am I doing here? Why is this happening? I was happy, and everything made sense, and now nothing does. I can't believe there are flowers in my hair. And did you know, that Berut guy is some kind of royalty. He's a beautiful Fae prince; I told him my cabbie New Year's story.'

Theylin saw her teetering figure, sleep threatening to take her. He wrapped his arms around her, holding her close, and she was so pliable she didn't fight him and wrapped her hands into the material of his shirt.

He was so much taller than her it was a struggle to lean his chin onto her head, and he held her close. 'Do you know what a soul spirit is? Not many of my kind have them. In this world there are still old spirits. They aren't gods exactly, but they are as close to immortal as you can be in the corporeal world. Seraf is a fire deity. She found me when I was in the Temple. When I was young and full of rage and confusion, I was kneeling in the Temple sands. I was defiant to the gods but not even knowing what to ask for. She rolled in that day, bursting into the arena. It was as if she gave the fire direction in me. There was all the acceptance and direction I would ever need in this world.'

Amara sniffled and took some deep breaths while she pressed herself into his chest. She looked up at him, and green eyes full of compassion stared down at her. 'She's like a soulmate?'

'She's a blessed guide and a best friend. She's saved my life more times than I can count, and not just from weapons and violence.'

'Must be nice. Am I to take it that she reflects your untamed wild side?'

Theylin was smiling now. Still holding her, he gave a subtle shrug of his shoulders. But his eyes glittered with all the mischief that he had gotten into. *Part Wilding indeed*, Amara thought. She realized she had been in his arms for several minutes in the quiet, so she slowly pushed her hands against his chest so that there was space between them, but he wouldn't release her completely.

'Keirin should never have brought me here. He knew. He knew all along that I was in danger at home, he's hiding things from me. I don't even know who these people are. I don't even know what I am. Theylin, maybe this was all a mistake?'

'Seraf let you touch her. I trust her. And if she accepts you, there is no way anything will go wrong during your Awakening. The gods will be kind to Fae with golden hearts.'

Amara let out a breath she hadn't been aware of holding, and finally her shoulders slumped. 'That's good to hear.' She believed him. This green-eyed man in front of her, she believed him and was sure he would keep his word. He was boisterous and jovial, but she thought deep down he might be an old-fashioned gentleman. She saw the force of him.

With a final squeeze to his arm she kissed his cheek and started to close the door. 'I'm going to get some sleep. It's been a long day. What time do we start towards the city?'

Theylin absently ran his hand through his hair and thought a little before answering. He finally released his hold on her. He shouldn't be this close to her. He shouldn't be making promises to her when he knew that their paths would be parting so soon. He never held back from telling a woman he found her beautiful or intelligent or riveting. He didn't feel he should have to, as long as he was also letting her know that he didn't expect anything in return for the compliment. The reward was being witness to everything she was or would be.

Amara was meant to be work, a duty that he had completed. He should let Keirin take her to Rehna tomorrow and should himself head towards the eastern forests where most of the reports were coming from. He hadn't even checked in with Venti in a month; a report from her was overdue. The Huntress was better than him in so many respects expect for her attitude, he had to check if she was terrorizing the east lands. Venti's safety also flitted through the back of his mind. He looked at Amara and saw the expectation that he would be with her.

'Early, as soon as the sun is up. We don't have cars the way you do. But there are transports that I will arrange. Get some sleep, and I will see you in the morning.'

CHAPTER 14

KEIRIN HAD TOSSED AND turned all night in his bed. He and Risa spent enough time at Theylin's home to have their own rooms, comfortable and designed to be a second home. Keirin's room was right next to his sister's, and that meant that he had been acutely aware that he lay one thin wall away from Amara. He kept thinking of that dark fabric falling over her skin. He had always seen that both his sister and Amara were short and dark-skinned with dark hair, but he had never looked at that dress as something delectable.

Even more unnerving was his reaction to coming up the stairs and finding her in Theylin's arms. He had been coming to apologize. He had wanted to say he was sorry for all his comments, for the upheaval that was happening to her life, for all of it. Instead, he stood on the stairwell not wanting to interrupt them. He also couldn't explain the way he could breathe again when Amara didn't invite Theylin in to spend the night.

He rolled over in the sheets till his feet were on the floor and he was leaning against his knees, rubbing his face, and feeling more tired than when he had gone to bed. The sun was starting to shine through the trees, and there was a warm orange glow to his small room. Theylin had offered him one of the larger rooms, but he wanted to be close to his sister and didn't need more than a bed and closet. After several decades the staff had stopped pestering him to take one of the large estate rooms; his current room was meant to house the maid or lady-in-waiting. The small space that barely fit the bed normally gave him a sense of safety and peace, but not today. He slept in loose black cotton pants and nothing else.

'You looks terrible. Why you no sleep?' He heard from the foot of the bed. No matter how many years passed, that pixie managed to make him jump as he popped in and out of rooms—and worlds, apparently.

'Jess?' He asked rubbing his eyes.

'Looking much better now. Colour in her cheeks. She not a bad human, you know. No Amara though.'

'Well, if you're expecting a warm welcome this morning, Amara's in no mood to see me. I just felt like I was deceiving her. She accused me of manipulating her last night, and she's right. I was supposed to protect her. From everything Fae. That was the one thing that I was supposed to do for her, and instead she's being brought into a nest of politics. What if this is happening because of us, Ribben? What if she's manifesting her Fae side because we were too close to her all these years?'

He pulled on a white cotton towel hanging at the end of the

bed and stood to go into the shower, leaving Ribben to sit wide-eyed on the bed. Ribben didn't say anything; he just listened to his friend talk.

'And my father knows something. He's not telling me why he wants her here in Beluvial. Risa would know. She's more like him than I am, knows just how he thinks. She needs to come back from this blasted tour of the South Seas. Those Fae might as well be in another dimension,' he mumbled as he turned the hot shower on and steam filled the air of the small bathroom. 'You should have seen Theylin putting the moves on Amara last night. Typical godlike charm; disarming women is like a sport to him.'

'The fire hair lord just wants her to be safe,' Ribben said, pulling at a string from the cotton bed sheets, his attention keenly examining them instead of looking at Keirin. He was still quiet, knowing that the conversation wasn't over.

'We have watched her forever. She was always just human and normal and a little foolish. Her taste in men was always terrible. I have to say it's kind of refreshing to see that she didn't throw herself into Theylin's arms or his bed. Not that it's any of my business.' Keirin was saying this all while drying himself off and starting to grab the chest drawers open and closed, pulling out clothes with more force than was necessary. He finally slammed one shut, making Ribben jump as he kept looking at the tall Fae drawing on a pale blue long-sleeved shirt with a pair of dark slacks.

'What? Ribben, you're never this quiet. Surely you have some smart-arse remark to make,' Keirin said, shoving clothes back in the drawers.

'You jealous bad, KK,' Ribben said, shaking his head.

Keirin's mouth opened and closed several times, with his eyebrows drawing together as he sputtered in front of Ribben.

'You ask, I talk,' Ribben said hopping to the floor and sauntering a few steps before looking back. 'Amara is up now, so I going to tell her myself that Jess is OK. You try and not look so green when you get breakfast food this morning. Not good look for you.' There was more than a little amusement in his voice and then he nixed out of the room.

Keirin heard a short shout from the adjoining room and assumed that Ribben had managed to scare someone else this morning. Then there was a string of laughter and giggling, and he wondered what they could be talking about so happily. Ribben was wrong. He'd seen Amara when she was five and making mud cakes in the dirt. He'd seen her go through puberty, when she had zits the size of volcanoes. She was a baby. A human baby. A human, but now probably Fae baby. Of course he would be protective of her, and it would be strange to see her with Theylin. He'd hated seeing her with Derek. He had loathed the human. Surely this was just the same thing.

He pounded down the stairs, desperate for something hot to drink and some form of breakfast. He walked into the dining room and saw Theylin leaning back in a chair, his feet crossed and propped up on the end of the large wood table looking crisp, relaxed and fresh for the day ahead. It was infuriating. He pulled out a chair and slumped himself over the table.

'Tough night, brother?' Theylin asked, swirling a mug of hot liquid.

'You're impossible. Please tell me there's something good for breakfast.'

'Porridge,' Theylin said with a shrug.

'Like this morning could get any more annoying. Ribben is back, helping Amara get ready apparently. We need to get moving. I have to get her to my father. I was thinking we'd use the riverboats. That will take us to the centre of Rehna, and Father can meet us. That way, he won't have any time to manipulate anything.'

Jennas slowly crept in and slid a plate in front of Keirin with scrambled eggs and buttered toast. He looked at the pile of eggs topped with green herbs and then looked a sincere thank-you at the girl, who winked at him. He picked up a fork and started to devour the eggs.

'I'm going to be joining you. I have already arranged for my family boat to take us. Uncle Darius will be ever so pleased to see me.'

'You don't need to do that. You have met the commands of the Mehsari; I can take Amara from here. It will be safe during the day. Thank you, though, for everything,' Keirin said between mouthfuls of eggs. 'Besides, I know you have the estate and the east lands to see to. Venti must be chewing men alive. That woman scares me. Sometimes it's a stunning thing to behold; sometimes I just want to run screaming.'

'Venti has been asked to make an appearance in Rehna; it's been three years since she was trialed and evaluated. I sent the letter two weeks ago. I think it best if I see you both to the city. With everything that's going on, I need to pay a visit to the seat of Onyx house,' Theylin said while getting up and swinging a large coat on. The tan weathered material had a thick heavy neck; it was lined with wool and tied to the side. He was heading out to see Seraf. Fire deity or not, she would not come into the stables or the house. He was sure after many centuries that she had another form, but he had not seen it.

Keirin rubbed his chin, feeling that he should protest against Theylin coming. He didn't know what to say. He never saw his friend volunteer to come into the city and certainly not to willingly make an appearance at his uncle's house. There was so much tension there; Darius all but despised his nephew. Most didn't know it was Theylin who should be living in the city, lord of that house. But he didn't want his father's heritage.

Keirin just nodded as Theylin slipped through the doors of the house, through to the kitchen where the servants were still cleaning and prepping for the day. He smiled and winked at Fae Genwaren, who was the robust house cook that had watched him grow up. He stole an apple on his way out the servant's door with his hands in his pockets, bracing himself for the cold air. This was the fastest way to get to the alcove in the woods where he often found Seraf foraging. He wasn't sure if the place had always been beautiful, or if it had become that way because of her presence.

He walked with fast wide steps across the dirt path which led outside the stone walls surrounding this side of the manor straight into green woods. He could walk the path blindfolded and soon made it to the glade. The sunlight streamed in through the cold winter air, but he wasn't cold. He'd tied his hair up today with leather and walked till he came upon Seraf lying on the cold wet grass and as he approached, she started rolling. Her legs were in the air and she was kicking and rubbing her back against the ground, and he started laughing her.

'You're in a good mood.' He walked towards her and then shuffled onto the ground next to her where he took a seat leaning against her. She was on her stomach again, with her back and front legs tucked into her. Theylin leaned against her shoulders. She curved her large neck and brought her head around so that she was nipping at the material of his pants leg. He reached out and gently petted her muzzle.

'I'm going into Rehna. I think Amara needs my help. I trust Keirin, but I don't trust what's happening.'

The great horse lowered her head slightly but kept her green eye fixed on him. She agreed with him, he could tell.

'I missed you. The human world was strange. There's so much there, but I didn't think there was substance, you know. The food may as well have been air.'

Seraf huffed out some air and then looked forward. She had never been to Earth, and Theylin could tell that she had no interest in it. 'Do you know what is happening, the blight that is in the east? Some of the other cities in Beluvial have sent reports that they have seen the same thing.'

Seraf turned to look at him as he leaned against her. His head was laid back against her coat and withers. Seraf as good as sighed. *'Come with you.'* The words whispered through his head. It was a female voice, soft and sharp. Seraf wasn't human, and it was hard for her to communicate with him this way. They had learned to speak to each with many other cues, but when she spoke, he listened and didn't argue. He watched her a bit longer, lying with her breathing in the cold air. He couldn't count the number of hours he had spent with her, just lying in the woods or exploring the deepest parts on horseback. He had found a peace with her that he had not thought possible after the death of his mother.

His thoughts went back to the few years of his life that he

had been with her at this place, his grandmother's home. His mother had been high Fae, but his great grandmother had always been a wood sprite. He had met her several times over the centuries. At this point she actually looked younger than him. His grandmother had been half Fae and half wood sprite but had managed to gain influence and power. The blending of the two lines had somehow made her gifted. It had been years before he found out that her skill was killing from a distance, that she had been a highly paid assassin. Ironically, her daughter, his mother, was the gentlest person he had ever known. Her marriage to his father had been her one defiant act in a lifetime of goodness. And his father had fed her to the wolves. Onyx house had consumed her as far as Theylin was concerned; he had abandoned his birthright centuries ago.

Seraf could tell that he was getting quiet and melancholy. She shook her head and mane before she swung herself forward, getting her front hooves in front of her and standing up carefully. He was ungracefully slumped on the ground where she had been lying. She moved around slowly, flicking her long tail at him. She gave him a look that he knew all too well, that he was meant to be prepared to ride. He chuckled, grabbed her mane, and deftly lifted himself onto her back. With a deep intake of breath, he let his legs fall into place and turned with Seraf as she started to gallop towards the river that would take them to Rehna.

Just as Theylin's house had been described as a cosy woodland cottage, there was a similar failure of description of the 'boat' that was going to take them the city. It was easily five hundred feet long and extremely wide and low to the surface of the water, sitting serenely like a floating barge that seemed to merge seamlessly with the still swirling waters of the dark green river. The front of the ship curved upwards to form a coiling peak that ended in something that looked like a bird's head. The head was tipped in gold; the rest of the ship was a stark bright white with swirling symbols forming a trim along the wooden railing that surrounded the ship.

The front of the ship had a latticed roof covered in vines. During the winter there were no flowers, but Amara had been told that in the summer months dark purple flowers bloomed over the even lusher foliage. In the winter the floor was bare, but in the summer it was covered with pillows and throws so that you could sit under the dappled light that came through the vines. The feel of the boat reminded Amara of lounging in a Turkish restaurant. Like much of Theylin's house, the interior of the ship was panelled in dark wood, and the hallways were narrow and intimate. There were only four rooms on the boat, and one was for the caretaker who lived on board, Fillias Fae Mereck.

Amara had taken an instant liking to Fillias, because as soon as she was on board, he was cracking one joke after another. His whole demeanour seemed to put a person in better spirits. Every movement and tone of voice added a sense of levity and humour, and she couldn't help but smile at him. When the subtle swaying of the boat was coupled with Amara's night of drinking, she found herself desperate for crisp cool air and made her way to the ships steering wheel.

'How long have you been working for Theylin?' Amara asked while leaning over the railing to stare down at the deep blue-green water of this beautiful river.

Fillias glanced quickly in the direction of the other men

and quirked an eyebrow at them. Keirin cleared his throat and continued to lean languidly against the railings looking straight ahead down the wide winding river. 'Around 400 years,' Fillias replied. 'I was actually employed by his mother years ago. She wanted to be able to travel back to the city as often as she could. She had a love for it.'

Fillias was a tall man with sandy blonde hair that was thinning and coarse, but he was tanned and had deep crow's feet around his bright green eyes from smiling constantly. Amara couldn't help feeling like everyone's eyes seemed to shine outward. The only dark eyes that she had seen in Beluvial were Keirin's.

She hadn't spoken to him all morning as they had made their way towards the river. She had walked a long way with Ribben, who had chatted with her about Jess. *Chat* was the nice term; he had gossiped, as apparently Jess was seeing way more of a certain gentleman than she had let on. It made Amara happy, apparently the potential suitor had noticed how worn out Jess was and decided to show up at her house with chicken soup and a movie order. He sounded like a nice guy. Ribben said he was going to keep an eye on her while they were here in Beluvial, as he didn't have to keep an eye on Amara since she was already well taken care of.

At the end of the boat was the clicking of large hooves. Apparently, it wasn't common, but at times Seraf would travel on the boat with Theylin if time was important. She clearly wasn't happy about it, and she paced back and forth and from side to side of the ship swishing her tail. Amara stayed far away from the horse, sensing her tension. Seraf's coat kept reflecting the sunlight; the sheen of the coat varied as her skin rippled and twitched. Theylin seemed to be as relaxed as any man could be.

Amara kept looking between them as if hoping to see a visual display of their connection, of how two beings were meant to be bound together.

Theylin was leaning against the railings, as was flipping an object in his hands. He was picking at it with a knife when she approached and stood at the railing next to him. She leaned forward as if to peer over his shoulder at what he was doing with his hands. He glanced at her and gave a wan smile as he handed over the cool dark metal; it was a sharp serrated arrowhead.

'I know you're not from here, and Fillias will never complain, but in Rehna avoid asking questions of time. The Fae are touchy about age.' He turned back to the dark waters and looked out over the wide river. It was hundreds of meters wide, and the wind rippled over the water. Gusts of it were almost slicing into the water. Theylin glanced towards Keirin, who was still leaning against the bow of the ship with tight shoulders and his head hung low. It wasn't like him to lose control over his influence of the air around him. Or maybe today, he just didn't care about reigning himself in.

Amara flipped the arrowhead around and saw what looked like text scribbled on the dark metal in scratchy writing. The letters were all curved and loopy and could have been more of a doodle than a word. She looked a question at Theylin, as she ran her finger over the letters. 'Darius' was his response.

'Who is Darius?'

'My uncle. The head of our family seat, he perches himself in Rehna. Like a vulture.'

'So you're close then,' Amara said setting the arrowhead back in his hand. 'Can I ask why you have his name on an arrowhead?'

'One day, I'm going to pierce his black heart with it.'

Amara swallowed hard as she watched Theylin because he seemed to go very still, and she realized that there was no part of him that was joking or simply wishful. There was force behind his words. She watched him and realized that while Seraf was outwardly showing her dislike of being trapped on the boat, in the middle of the wide delta that was a river, Theylin was doing his own form of pacing.

'You need to talk to Keirin,' Theylin said with a half sigh, half frustrated grunt. He glanced over at the dejected Fae lord, as another gust of wind slashed over the water towards the boat and straight at Theylin. 'Damn it, I know you can hear everything, and I'm not wrong in saying you two need to mend the fence.'

Amara had a jolting moment of remembering that the dark-haired man at the front of the boat, who seemed to be making himself as small as possible, was in fact a being of great power. Lord of Air, Ribben had called him. He had said he could hear her anywhere, if she called him. No matter what world. So she decided that she was going to try something. Theylin had stormed off muttering that 'the wind was a whiny bitch' and headed for the inner cabins after nodding at Fillias.

Amara braced her elbows against the railing, and made no movements toward Keirin. With her fingers threaded in front of her she stared out over the water, which was much lovelier than the brown waters that she saw in most rivers. There was no sediment run-off from the shores, she thought, as she saw lush tall grasses and leafy shrubs lining the banks. Amara swallowed again and cleared her throat. She spoke in a soft whisper.

'Keirin, I got really scared last night. With everything. About everything. I saw my friend almost die, and I came to this place and … I'm not sure why I'm here; I'm not sure it was the right decision. I'm really not sure I'm safe.'

She glanced in Keirin's direction; he didn't move a muscle. He didn't change in any way to suggest that he had heard her, and she started to feel foolish. She looked back at the water thinking she had misheard him at some point. Surely he couldn't hear her anywhere. She sighed and moved her wind-whipped hair from her face.

'You will always be safe,' she heard whispered behind her. She glanced back expecting to see Keirin standing behind her, but he was still dozens of feet away, watching the winding river ahead of them.

'Don't promise that,' Amara whispered back. She wasn't going to buy that promise anymore. The small dainty flowers pulled from her hair were spilling out of her jacket pocket and she gently tucked them back in, curling them into a circlet that set next to the blue safe stone Ribben had given her. The air over the river was chilled, and she started shivering and pulled her jacket tighter around herself.

Keirin finally had the courage to glance back at Amara in her muddied blue coat. He saw her fighting against the wind and the cold. Closing his eyes, he took a deep breath and calmed the air just around her. Her eyes went wide; she looked around at him and smiled as suddenly the whipping cold air seemed to still. They passed a few moments looking at each other. Then Keirin nodded and turned back to the front of the ship. He should have felt relief at the exchange, but he was unsettled. What if he couldn't keep his promises to her?

CHAPTER 15

AFTER THEIR PEACEFUL PASSAGE along the smooth river, the banks began to widen. Many other rivers seemed to join in a delta to make it feel like they were on a great wide lake instead of a meandering river. As they started to get closer to Rehna, Fillias tried to tell Amara some of the names of the rivers; there were more than twenty bodies of water of varying size. Even though Amara was spelled and she heard English, there was clearly a different language here, an older, more beautiful tongue. The sound of it was velvety and flowing.

Fillias explained that the city of Rehna sat at the bottom of a valley where many rivers fed through high cliffs to reach the ocean. The river they were on was called Obenarin and soon they would merge onto the estuary that fed directly into the ocean. The fastest way into the city was to pass by the Seat of Pes and enter through the engineered locks along the River

Bestayan, a gentle river that meandered through the middle of the city.

The sharp tan and brown peaks of the towers reached high above the trees, appearing to extend into the clouds. The buildings had a curved design towards the ground. Shrubs and grass gave way to large conifers as they approached the sea and the shore become large cool grey stones along the edges of the river, which had opened up to a deep blue sea. Even though it was cold and winter, the sky was bright and the air was crystal clear. As they turned around the banks of stone, they finally saw the buildings of the Savier family home come into full view.

Amara could see a broad white set of stairs, that dropped straight into the ocean. There was a two-hundred-foot bank where the water was shallow and lapped over white stone, placed in stark contrast to the grey stones that lined the edge of the river. Amara stared at what looked like a beautiful castle rising from the edge of the ocean. Light blue domes glinted in the sunlight almost like mother-of-pearl. The rest of the building was an off-white colour with streaks of pink and warm orange faintly gracing parts of it. In all the dark green of the conifers and the dark stones of shores surrounding it, the home stood out as if it was meant to be in another land.

Theylin came out of warm confines of inner cabins to check on Seraf, who had finally settled down on a bed of dry hay that had been provided for her. Her tail was still flicking powerfully, but she had at least stopped pacing. Traveling over water was not her favourite thing to do.

Amara was transfixed by the building. Theylin walked next to her at the railing and pointed towards the white steps that the ocean was currently lapping gently against. Strong winds made choppy waves that rippled towards the shore.

Underneath the water, close to the white stone, a ripple of water was heading with intent towards the buildings. Amara squinted and couldn't understand what was so interesting that Theylin kept staring at it with a smile. Then from the stone bank Amaras saw a flash of a fin, followed by the curl of a scaled muscular tail that was a beautiful orange, white, and black. It was a patchwork of bright, beautiful colours that she had seen on koi fish in photos and paintings. 'That fish is huge,' she said, leaning forward in hopes of getting a better view. They were now close enough that Amara could tell that the fish was in the shallows of the purpose-made white marble seafloor, rapidly surging towards the steps that joined with the ocean.

Suddenly a figure slipped out of the surface of the water, dark silken hair breaking the surface. The creature looked nothing like a fish and very much like a naked woman. She was lithe and golden-skinned, so petite that the curve of her waist seemed impossible. Her black hair glistened as it ran down her back. Within moments she turned around to reveal an equally petite and elegant angled face with bright turquoise eyes that Amara saw clearly from a hundred feet away. The woman leaned back, her eyes closed, and turned her face up to the sky. Amara saw that beautiful multicoloured tail was attached to this beautiful woman, now leaning back on both arms, naked from the waist up and slowly swirling a tail in front of her.

'That's a … that's a mermaid,' Amara said, breathless.

'That's a Pes Savier,' Theylin said. 'Southern Ones. They aren't even Fae; at least, that's what they say. They don't have the same magic as we do. But they are secretive about their true Origins.'

'They call them mermaids on earth,' Keirin chimed in. 'Though they have been portraying them as pretty ugly and always evil.'

Theylin snorted. 'Well, I have to say, they have gotten it quite right then.'

'Mermaid. It's a mermaid.' Amara was still staring out over the water as a clear, translucent, and beautiful fluke flicked out of the water briefly. The tips were thin and trailing and reminded her of beautiful goldfish tails.

'Just because your ex was slightly … um … gods, she really was odd,' Keirin said, trying to wave politely from the boat's edge. 'I was trying to find something nice to say about Ursuna. You were with her for fifty years; you must have had a reason.'

'That is in fact Ursuna now, sitting on the basking deck,' Theylin said as he raised his hand to wave towards the delicate figure. 'It's actually a marble outcrop for the Pes to sit on; the ocean floor drops just beyond.' The Pes languidly leaned her head backwards in the winter light, as if the freezing water were a warm bath.

Theylin raised his hand, and a large gust of orange-green fire swirled upwards several metres and dissipated. Ursuna jumped at the sight of it, but she slowly raised her own arm in a slow return wave. She cupped her hands as well, making round swirling movements. Large floating droplets of ocean water beaded from the surface of the ocean until they quickly turned into a swirling smooth ball of water. This sped into the air above her, flashing a soft turquoise blue before it exploded, water droplets raining down on her.

'What was that?' Amara said, laughing at the beauty of their magic.

'A message between friends,' Theylin said, warmth and memory passing across his face. Amara had an uncomfortable moment of envy. In a few moments, Theylin had more warmth and affection for a woman no longer in his life than she had experienced in years. This must be how a successful relationship ends.

'I always loved mermaids,' Amara said, not having taken her eye off of Ursuna as she began to shrink into a small figure in the distance.

'I don't know if Pes and mermaids are the same thing. I mean Ursuna is beautiful, but that's an exception. Most of them are quite … fishy. All funny angles and big eyes, really.'

'She is the most beautiful thing I've ever seen,' Amara said, gripping the edge of the boat, looking star-struck.

Theylin gave a pointed look at Keirin, asking him without words if it was possible for anything more pathetic to happen than to be enamoured with a Pes. Keirin responded with a snort. 'You can't judge.'

'A long time ago,' Theylin responded wistfully, giving a final wave as the Savier Louse passed into the distance. 'When is your sister coming back from her meeting with the Southern Ones anyway? She's been living with the Pes for months now. Strange for someone of the air to be so comfortable surrounded by water, don't you think?'

Keirin had wondered the same thing about his sister for weeks. He had missed her immensely. Since he had come into his powers, his position among the rest of the high Fae had changed. Friends had vanished; invitations to great houses and events had stopped. He had been elevated to the highest positions of respect. But his people had started to fear him. That never happened with Risa. To her, he would always be her brother, and she would never be afraid of him.

'I swear my father wants her to marry one of them. He would never say it out loud. He would just watch all the pieces fall into place. He wants to know their secrets. Risa knows it as well. She should have said no to being an ambassador, should have stayed and continued her studies at the Citadel.' Keirin looked out across the water, now starting to ripple from a strong breeze coursing over the surface. 'I miss her.'

Theylin clapped a hand on his shoulder with a squeeze, 'Me too, brother, me too.'

Amara sensed that the weather had turned milder as they grew closer to the city. They were heading well up the River Bestayan, and Amara could see many fae made constructions. It was a system of canals, and they had already gone through several locks where they were rising higher and higher from the ocean's level. She found the land around them to be almost tropical; it was still lush and full of conifers and rich vegetation lining the shores.

Beautiful long, slender houses lined the canals, all in varying bright colours, peaches and greens and robin's-egg blue. Many of the roofs were thatched, with smoke gently billowing from chimneys. Large windows offered a view into sleek exteriors, all looking like Theylin's: slim, low wooden furniture and tables, and wall murals everywhere. Gold and green leaves grew along the walls, helping the houses fold into the foliage around them, as if they grew from the ground themselves. A few of the houses were grander, with large decks and large windows encompassed in log buildings.

They were getting closer and closer to the city and the houses were beginning to increase in frequency and arrangement. Amara thought it was beautiful. She should have been cold standing on the bow of the boat, but she knew that Keirin was doing something with the air to keep her warm. They hadn't spoken, but the tension between them had dissipated.

There was still a knot in her stomach as she approached what was looking to be a beautiful city. She had been here only one night, but her thoughts flashed back to her family and to Jess. She had told them that she had gone on a research trip for the university up to Scotland. A couple weeks she would be gone, working with a research group in a similar field. She knew they would be anxious. Luckily Ribben had said that he would use her phone to message them. She pondered how no one explained to her why that pixie could move between worlds, when she had to go through some kind of vomit-inducing dimension blender?

Images of the creature cowering above Jess skittered through her mind, and thoughts of that thing or anything like it coming after her parents steeled her resolve. She would do this ceremony and make sure she wasn't a target to attract anything towards them. And then she would go home. As lovely as this world was, she was going to go home.

Keirin was still lingering away from Amara, afraid to ruin their unspoken truce. They would be pulling into the closest city port soon.

'Why aren't you doing the mind-to-mind talky thing anymore?' she asked, suddenly standing next to him. He jumped and grimaced at her. How the hell had the woman learned to move so quickly? Sneaking up on him wasn't an easy thing to do.

'It's not considered polite,' he said, arms leaning into the wood railing. She stood next to him with hair in her face, expecting more. Her grey eyes were asking him to speak more, to fill the silence. She was extending an olive branch, and he shouldn't pull away. 'There was a time when the Fae were more connected as a people. We were more like a hive. So within close proximity we can still communicate with each other. Most times it's everyone in a space of thirty or forty feet. Speaking with more individuals like that isn't something that's normally done anymore because you may end up sharing your most intimate thoughts with perfect strangers. If Theylin and I had known that you would also able to speak and think along those mental channels, we wouldn't have spoken to each other that way.'

Amara started to stretch as she thought about what Keirin said. Hive minds were something she was familiar with when it came to bees. She started to wonder how different the Fae really were, even if they looked so similar to humans. Keirin and Theylin were lovely to look at, but there were no pointed ears, no signs that they were magical creatures. Overheating, she sweated and fanned herself, finally having to remove her jacket. It was the middle of winter, and she could swear the further and further they went up the river and the closer they got to the city, the more she felt she was overheating.

'I am roasting. I mean, are we heading up the river or to another continent?' Amara asked, starting to peel her sweater away as well. Looking out at the houses and buildings along the river's edge starting to change as well. Before they appeared to be beautiful forest cabins and stone cottages. These houses started to look distinctly like they were from another era. There were white columns and tiled roofs, balconies with hanging gardens. Even more lovely were the glimpses that she could see inside the homes. The walls were painted solid colours, vivid purples and greens. The walls were covered by more colourful murals, every inch of them bursting with colour. She could see figures and animals. Again they must be telling some beautiful story. Deep-coloured curtains of crimson and royal purple, sea greens and soft pinks all seemed to be swaying in the balconies that seemed to be open to the cool air.

Theylin stepped out from the sitting area of the boat in a soft green shirt that was V-necked and revealed more than a little of his muscled chest. He walked out throwing a light jacket over his shoulder, looking grumpy.

'This is why I can't come to this city, K. It's like a sauna. I mean have they broken the environmental controls? Why by the gods do these people need the city to be so warm?'

'Environmental controls? For the whole city?'

'There are ways they can adjust the temperatures. Yes. Keeping it this warm increases the growing season for many of our foods, and yes, it's more pleasant for the citizens,' Keirin said, eyeballing his friend. 'Fire elemental, my ass,' he muttered.

'I heard that!' Theylin punched him in the shoulder.

The friends chuckled at each other as Amara started to undress in earnest to stay cool. 'How can they do this? Heat a whole city?' She started to see people standing outside in long cotton dresses, light shawls around their shoulders. A golden-skinned woman leaned over with a beautiful blue glass pitcher, the long neck helping her water plants on the balcony that were stretched out over the water's edge.

More and more boats were moored to the edge of the banks, all of them smaller or larger versions of Theylin's with curved wooden bodies, colours varying from soft golden tan to dark cherrywood. The curved heads of the ships seemed to change; some were animals and some were the naked torsos of beautiful women.

Everyone looked human, of different sizes and shapes. What Amara saw most was the beautiful diversity. Where she had often felt like she stood out with her dark features, she had seen people of all shapes, skin colours, and sizes starting to stroll the streets next to the river. She started to see markets and shops and small harbours.

'We are almost at the centre of the city.' Theylin pointed ahead. 'They constructed the harbour so the canals spread out from the centre—twelve canals for the twelve houses that founded the city. Each of them are still owned by the houses in name, but they are freely used by the people. Today we are going to dock in the eighth passageway and make our way to Onyx house.' Amara could see a huge harbour opening up ahead. It was several miles in length with hundreds of beautiful boats. Some with sails were coursing at all angles, but somehow avoiding each other, sometimes by inches.

'Does Keirin's family have a channel here?' Amara asked, taking in the rush and beauty of the city around them. She had seen from a distance that the city lay in a valley that was so deep it appeared like a crater. Outward from this central harbour the walls of the valley rose steeply, and where she might expect to see skyscrapers and tall buildings, she saw huge, ancient trees rising up, and in those trees were lights and homes. Below them as well were homes of varying round shapes and sizes, but all seemed to be made of log and plank and vine, and the roofs were all covered in some form of lush vegetation. Some had large leaves the size of beach towels, and others were tall grasses.

And within all the green she could see colour everywhere, silk and sheer sheets of cloth tied up to all the branches, hanging from the windows. Warm sunflower yellows, saffron oranges, purples and soft blues, and all of the houses were covered in variations of the same filigree design of leaves and vines, some in silver etched into the soft wood and some in bronze or gold. The designs made her think of Viking or old Nordic designs she had seen in museums, but all of these designs were finer and more detailed, and they didn't maintain strict symmetry to borders or squares. It was as if they mimicked a living growth over all the buildings.

'Keirin's house isn't considered to be one of the twelve. The titles are old and really just hold prestige in name. There is still power and money there, but the ruling council, the Mehsari, are selected based on election by the people. They rule based on being wisest and oldest of us. It's a position of service, my grandmother says. She will likely be the one greeting us at the docks.'

Theylin reached over and casually drew Amara in front of him as they started to pull into one of the canals and pointed towards the end of the canal. What looked like a small group of boys dressed in brown smocks jumped from the canal walls head first into the water. They broke the waters surface smoothly, but when they their heads broke the surface Amara was stunned to see their forms had changed. Sleek wet heads that looked like horses appeared but as they dove head first into the water and assortment of coloured fish tails broke out of the water.

'Hippocampi children sometimes work the docks for extra money. They look small but they could pull twenty of these boats.' Theylin explained as Amara beamed trying to look over the edge of the boat to see them. They looked like seahorses the size of large dogs and were circling the boat, easily seen in the clear waters. The boat was suddenly dragged smoothly across the bay into one of the canals and pulled to a stop. Two of the Hippocampi stayed in the water, shades of dark blue and purple peppered their flanks and fins. One the boys scurried up over the railing of the starboard side of the boat, bright brown eyes shining at the crew. Fillias clapped a hand onto the boys shoulder, knowing his name and passing a few silver coins into his hand, earning a wider grin. With the help of the other boys, now in human form a heavy plank was lowered. Small steps at the water's edge lead up to a canopied city street. The canopy was made of heavy purple cloth, intwined and stretched between massive trees that were the size of tall buildings.

At the top of the stairs waited an older woman with cream yellow hair rolled into an intricate bun on top of her head. She was draped in a long dress of varying shades of blue, and Amara could see as they pulled closer that she had the exact same colour eyes as Theylin, and they were staring a hole right through her. While she found Theylin full of warmth, the eyes fixed on her now were like ice going through her veins. The woman was smiling but it didn't reach her eyes. She wasn't tall like Theylin and in fact had a homely roundness to her as she stood with her hands clasped in front of her.

The boat was docked next to the tall stone stairs, and Seraf launched herself onto the landing. There was a huge leap and a clatter of hooves as she found her footing and bounded up the stairs, barrelling past the woman, who went from a regal statue to a windswept and sputtering heap on the floor. The next beautiful sound that Amara heard was Theylin's laugh echoing between the walls of the canal. Seraf pranced her way down a narrow street, seeming to know exactly where she was going and clearly pleased to be on firm land at last.

'Will that creature never learn some manners? Gods above, I know she makes you happy, child, but sometimes I just want to give her a swift kick,' the elderly woman said, irate as she started to shuffle herself up from the ground.

'She didn't mean it, Nana. It's just hard for her to be on the water. She gets really seasick,' Theylin said, reaching down to take her hand and pull her up into a hug. He leaned over her and held her with genuine warmth, and when he released her, there were tears welling up in her eyes as she peered up at her grandson.

'Tiamerasa Fae Marcus, please meet Amara. She is Earthborn and seeking the blessings of this world.' He smiled at his grandmother, the look imploring her to please be gentle.

'I am well aware of who and what she is,' Tiamerasa said without any intention of listening to her grandson's unsaid plea. She walked forward to eye Amara, who had now gotten to the top of the stairs and stood next to Keirin with her duffel over her shoulder. Keirin stood slightly behind her but looked nervous while the silence stretched out, and the green stare bore down on Amara. To her credit she didn't so much as shuffle on her feet and stared back with cool grey eyes.

'I take it this was your father's doing, Keirin. I knew there was some human family; there have been stories for years of his obsession. I would have thought that he could finally put that side of his life behind him. He was the one who gave up life on Earth; why does he insist on bringing parts of that soiled realm here?'

'Did you just call me soiled?' Amara said, taken aback.

'Tia, she is coming into her powers; she is Fae,' Theylin said in a steely voice. 'She is owed the respect of our kind.'

Tiamerasa's eyes sliced towards him in shock at his tone towards her. A few blinking seconds later, she turned with a smile towards Amara, and it was like a switch had turned on and off. One minute the woman had been sneering down her nose at Amara, and the next she seemed to be nothing but a sweet welcoming grandmother. 'I will escort you to the Onyx family home. It may not be mine anymore, but I still have rooms there. You will be welcome, no matter what my son Darius says.'

She started to pace down the narrow streets that were lined with delicate wood balconies on either side. The walls had a rough appearance as if made from sand and cement, all the same tan colour. All the women wore long dresses synched at the waist just below their breasts; the material looked thick and heavy but somehow breathable. Over their shoulders were a variety of shawls and necklines. Amara thought them all simple and beautiful at the same time. Some of the patterns were plant and animal themed, others wore materials more like lace with geometric patterns.

In a stark difference to the wood folk that Theylin had introduced her too, everyone here looked human but living in a culture thousands of years old. The clothes weren't quite Roman or Egyptian, but that was definitely what Amara thought of. She saw a woman in a beautiful dark purple pleated dress that fell beautifully to the floor and dragged slightly behind her as she started pulling dried flowers and herbs down from the wires on the canal wall. She started to feel more masculine than ever in her jeans and boots. The streets were all paved and covered in flat stones, the walls were painted creams and light blues and had a rough texture.

They walked for several minutes turning down several narrow streets and Theylin was nodding to many individuals and addressing them by name. Everyone would greet him with a gasp and large smiles, all expressing their joy at seeing him. How long it had been since he had graced them with his presence. Offer after offer poured from them for him to eat at their tables before he left. Amara hung back with Keirin and was given a glance sidelong from many individuals but no one would look at her for too long. To her surprise, hardly anyone spoke to Keirin. There were many formal greetings, but where the fire lord seemed to receive unbridled worship, everyone appeared to give the Lord of Air a wide berth.

'We are going to part ways here and see you at the Temple in a few hours,' Keirin said. 'I've already sent word to my father to prepare the Mehsari for a formal chambers meeting. We will stay at my family town house.' With that he turned left down one of the wider city streets. There were still just houses and balconies and doors but the space between them appeared wider.

Theylin gave a wide yawn and looked at his grandmother with a grin. 'Just me and you, T; whatever will we get up to?'

'You will come with me to the family seat. I have words for my son. Your room has been ready, as it always will be. And you, Air Lord, don't think I don't see the slight you send to my line by saying that this one should stay in a paltry townhouse when an ancient family would have housed her.'

'Tia, can we please leave the politics be? He is just doing as instructed. You know that I was only there as a protector to get her through the gates; you were in that meeting. My role is done.'

Amara felt a knot develop in her throat as she heard Theylin explain away his presence and the task that he had now completed. She turned her eyes towards the ground and gripped the bag she held a little tighter, trying to cover her disappointment. He had promised to stay with her the whole time. She bit her lip, realizing that she already trusted Theylin, but Keirin was another matter, and she certainly didn't want to be alone with him.

'Maia Tia, please forgive me for my unintended offense. Amara needs to meet my father. I had not thought that you would want to host her. Onyx house is not known for their love of humans.'

Amara was getting more irritated by the moment at being spoken about as if she weren't standing right there. There was a cool silence, and Amara was about to speak out when Keirin gently took hold of her hand behind him in a plea to stop. Tiamerasa was still staring at him with her hands folded, clearly deciding something significant that Amara couldn't fully grasp.

'You are forgiven, Air Lord. And you are right, Darius would have thrown a hurricane of a fit for a human to be under his roof. Though his son would have been pleased to see one in real life. The young ones think you are myth, you know.' she said, finally addressing Amara.

'A good myth?' Amara asked quietly.

'A sad myth,' Tiamerasa answered as she turned away and planted her hand on her grandson's arm requesting he follow her. She started to walk down the path to the right, long robes whipping around her, without glancing backwards. Theylin paused for a second and then reached forward to wrap one arm around a surprised Amara. He tugged her close so that she was tucked against his chest with her head under his chin. After a moment she gave in to the embrace and chuckled, wrapped her arms around his waist, and leaned her head back to smirk at him.

'See you soon, then?' she said.

'Count on it,' he said as he released her and started to run down the path to catch up to his rather sprightly grandmother. Amara found herself wondering how old the woman actually was, amazed at the speed with which she could move.

'We had better get moving, Amara,' said Keirin. 'It's been a long day for you, and we still have to make an appearance today. It's going to be a bit taxing.' Despite his best efforts, his words came out with a bite that he hadn't intended. This always happened with Theylin. *He says three words to any woman, and she's ready to bare her soul and fall headlong into his arms.* Well, he wasn't going to get involved in it. His world was literally sick, and he was spitting and bitter over a hug. *Damn that pixie!*

Amara started to half sprint and half walk to keep up with Keirin, who was now moving at a breakneck speed along the stone paths. They came out of one side street and into what looked like a massive open plaza. Amara just stopped and stared for a moment, as she had never seen anything like it.

In the middle of the massive open plaza were white arches that stretched into the air, they looked like they were made of what she would have thought was white marble. Since she had been in this world, she had only seen products or clothing that would have been made before the industrial era of Earth. Everyone was in clothing and cloth that looked like it was lovingly made by hand. They were thick and luscious materials with beautiful accessories that adorned the arms and heads and ears of everyone around. Chain linked rings and thick metal bands adorned everyone. Nothing she would think of as modern or electrical. No cars, no watches. No electric street lights.

Here the streets were lined with stalls selling a plethora of goods. Sweet balls and glazed breads, buckets of colourful spices. Copper toned jewellery, and pieces all made in a shiny blue metal that Amara couldn't help adoring. Without much coaxing Keirin bought Amara a pendent that was a solid blue circle engraved with a delicate pattern, a knot for protection. Amara melted as a he passed her a sweet ball of fruit coated in pink and green nuts, some of her hang over finally passing as she embraced the bustling market.

But there was an ocean of people in front of her with thronging displays of goods: clothing, small toys, household items—there was a stall full of chiseled and engraved mirrors. Some were simple and others elaborate. Some held the same curved lettering she had seen on Theylin's arrowhead. Communication mirrors. Before she could pick one up Keirin dragged her along and she could have sworn she saw words moving across the mirrored surfaces?

It seemed like a thousand stalls lined the street, bustling with people. She also saw strange things that she didn't have a name for. She saw a man reaching into baths of water and drawing out long blue florescent string, it looked like seaweed that was glowing. Keirin explained that their technology wasn't far off from human computing systems, but that it had been developed using a form of plant that carried messages much like nerve conduction. Above the city she could swear she saw a pulse moving through the air; it wasn't sound or light, but it thrummed through her. And as she looked up, she saw small silver and red metal birds floating through the air, hundreds of them flashing in the light.

Keirin followed her stare. 'Courier Besmots. They send parcels and sometimes handwritten messages between friends. Mirror magics are not foolproof, and someone could be listening.' Keirin chuckled at the pleasure he saw on her face, reaching behind him to take her hand so that he wouldn't lose her in the crowd.

Looking out over the crowd she realized that the Fae seemed to embody all manner of people. She saw every shape and colour she could think of and varying shades of skin colour. On the faces of some of the women who had pale yellow skin she saw dark red dots in a triangle on their foreheads; a single dot on the bottom and two on the top. They dressed as everyone else, in dresses that reached to the floor, with layers and colours and low necklines. She saw men who were so dark their skin colour was almost shimmering blue in the sunlight, and they were striking. They seemed to be standing taller than all the rest dressed in red robes over tan tunics with sandals on their feet.

On the other shore of the narrow canal that cut into the open-air plaza she saw buildings that could only be temples. All of them were beautifully adorned with coloured silks and precious coloured stone inlays in the walls. Some of the buildings had large Greek columns in front and others had stone walls that were drilled to look like they were lace cloth made of stone. The illusion was so fine and real that Amara almost reached out to touch it and wondered if she could break the stone with her hand.

She stopped when she realized she was reaching into the air from hundreds of feet away, and Keirin was staring at her actions. 'What are you doing?' he asked.

'I'm sorry. I—That Temple. I just wanted to … I don' t know why, but I was reaching for the stone entrance. It looks like it's a thin layer of cloth.' Her last words were quiet and fading as she stared at the entrance. This building had a yellow gold roof that fed into six high towers fanned out like a star; their peaked roofs looked like teardrops. The rest of the building was white marble decorated in the same fine stonework as the entrance. And along the walls etched into the stone were the oldest of fae stories of Heroes and Heroines that were all standing tall and pointing in the silhouettes to the entrance, inviting others to enter.

'The building with the yellow towers, you wanted to touch that one?' Keirin asked, surprised.

'What is it?' she asked as he stood staring at her. 'It looks like a Temple.'

'That's where you will have to go … that's where the Awakened Fae find their powers if they are going to receive them.' He studied her for a moment and then stepped, closer to her, taking her arm gently in his hand. 'Are you sure you're all right?'

'It's been a long day already. I think maybe I'm just tired and need something to eat,' she said, turning to him with a smile.

Keirin didn't believe her for a second. He had seen the instant pull she had towards one of their most sacred buildings. He hadn't meant to take them so close to it, but cutting through the common market was the fastest way to get to his family's home in the city. They didn't live in the old quarter where the oldest families had their ancient seats. His father had never held one of those names or titles, so they had a small townhouse nestled in between the old temples, in the narrow suburb between the fae-made inlets and the sides of the valley.

After only a few streets the sound of the busy plaza died down, and the streets grew wider. Soon the buildings were placed further apart, and large trees and green foliage seemed to be invading the space between them. The streets were still built of smooth stone, but where there had been narrow paths that only allowed a few people to walk together, now the roads were broad.

'They call this area The Pinch,' Keirin said.

'Why would they call it that?'

'It's the only stretch of flat land in the valley, the sides of the valley rise up sharply on one side, and the old city canals straddle it on the other. So it's a piece of land that is pinched in between the mountains and the water.' He started to slow down in front of what was a sharply designed townhouse. The building was made of beautiful wood. Along all the edges and trim was beautiful gold filigree. This time Amara was sure that she saw Egyptian hieroglyphs along the floor tiles leading to the wide double doors at the entrance. She couldn't believe the weather that she was experiencing here. The air had been freezing outside of the city, normal for this time of year. She was assuming that they had seasons just like earth, they appeared to have a sun and a solar system. So why was this place almost temperate?

'How is it so warm here? Every mile we got closer to the city, it got warmer and warmer.'

'Do you feel the pulse?' He said, opening the front door and dumping his bags onto the dark wood floor. In front of them was a courtyard open to the air with a shallow but beautiful circular pool in the floor. The pool was filled with turquoise and cobalt tiles that made a mosaic that looked something like a bird. She noticed that the dark red wood was accented by lovely blues and greens throughout the house. Just like Theylin's house, it wasn't huge or richly decorated, but the walls were once again vibrant with colours and designs. Tables meant for lounging and shrubs and green plants lined the edges of the courtyard.

From one of the doorways furthest from her Amara saw a tall man step forward. He was striking in his appearance. Where Keirin had an dark and alluring quality, this man was purely seductive. His eyes were hooded and had an angular shape, dark brown to the point of being black, and they pierced through her even as he smiled at her. This she knew had to be Keirin's father. She saw now where Keirin got his golden tones and dark hair. His father had a slightly smaller frame, almost feminine, and the long dark hair also made him seem delicate.

'Welcome, Amara Fae Baelin,' said Mehkar. 'I have been waiting a long time to meet you.'

'I'm OK with just Amara, thanks.'

'As you wish. I'm afraid you will not have long to place your things down and settle in. We have to meet with the Mehsari, and the Temple will be opened for you as the sun sets. That was the way with your line. They always entered the Temple at twilight. The beginning of dark things, they would say. Keirin was there at high noon. That was a day.' He smiled white teeth at his son.

'A few hours is cutting it tight, don't you think?' Keirin said with a frustrated sneer. 'Let me guess; this is part of their plan to keep her from the Temple.'

'No, it was my request that we do this quickly. Amara, has it been explained to you what will be happening today? Has my son explained what you will be asking to happen?'

Amara glanced between the two men, trying to read between the lines. Keirin was shuffling in one spot and looking at everything but his father. His father was talking to Amara but clearly giving a disapproving assessment to his son. She looked a question at the older man and shook her head no.

'Right. Firstly, it would be our honour to provide you with the appropriate attire for this kind of ceremony. It is sacred to us. My daughter Risa will help you.'

'She's here?' Keirin shouted. In a second he was bounding away from them through an open doorway and yelling his sister's name.

Mehkar chuckled and shook his head. 'There isn't anyone in the world he loves more than Risa. You have to forgive him. She's been in the South Seas with the Pes for several months. She only arrived today, and I didn't tell him that she was coming. He had enough to do.' Amara took that to mean babysitting her.

'So let me explain what has to happen. You have become aware of your Fae heritage, yes?'

'Painfully so,' Amara answered clearly and with focus.

'That was unfortunate.' He walked over to Amara, who was holding her winter jacket awkwardly, wondering where to put it.

Mehkar reached out and took the jacket from her and paused for a second, taking a large swallow as he looked at her. 'You have his eyes. He had those same stone grey eyes.' For a second Amara could almost see the memories flooding through his eyes.

'You knew him?' Amara asked, finally excited about something on this journey. 'What was he like?'

'Funny. He never failed to make me laugh. He was one of my truest friends. I miss him to this day. But then again, here you are, so he will never really be lost to me. Remember that he never for a moment regretted walking away from this world. Not just for the human woman he loved, but for all children and family that he gained as well. You were all worth everything to him.' He paused and then placed her coat over one of the low-lying lounge sofas and motioned for her to sit down.

'May I ask, how can I be one of you? From what Keirin said, I'm generations away from being Fae; I must have so little of your bloodline. Why is this happening?'

'That is a good question. I don't have a simple answer for you. I see that you are educated, and humans are now becoming aware of the code of life, the blueprint as it were.'

'You mean DNA?'

'Yes, exactly that. And you are aware that all of these small parts—well, they make up what we are, even the smallest parts. In you that one part that sparks off the power in us and allows us to connect with Deity is still present. It has not changed or mutated in all these generations or been lost—a small miracle, really. There is a prince among the Orchidru who has been searching for decades for a way to access power, to see if it is simply dormant in their blood or needs to be replaced. He would find your existence fascinating. I wouldn't have thought it possible, but here you are. Clearly Fae.'

Amara sat for a while trying to recall her basic genetics classes that she had at the beginning of university. She thought she understood what he was saying. One gene. Sometimes a disease came down to just one gene that was expressed. Sometimes the gene had to be in the right place at the right time. 'But I still don't know what that means. I express some dormant gene, and then what? I smell different. How does it change me?'

'From what the scholars tell me, it's a hormonal thing. It is something to do with the right age and release of hormones into the bloodstream turning on genes. You can think of it as Fae puberty.' Mehkar chuckled at his gross oversimplification of a privileged and sacred conversion for their people. 'It is not a change in you; you were always this, it was always inside you. What is happening to you is a mystery to our kind still, a conversion of faith. Even though we have the science to say what protein makes what change in the body, we still don't really know. We are allowed to connect with Deity. We manifest powers that we know are given to us by our gods, gods of this world that have always been and always will be. When you are at the Temple, you present yourself to them. One will see you and hopefully accept you and possibly grant a gift. We call this an Awakening. Even among the high Fae, not all of our kind have this event. For some it is a simple acknowledgement. They describe it as knowing that they were seen by a higher power, protected and known to it, but no powers come to them. Others …. Well, the Awakening process can be a spectacle for those that are truly touched and connected to deity.'

'But ….' Amara couldn't ask the question she wanted to. She

could see that for Mehkar this event held much importance—it was part of who and what he was, part of his beliefs, and she was here to turn it down. All she wanted was to be purely human again. She had come determined to refuse this gift. Confusion danced across her face. 'Keirin told me … he told me that I was here to refuse it, so that I could go back to my life. I can do that, can't I?'

Sadness crossed Mehkar's face. 'Yes, that is your right.' He turned away and folded his hands together as he sat next to her. 'I would encourage you not to, my dear.'

'I'm sorry, but I have to. I belong back in my world. I mean, this place is beautiful, I can't deny that, I just want to see it all, but I don't belong here.'

'If you came through the gates, then you belong here. I ask you to think on it. Do you not believe in God, Amara? In those powers that govern the universe? In the power that connects and ties together all things? Would you want to be cut off from that even in the smallest way? There are those who spend their whole lives seeking the closeness that we are privileged to have with Deity. We have yet to see which god grants power to me,' he said, looking gently at her.

Amara sat quietly, feeling both nervous and terrified at the same time. 'What did you say?'

Mehkar looked unsure. A few breaths passed before he quietly responded 'We don't know which god will grant me power?'

'Why would the gods grant you power at my Awakening?' Amara asked inching away from Mehkar.

Did she believe in god? And if she did, was she actually ready to face a god? Be seen by one? Judged by one? What did these people really want with her? She started to feel ill and lightheaded.

Mehkar reached out and took her arm. 'You don't look well suddenly,' he said as he put a hand on her back and starting rubbing slowly.

'Baba, what have you done to her?' a light voice whispered from the hallway. Amara looked up to see the slightest figure standing in the doorway. Where Keirin had not fully taken on his father's dark and rich looks, there was no denying that this child was Mehkar's heir. She had the same beautiful dark almond-shaped eyes and pin-straight hair that fell just below a small chest. Her frame was sleek, with just the slightest curve to her hips, and surprisingly she stood even a few inches shorter than Amara. She wore a white cotton dress that was tied around her neck and a gold armband encircling her right bicep. While everything about her was plain and understated, she managed to make it look elegant.

The girl came forward and leaned in front of Amara to peer more closely at her. She didn't look older than seventeen. 'She looks like she's about to hurl,' she said, accusing her father.

'It's about the gods, dear. She didn't know they were real and at the Awakening.'

'Oh, right. Don't worry; I was just as green when the morning of my ceremony came. Keirin said it would be easy, but I almost didn't make it to the Temple. In your defence, I had a lifetime to learn of it, not just a few days.' She took Amara's hands and gave them a squeeze. Her warm amber eyes were bright and full of sympathy. 'Keep breathing. It's not a scary as it sounds. They act like the gods are going to come down and spank us in the arena or something, but it's more subtle than that. It ends up being beautiful.'

Risa looked so genuine and honest. She looked so much like Keirin that it comforted Amara enough that she started to take breaths.

Amara looked at her and smiled, and for a few seconds everything went still, and she was sure that she was going to be OK. Then she started seeing stars, and her vision was blacking out. She knew for the second time in her life she was going to pass out.

CHAPTER 16

THEYLIN STARTED TO WALK down the well-lit stone hallways. The stones were warm and inviting, a soft grey colour that always seemed as if it had absorbed the light around it. Where some of the Fae didn't like using energy sources for lighting, his uncle had been quite adamant that the whole of the large house be set with great burning Turine lights that shone a vivid white. He always found it so much colder than the candle and gas lights that they still used in his country manor.

He walked straight towards the room that he had occupied on and off since his childhood. He had tried a hundred times to give the room up to his uncle, but this his grandmother had adamantly forbidden. He was always housed in the largest room of the entire manor, the master bedroom—something his uncle resented with every breath he could take.

He walked into the large spacious circular room with

arching ceilings made of stone, it looked like the ceiling of a cathedral with intricate designs painted into the walls, trimmed in brushed on gold and a soft sky blue. Since childhood he had always loved staring at the ceiling when he had lain in here with his mother as she read him story after story of the Fae that had come before him. The mythology he didn't know, but he could never get enough of hearing her bring the stories alive.

Theylin laid down his things on the back of a too-ornate brass chair and started to kick off his shoes and clothes as he headed for the large bathroom with stone walls and a walk-in shower. The day of travel across the water always left him feeling as though he had salt on his skin. It brought a smile to his face to think of seeing Ursuna today in the water. He'd ended so many nights with her feeling the same way, like there was salt tickling his skin. He wiped his face with a damp clean towel and started to get undressed from the clothes of the day. He was sure that being in this house would be the same as always; the same resentment, the same old wounds. It was so toxic that just the anticipation of it nauseated him. How he hated his uncle.

He hated even more that every time he saw him, it was his father's face he saw, his father's twin. Birth was rare for the Fae, but the birth of twins was even more so. It had been a great pride of Onyx house to have produced twins, and when both them went through the Awakening ceremony to come out with gifts from the gods, they brought prestige to their family. Both were granted dangerous gifts. But still, the half-breed nephew had outdone them both by having a demigoddess claim him as her own.

It was that day that his grandmother had announced that he was to become the head of House; the title would fall to him even though his mother had not been full high Fae. He had not been joined with Seraf for more than a few hours, and he turned down the title and spent the next ten years wandering the continent with Seraf. He told them to do whatever they wanted with the title. Darius could have it. Any of his many social-climbing cousins could have it. He had just been lost in the bliss of Seraf and finding a being who released the rage and anger in him in the best way, by teaching him to let it go on his own. He came back a changed man after those years.

A knock on the bathroom door startled him from his memories. 'My Lord, I'm sorry to disturb you. Your presence is urgently requested.'

Theylin turned and opened the door, almost knocking over the servant girl, sending her stumbling backward. 'Tell him I'm coming in a few minutes unless he wants to see me naked,' Theylin said, starting to throw clothes onto the bed to change into. He looked over his shoulder to see the young girl staring at him, grinning. Ariah was only one hundred years old but she had never seen the fire lord in person as she had only recently started working in Onyx house. She had been nervous to hear that he had finally arrived in the city, but her stumbling words and hand-wringing vanished at the sight of this tall man. Even though he was lean, he was muscled, with narrow hips and a very obvious red trail of hair running from his belly button that disappeared under his trousers.

He fixed her with a grim look. 'Is there more to this message?'

After a stumble with more grinning, she gave her apologies and started for the door and closed it slowly, still smiling at Theylin. Then he heard her running down the hallway yelling, 'He's beautiful!' in the distance. Theylin wasn't unaware that women found him attractive, but he had to smile and feel a bit pleased with himself that even the young ones were still taken with him. Seraf would have snorted in disdain at his vanity.

He pulled on a grey shirt and loose trousers. On top of this he donned a white floor-length robe that had long, wide sleeves. The attire was formal, but he didn't want to face Darius without weapons. Even clothing and status were weapons in this house. The white robe was trimmed in blood-red lace patterns consisted of swirling and curved designs depicting horses racing through them. He wished Seraf was in the house with him. But the last time that she had met Darius, she had nearly plunged a hoof through his head.

Theylin headed down the stone hallways to what he knew was the den. It had been his father's bedroom once, before Darius had it redecorated and repurposed. He walked into the room and saw the large wooden desk covered in paperwork. It looked like dozens of maps and scrolls of literature. Two large leather armchairs flanked the desk, and his grandmother was comfortably tucked into one.

With his open hands on the large wooden desk Darius stood leaning over the table with his head angled downwards and long dark red hair falling over his face. Where Theylin was warm and wholesome with his cleft chin and good looks, Darius was sharply beautiful. He looked like a man just heading into his forties and was still young, until you saw his eyes. He had dark grey eyes that seemed almost dull in appearance. His face was longer than Theylin's with a narrower chin. Their large bow mouths marked them as closely related.

'Nephew. Kind of you to grace us with your presence,' he said without looking up from his desk, and then he let out a frustrated grunt as he swiped some of the maps onto the floor. 'Damn it to the underworlds, have you nothing useful to add to this house except your fur-covered beast?' he said, turning his eyes full of anger towards Theylin.

And so it begins, Theylin thought. 'Good to see you too Darius. Tia, you are so right. I have been missing out on these beautiful family moments living in my hovel in the woods. Why didn't I come sooner?'

'And the whole of the city saw you saunter in with what I'm told is a *human.* This is what he brings to us. Filth. We all know what they do to everything they touch, and he brings it here.'

'She's come to have an Awakening, Darius,' said Tiamerasa. 'By our laws that makes her high Fae. If she comes to our home, you will treat her as such.'

'Comes here! She's not setting foot in my home. It's bad enough that I have to put up with my half-breed nephew and his mongrel horse coming and going as they please.'

'That's enough!' Tiamerasa screamed as she stood out of her chair, and to her credit the sound was so loud and so piercing that Theylin saw Darius flinch. A second later he let out a deep breath and turned around. His eyes settled on Theylin, who knew better than to interfere with what the dynamic this mother and son had been nurturing for centuries.

'She is something. I thought it was a pet obsession that Mehkar has had for centuries. I laughed about it. But I've seen her, Darius. She's something valuable; power knows power. That girl has a value that I haven't begun to understand, and we will not be kept from it.'

There it was. Soon would come the requests. Theylin put his hands on the back of the chair, mirroring his uncle's posture only minutes earlier. There was no escaping the politics of his family. He loved his grandmother; she was an unstoppable animal when it came to hunting down power, wealth, and leverage. She was the definition of what a child of the Onyx line should be. He had loved her so much as a child because she never ever rejected him. But as he got older, he saw the politician more often than the woman. Respect her or fear her, he could never settle on one or the other.

'*She, it, her* has a name,' Theylin said. 'She's a good person. She's come from everything she knows to save everything she loves in the other world. There's nothing for you to gain from her. She intends to denounce any of her powers at the ceremony today.'

'She could not be so stupid,' Tia said with shock on her face. For all her power and prestige, there was one thing that Tia had never achieved. She had not been presented with anything at her Awakening ceremony. Rumour was that the Temple had been paid by Onyx house to even have one. She was blessed, as anyone was when they entered the arena, acknowledged as one of the gods' children, but she was never given any gifts; she left the arena unchanged. She could not comprehend anyone giving up what she could never have, could never buy, could never accumulate enough power to blackmail someone into giving her.

This was where Theylin laughed and chuckled. He could read it all over her face. 'Why have you summoned me here? I have to appear at the Temple. I promised her that I would be there as a witness for her.'

Tia wrung her hands in front of her. Darius still stood with his back towards his nephew. 'Keep her close. Find out what is going on,' he said quietly.

'What do you mean, find out what is going on?'

'The boy has all the finesse of a Wheralia in a glass room,' he muttered.

'The girl is important. Mehkar has been hiding something from her. We finally have a seat on the Mehsari and maybe she is key to ….' Tia couldn't finish the sentence as she saw the anger overcoming Theylin's face.

'You think I'm going to be your spy?' Theylin spat.

'You're not spying; we just want to know what role she plays. You have to admit it's suspicious timing. Just as we hear report after report coming from the outer territories that Fae are dying, people are vanishing, and some kind of sickness is spreading, the main priority of the Fae Boron family is to bring a human girl to this world to—'

'Those people are my family!' Theylin bellowed at the top of his lungs.

Tia was stunned, and Darius turned around from his window with a knowing smile. He folded his arms over his muscled chest as he looked his nephew square in his eyes, always seeming to enjoy getting him to shake off his carefree appearance.

'The Fae Borons took me in after she died. Don't you ever forget that they are my family as much as you are. I will not even entertain doing anything behind their backs. This conversation is over. Tia, I love you but … this is too much, even from you.'

He turned on his heel and heard his uncle's barking laughter. Tia was sputtering behind them, and his uncle's merriment grew louder as he stormed down the hallway. He saw several of the servant girls, including the one who had been in his room, huddling around the corner where they no doubt heard every word. Ariah was star-struck as she watched him head straight down the stairs and to the courtyard, where they could already hear Seraf walking back and forth impatiently for him.

Just before he could enter the courtyard he stormed straight into the only other person whose presence made his skin crawl. Chandara. She was wearing a skin tight pantsuit holding a folder of papers. No doubt she was reveling in being voted into the Mehsari as the new representative for Rehna. 'Theylin!' she cooed as her eyes danced over him, making him as uncomfortable as the day she married his cousin. She had walked away from Keirin for a title and the bloodlines that Onyx house could offer. When she had not been able to create and inkling of attraction in Theylin his cousin Beraphon had been a lovestruck substitute.

'Slinking back to Darius for more orders?' Theylin quipped without remorse.

'Well we are all running around in circles hearing about this awakening, for a human no less. Will you be joining us in family box in the temple?' Chandara asked without the slightest inkling that Theylin's jabs affected her.

'Alas I will have to give my regards to Beraphon later, I will be with the Fae Borons.'

Chandara pouted for a second and sighed knowingly 'Of course. We shall miss Beraphon too, he is North of the city. You know him, always researching some new form of wood magic.'

'A shame.' Theylin said eager to go.

'Will we never be friends?' Chandara asked as Theylin brushed past her. He stopped a moment and thought of old days, when he was sure she had loved Keirin. Of nights all together laughing in the woods, of sharing in her joy as she had convinced him that she loved them both.

'We are creatures of so many years Chandara. Our memories are long. But for what it's worth, I truly wish you happiness. I just don't know how to be part of that happiness anymore. But may the gods bless you both.' He left Chandara wide eyed in the darkness of the doorway.

He entered a small courtyard with stone tiles. He walked towards Seraf with purpose, his hair loose and blowing in the wind, and she could sense his need to be gone from this place, to be outside of all the oppressive memories that flooded him, and mostly to be near Amara again. He was already worried about her and what would happen with the ceremony. As the light from the evening sun was glowing a red orange, he knew he didn't have long to be at the Temple.

Seraf was seven feet tall at the withers, and most men could barely reach to touch her full height. She had long since learned to lean down with one leg forward to allow Theylin to grab her mane and pull himself onto her back. He leaned forward and swung his leg over her, and instantly she was cantering out of the house. They knew each other so well and moved so in sync that it had been centuries since they had used a saddle.

On the street more and more people were gathering outside their houses to see Theylin ride past them. It wasn't often that the fire lord rode through the city. He looked like a god on her back, and many had no doubt that Theylin was exactly that, a god amongst them.

Amara woke up in a soft bed with white cotton sheets, in a large room with dark blue walls. She looked around to see that the room opened up to a large open garden that allowed the evening light to stream in past delicate white pillars. There was also a massive stone bathtub. She breathed in clean air, and there was a scent to the plants that lined the courtyard that she liked. Some kind of crisp sweet spice that was refreshing.

Then she shot up straight out of bed and remembered where she was. In Keirin's house. In some other land, about to perform some crazy ceremony. What was she thinking?

'Take a deep breath. You gave my sister quite a scare. She has been giving me grief for the past couple of hours, saying that I obviously haven't been taking care of you,' Keirin said from the chair across the room. Amara began to throw the sheets aside so that she could get out of bed, but then another wave of dizziness hit her, and she swayed on the edge of the bed.

'Gods, you have to take it easy. She will kill me if you faint again.'

'I don't faint. Since when do I faint?' Amara moaned as she reached out to take Keirin's offered hand.

'There was that time at the sleepover.'

'It's so weird that you know that,' she said, putting her head in her hands and groaning.

'I still think that you must have not eaten or something. Who faints at seeing a mouse?'

'Keirin, do I have to do this today?'

Keirin looked at her and cleared his throat. 'Your arrival at the Temple was announced in public forums. If we don't do it today, the Mehsari could find some loophole in our laws to prevent or delay it. I'm sorry; I didn't know that journey here would be so hard for you. If I had known, I would have given you a couple of days, but I thought the sooner you turned down your powers, the sooner you could go home. I wasn't thinking about you.'

He sounds genuine, Amara thought. Her head started to clear, and she took deep breaths. She loved that smell in here. There were thin curved pillars between the bedroom and the open-air courtyard, and in the soft evening light she couldn't help but find it beautiful. She was still in her winter clothes, and it was too warm and humid. Keirin was still looking concerned as he sat on the bed next to her, and for a minute she decided that she was just going let herself take the help. She leaned over and placed her head on Keirin's shoulder and rested her forehead there while she kept breathing in the sweet air. He smelt the same way, something spicy and crisp.

Keirin went still as Amara leaned onto his shoulder, and he kept hold of her hand. His forehead wrinkled, and he decided that he would just stay still and let her take whatever comfort she wanted. He had seen people do this before. He knew that if they were lovers, he would wrap an arm around her and tuck her into his shoulder or lean his head on hers. He took a large swallow and continued to look down, her hand in his. It had been almost a century since he'd been intimate with a woman. Chandara had ruined him. He knew he shouldn't be such a coward, even as he started to shuffle himself away from Amara, and took her by the shoulders. She groaned again and looked at him as if he were an alarm clock that she was about to smash.

'We only have an hour. My sister is happy to loan you a dress; she has set out a couple. I'm going to leave and let one of the maids help you change. This is my room, and no one else has access to the garden.' He let go of her hand and got up from the bed and started backing towards the door.

He saw it on her face then, the withdrawal and the retreat. She realized that she had invaded his personal space and wasn't wanted, and now she was embarrassed. She put her hands between her knees and turned her head away, nodding in acknowledgement of what he was saying.

In a few seconds he was out the door and saw one of the housemaids approaching with a worried look. 'Is she OK?' she said.

'Beena, could you help her please?'

'What did you do? You look like you're in need of a drink, you're so shaken up.'

'Please, Beena, I'm fine, but she needs your help to get into the clothes.'

'You are too old to be calling me that.' She pecked him on the cheek and walked into the room. He loved that woman, who had lived in their house since he was a young boy. Beena was what he had called her when he couldn't pronounce Behnariva. He should call her Fae Marivan as a formal name. But that wasn't how you addressed family.

Amara saw the maid slip in, a round woman with a warm, caring face. She had blonde hair that was almost white. It was slicked back and braided at the base of her head. She walked over picking up several of the dresses and laid them on the bed.

'I'm sorry, dear. I told them you were too weak to be doing this, but they insisted. Said it was a matter of life and death apparently. You would think surely they would let you bathe, but no. I tell you, that boy never changes—so impatient. Though I've never seen him sit still for so long as he did when he was watching you.'

'Watching his prize, you mean?' Amara said, finally standing up. 'I'm really capable of dressing myself. I didn't grow up with servants; it's really not necessary.'

'You will need help with the laces, dear. None of these dresses has a back. I'm glad to see that your build is the same as our Risa, so the dresses should look as lovely on you as they do her. Now do you know what kind of elemental your family tends towards. She's left out some colour choices here, but people like to choose one that suits their coming gifts. My favourites are the dark blues and greys of the water gifts. Of course, an emerald green for earth gifts and there are those in the deep reds and oranges, but the fire gifts are the rarest. She's left out one of everything. What is your choice?'

Amara finally looked the all the beautiful dresses lined up across the bed—all of them floor length in varying materials, silks and cottons, chiffons and some heavy velvets. All of them were also designed with intricate ties and additional pieces of cloth to wrap around the shoulders and waist.

'None of these.'

'What?'

'I'm not wearing any of these. Can you please bring me my things? I've got a dress in there. If I'm going to make a spectacle of myself, then I'm wearing my own clothes.'

'But, my dear, this is a formal event. You're going to be in the presence of the gods.' Beena's voice went a little shrill.

'They must have seen worse, being omnipotent and all. Now, thank you so much for your help. I just need my bag and my things, and you know what? I see a tub out there in the courtyard, and I'm going to take you up on that bath.' Amara wasn't sure if it was the warm air or that power nap she had taken after fainting, but she decided a hot bath was all a girl could need.

She turned around and started peeling off the too-hot sweater as she walked towards the courtyard. This was decadent, a large tub out in the open air that was just for this private bedroom. The man had taste. She turned the dial, and hot water started pouring into the tub lightly steaming. Amara smiled and looked defiantly at the maid and started to undress, throwing her clothes to the ground.

As the maid started to scurry out Amara was already sinking naked into the water, and the maid shut the door quickly. Keirin was still leaning against the wall outside the door and started. He looked at the maid, who had started to laugh. 'I don't know where you got this one, but I like her,' she said as she started to head down the hallway to retrieve the clothes that had been left by the door. 'And don't go in there; she's naked as a newborn. Taking a bath.'

'A bath! At this time? We are going to be late. Do you know how angry they are going to be if she isn't there at the appointed time?'

'Apparently that's not her problem,' Beena said with a chuckle. 'And really, the woman travels all the way here from I don't know where, her clothes are strange enough, and she faints—and you're pushing her to get to the Temple. Where are your manners?'

'Now is not the time,' Keirin said now rubbing the heels of his hands into his eyes and gritting his teeth. How was he in this scenario? A naked woman bathing in his favourite private bath, the most ancient and most honoured elite of his world waiting for him to present her, and of course all he could think about was why he couldn't be more like Theylin and just act like a normal, suave, lean-into-the-moves kind of guy. Gods, why don't powers ever help with girls?

'Why are you making that face?' Risa asked

'No one is making a face,' he said, drawing out each word without opening his eyes still grinding his hands into his face.

'You're making that face … that girl face. Do you like the human?' she said with an excited shout.

Oh Gods, I could die. How does she always know?

'You're making that noise. That I'm-completely-right, moaning noise! You like her! Wow, she's really different from … well the others.'

Keirin slid to the ground so that his elbows were on his knees. 'Risa, for the love of the gods, please stop talking. I beg you.' He knew their gifts were air elementals, but surely she needed to breathe like the rest of them. He laid his hands on the ground next to him, and Risa scurried in to sit close to him with her knees drawn up to her chest.

She started doing her thing. It was such a subtle gift that she had been given from the gods, but Keirin thought it was one of the most beautiful things that he had ever witnessed. She breathed next to him, looking at him, really looking at him as she had done all of her life, and he felt the ache of his confusion ease, the pain of his past being pushed away. Suddenly life was clearer, and he was breathing with the steady rhythm of someone who was once again grounded to the earth. He looked at his sister and smiled. 'So, thanks for that. Be a good sister, and go in and help her.'

She smiled at him. 'Anytime.'

Beena showed up lugging with her the duffel bag that Amara

had brought. Risa looked at her and nodded as she stood up, took the bag, and slipped into the bedroom, leaving Keirin on the floor.

Amara sank deeper into the hot water and sighed with relief as the steam swirled around her. She was aching and sore from dancing at Theylin's the day before, and her head still felt fuzzy. She pushed her feet up onto the end of the smooth stone tub and rubbed her feet against the edge to massage the sore spots. That sweet spicy smell was getting stronger as the evening light was dimming.

'You look way too comfortable to be disturbed. But you really should be getting excited about your big day,' Risa said as she walked up to the edge of the tub and sat on the edge. Amara thought about covering herself up but then she thought, *The hell with it*; if Risa was OK with her naked body, then why should she be bothered by it? She sat up in the tub so that her torso was out of the water her the hair on the back of her neck was curling softly.

'This is crazy. This whole thing is crazy, and I should have never come here,' Amara said, pulling herself out of the tub and letting the water drip all over the stone floor. 'Where does he keep the towels in this place?'

'The shelves by the bed; you will find a robe as well. He told me about the attack on your friend, that you are here to keep your friends and family safe. There is nothing crazy about that.'

Amara opened a white cupboard and found shelves with clothes and robes and towels. It all smelt like that spice that was spreading through her, making it easy to breathe. She wrapped herself up in a towel and sank down on the bed and started to open up her duffel bag to pull out the one dress that she had packed. It was a skin-tight dress that hugged her hips and ended tightly around her knees. It was a butter yellow and hugged her waist and chest. The top of the dress was delicate lace that crept up to her neck while leaving her shoulders exposed and had one velvet button on the back. She shook it out onto the bed. She loved this dress. She felt elegant and sexy all at the same time.

'That is an interesting choice,' Risa said, suddenly standing close to the bed. 'I didn't think Earth fashions would be so … appealing. Would you mind if I asked the tailors to fashion something similar for me?' Amara jumped a little. Risa didn't make any noise when she moved.

'How is it that everyone here seems to know about Earth, but none of us know about you?' Amara asked as she continued to dry herself off and this time she motioned for Risa to turn around so she could have some privacy while she changed.

Risa obliged her and turned around while still talking. 'You're as much of a legend to the rest of my world as I expect we are to you. I'm more familiar with your world because Keirin has been going over there for so long. I used to worry about him; all the time he'd be gone for days, and sometimes he's come back … a little haunted by what he learnt and saw.'

Amara pulled the dress on over her legs and fastened the button at the top of the lace neckline. She had always loved the figure-hugging material and started to brush her thick, straight hair out with her fingers as she looked around the room for a mirror. She wanted her boots. OK, maybe they weren't the most feminine of choices with a pencil dress, but they were comfortable, and she knew she wouldn't fall over in them.

'So what do they say about humans then? Am I what you expected?'

'You're not really just human, you know. But you're definitely not what Keirin has been describing for all these years.'

'Yes, I'm well aware of my chore status to that bag of wind,' she said, still looking around for a mirror.

Risa snorted and laughed. 'What are you looking for?'

'A mirror. I just wanted to fix my hair and put on some makeup.'

'Yeah, we will have to go to my room for that, Keirin doesn't have a mirror in here. He says he's too pretty to need to check out how he looks. I'd love to say it's arrogance, but he's kind of right; rolls out of bed with killer hair. Which, by the way, you have right now, and we don't have time for makeup. Let's go.'

Risa grabbed Amara's hand and yanked her towards the door and out of the room, and they both almost tripped on Keirin who was still on the floor outside.

'What are you wearing?' Keirin said, eyeballing her up and down.

'Whatever I damn well want!' Amara said with force.

Risa gave Keirin a look to say he needed to be quiet and not push an already stressed-out woman too far.

At that moment they all heard hooves outside on the road, and Theylin was yelling from the road in greeting. From somewhere in the house Beena was calling back at him. They all looked at each other when the words 'No hooves are allowed in the house' were screamed at the top of someone's lungs. Risa burst out laughing and they all started running for the front doors.

CHAPTER 17

AMARA HAD WALKED QUIETLY behind Seraf as Theylin sat on her back and led the way; Keirin and Risa flanked her. From the very beginning of this walk, from the townhouse back towards the Temple, a gentle quiet had prevailed. People were gathered along the streets and market stalls were closing early. Many of them knew immediately that it was for her. Seeing Theylin on his great mount, they knew that the Temple would be opening its doors this evening.

Every alcove of homes had a glass panel placed upon a wall or public meeting area. Through common magic an announcement had been placed hours ago, that there would be an Awakening ceremony. Mehkar had made sure to leave out the origins of the person being presented to the gods, but someone among the Mehsari must have leaked that she was human. Within hours word had spread throughout the city, and even some of the surrounding regions had heard of her.

It had been twenty years since an Awakening had taken place, and the city was beginning to slow itself down for the resulting festivities. For at least a day and a night, work would cease, and there would be food and drink for anyone who wanted it. The people were prepared for the gods to walk among them; it was something sacred, to be celebrated—a reminder that they weren't alone, that life was an ever-growing cycle.

Mehkar had been at the Temple for hours preparing it for the ceremony. From what he had researched, the Baelin line used a deep crimson as their house colour. So he'd asked for blood-red Tellana flowers to be bought and displayed around the Temple. They had soft petals and spiralled out from a black centre. The petals grew perfectly in sync with each other so that together they formed a tunnel, and the dozens of tubes together formed a pleasing shape. Hundreds of them with their dark green leaves were hung over the entrance of the Temple and dozens more were hung over the small white central Temple.

The outside of the Temple had been built hundreds of years ago, a renovation of what had been. The stone walls had been turned by old magic so that solid pieces of stone had became bendable and moulded into lattice sheets, geometric shapes spun out within pieces of stone that were stretched to paper-thin sheets. Stone flowers were so lifelike that people would often have to reach out and touch them to believe they were pink or white stone.

Mehkar's favourite part was the entrance, shielded behind a solid wall of lattice that was designed with lace stars and leaves. Through the holes of the lattice, one could see an archway that led straight onto the sand arena. At the end of the oval arena was the real Temple that was housed here. Round and elevated on stone steps, the domed structure could house no more than a few people at a time. Stone pillars surrounded a central floor, supporting the white dome topped with polished blue stone. Inside burning herbs and incense were kept day and night. The polished stone floor was covered today in the petals of the deep red flower that Mehkar had ordered. This was the most sacred area in Rehna, in the whole of the continent. Gods had descended the stone steps onto the sands of the arena, and the same was expected to happen today.

Mehkar heard the company coming ten minutes before they arrived. The swell of people at the Temple doors suddenly increased, and he heard drums starting to beat, signalling the arrival of the one soon to be touched by the gods. Memories of his children entering these same Temple walls flooded back to him. He would have loved them just as fiercely if they had left this place with nothing but a nod from the gods. He was proud of them both for being so embraced. People still talked of Risa and her flood of yellow butterflies, and the way she laughed with pure joy still rung in his ears.

He turned to see a great horse through the shielded lattice wall that separated the outside world from the inner arena. He walked around the wall just in time to see Theylin jump off Seraf. He had never been a lover of equids, and even though this one was a demigoddess, she had never been more than part of the scenery to him.

Mehkar couldn't take his eyes off of Amara. Keirin had always described her as an ordinary human, but he couldn't see it now. She was glowing in the Fae lands; her skin was a darker golden brown than his own, smooth and flawless. Her lips were naturally a deep mauve, and he found her large grey eyes alluring. He wondered how anyone had mistaken her for just human. She was surely more voluptuous than most of the Fae, but that was seen as a sign of great fertility and beauty here.

What he could not believe was what she was wearing. 'I don't think either of you impressed upon Amara the immense significance of what is going to happen today,' Mehkar said scowling at her dress.

'Oh, go do one!' Amara scowled in the entrance of the Temple.

'Amara, this is a holy place,' Theylin chided.

Amara stood taking in deep breaths. She was huffing air out of her nose and looking at the floor and started staring at small deep red petals. She thought for a moment that she was yelling at Mehkar, but really she was yelling at herself.

For days she had been pulled from the life that she knew, struggling with who and what she was. She missed her family, missed Jess, and was sick to her stomach at the thought of something happening to them. She had been dragged around, ordered here when she was exhausted, and she had been making herself small for these people, listening to them make a spectacle of her because she was just human. She was tired of being worried, so fed up that when she dug deep, all she found was a single-minded will to finish this.

She let out a single breath, and on emptying her lungs, she felt something wash over her, a pull and a calm.

Keirin was standing very still next to her, knowing that she was a woman on the edge of all her reason. He pulled her jacket from her shoulders and without her noticing pulled Ribben's small safe stone from the pocket, tucking the stone into his own trouser pockets. Ordinarily he would have discussed it with her, but she was in no mood to hear anyone out. Bringing magical relics or objects into the arena for an Awakening was frowned upon. The gods only knew what would happen when there was an unintentional mixing of magics.

Amara looked up and felt a beckoning and yearning that washed away all the other emotions she had been struggling with. This was her ceremony. And for the first time it wasn't something to endure; it was something that she needed. She wasn't going to be complete until it was done. She looked out at the small white Temple covered in deep blood-red flowers, and suddenly she needed to be there.

'I have to go there,' she whispered.

Keirin looked at her, confused, because he was sure that she was about to explode, and surprised at this change of attitude. He pulled her arm so that she was turned towards him and looked at her. 'Are you sure you're all right? You're looking odd.'

At the moment she was turned towards him, she whipped her arm free. 'If you do one more thing to piss me off, I'm going to kill you. I don't know how to kill a Fae, but I'm an innovative girl, and I will figure it out.' She spat the last words slowly and leaned into him.

'KK, she mean it.' Ribben giggled from the background.

Amara turned and all the anger she had melted at the sight of the little blue pixie. 'You came?' She knelt down so that she was at a height to look him in the eyes. 'Good, you can tell hot pants here to leave me alone.'

Mehkar started coughing violently and turned away while Risa and Theylin smirked at each other. As Amara reached out to hold Ribben's hand, Keirin made a high-pitched noise and started heading for the side doors that would take them into the arena, muttering something under his breath.

'Amara, it's time for the ceremony,' Mehkar said gently.

'Great. Let's get on with this peep show. Point me in the direction of the gods; it's time for them to meet one of their grateful creations.'

'She scares me a little. Are all humans this pushy?' Risa asked, glancing at Theylin for guidance.

'I don't know, but I like it. I was petrified entering this Temple,' Theylin said, grinning at Amara.

'Take the doors to the right,' said Mehkar. 'They lead to gates that will place you in front of the sanctuary. You will be right ahead of it, and you walk into the centre and ... well, present yourself to the gods.'

'OK, go through some doors and then stand in the centre of what looks like a sandbank. Really sand? It always gets in my shoes.'

'We will pass on your notes to the Temple elders,' Mehkar said dryly as he bowed and exited through the same doors as Keirin and was followed by a winking Risa.

Theylin leaned into her and placed a soft kiss on her cheek and pressed her forehead against his. 'I'm right here, whatever happens. You're a million times braver than I was.'

'You're the only one I like here. Besides Ribben,' Amara admitted in a rush and looked away towards the floor. Then she smoothed her dress down and started walking towards the dark entranceway. It smelt cool and wet within the walls of the Temple, the chamber was lined with vines growing all over the walls and areas were covered with leaves. She stood at the front doors and was looking at the flower-covered small Temple. The moment she was standing in the doorway, her stomach dropped at the sight of what must have been several thousand people sitting in the large amphitheatre that ascended upwards in all directions. In view of the seats, sat a small white temple like an island oasis in the arena sands. The small temple was the ancient point that gods and Fae met and communed, and the larger temple had been built around it.

In her whole life, she had never wanted to be the centre of attention. She didn't want fame; she wanted her own quiet piece of the universe to make her own. For several moments Amara was frozen to the ground as the roar of the crowd greeted her. People were dressed in brightly coloured clothes, their hair in intricate braids and piled in curled bunches on their heads. Copper silver and blue metal jewellery glinted in the fading sunlight. She could see a small ground-level chamber that looked out onto the sand, and Keirin and the others were all piling into it. By the look of the opulent chairs and heavy curtains and tapestries that made up the ceilings, it must have been some viewing area for the elite.

Taking a deep breath, she started to walk towards the centre of the arena. Her gaze fell onto the ancient stone Temple that stood at the other end of the sand arena. It looked out of place, rough and ancient, covered in beautiful blood-red flowers. The domed roof glinted a pearlescent blue, but all other colours had faded away leaving white stone.

The same pull that she had felt earlier started to wash over her. Her head was fuzzy but she felt languid and calm. The air smelt rich with the perfume of the flowers, sweet and crisp. She felt like she was floating instead of walking.

As the rush of euphoria swelled in her, Amara found herself kneeling in the great sand-filled arena. Her movements were dreamlike, and panic was washed away by a giddy rush to surrender to this place. She felt the urge to kneel directly opposite the small open Temple. Gripping her hand closed, she looked down to see dripping blood and watched the dark red droplets fall towards the white sand. A deep gash marred her hand, that had appeared of its own accord. She didn't know if she had willed it to happen, because she herself wanted it or because the life of this place had exacted its price from her. Her blood was splashing out in odd shapes and trickling over the dirt. A sacrifice. They hadn't told her what to do, but since she had strolled through the beautiful arched doors of this Temple, she had felt a pull; a yearning to be close to this place.

As the blood fell, she could hear her heartbeat thundering in her chest. She was calling out—not just with her mind but with her soul, with everything that she was. She was calling out to the universe to be seen, to know, to be heard in this place that seemed to be stripping her bare. What was this place? She was breathing, but the air was thick. Was she yelling out loud, or was the screaming all in her head?

At the sidelines Theylin was pinning Keirin to the wall of the arena. 'Let me go, dammit! Something is wrong! It's not supposed to be like this; she's not supposed to be bleeding like that!'

The crowd of thousands that were in the stone seats of the Temple had come to see the human, but they weren't expecting this. Amongst the crowd was Erid who leaned forward, intensely watching the small woman. Being here brought back memories of his own time in the arena, and he didn't envy her. He had been shaken to his core; the girl he saw before him looked like she was already broken, walking like someone possessed.

The noise in Amara's head became louder. The rush of blood through her body became unbearable; it didn't burn, but it felt like it was going rip through her. She started to arch her head backward, her straight dark hair falling away from her face as she held her right hand outstretched. The blood was now sitting in a perfect round puddle in the sand. Where it should have been soaking into the ground it sat pooling and started to rotate and swirl. The blood stopped flowing from her hand, and as soon as she opened it, she sat with it palm up to the open twilight skies above her. The wound in her hand was now gone.

'Keirin, does her line have blood magic?'

'What the hell are you talking about? No high Fae has blood magic.'

'Then how has she healed? And it sure looks like her blood is full of magic to me.'

From the back of the viewing booth they stood in, Mehkar was staring out intently at Amara. His lips were tight and thin, and he was waiting with his fists clenched together. His eyes never left her or the beadlike pool of blood that was ebbing and swirling like liquid mercury on the sand of the arena. Keirin, who was still struggling against Theylin to open the gates and get to Amara, stopped altogether when he turned around and saw his father's face.

'You know what this means!' Keirin said, turning to face his father squarely. He walked over to stand right in front of his father, peering down on him from his height. 'Tell me right now: what is she? What is it that she has that you and everyone else here wants? I've felt it since she got here. She's not like the rest of us.'

'She's more,' Mehkar whispered. 'More than both, and neither.'

'This is not the time for riddles. She's having the most disturbing Awakening I've ever witnessed, and I promised that I would keep her safe!' Theylin shouted with such force that even Keirin jumped and flinched. Keirin realized that the one who was close to losing control was Theylin. He was radiating heat, and the air next to his skin started to swirl and bend light the way a mirage does in the desert. Theylin moved steps closer to Mehkar, who didn't budge an inch as heat started to make him sweat.

'Easy, Fire Lord. I've died under the Egyptian sun and can bear more than you know of the heat,' Mehkar said, his eyes going to a familiar yellow gold.

'This is not the time to be challenging each other. Father, if you love me, then you will tell me what is happening to her,' Keirin said his voice breaking as the last words of his plea left him.

Mehkar turned his yellow eyes on his son, seeing in that moment more than Keirin wanted anyone to know. His father saw his panic, saw that he was close to losing control and not because of the chaos that seemed to be unfolding in the arena in front of them but because of who was at the centre of that chaos. Her, Amara.

'Keirin, she will be all right, but she's not going to have the same Awakening as the rest of us. She's something older than even the Mehsari remember. There are old scripts that speak of the Baelin line having an ability that went beyond being Fae.

They called them World Builders. They called them Bearer of the Lifeblood. Ever since the taint has started creeping into our land, I've been looking and looking for answers. And everything points back to this line of blood, to those who break the rules that govern all the worlds.'

Mehkar reached out and grasped Keirin's arm, and in the same breath, Keirin breathed deep as if drawing more than just air into his lungs. 'You have known me long enough to know that I would not allow harm to come to her, my child. I admit I wasn't aware of the theatrics, but she will be all right. There are just no living records of how Awakenings go for this kind of elemental. They have long since died out.'

'What do you mean this kind of elemental?' Keirin said. 'She is of water. I saw it; I saw it pull towards her that first day that Ribben made me check on her, swearing she was close to Awakening. I looked in our way, Father, and I saw it all pull towards her.'

'In our way?' Theylin asked, looking between them in confusion.

'Keirin, I looked too,' said Mehkar, 'but it's not just water. It's all pulling towards her. Look now.' Keirin took this moment to look at her with a sight that his father's blood gave him. He walked to the white marble banister and gripped it as he opened up his mind and was flooded with detail. It was all pulling towards her. All of it, all of creation that was in her vicinity, earth and air and water and everything that was matter was pulling towards her in the most minute way, and no one else would be able to see it because Keirin could see the molecules shifting ever so slightly. What was she? No one did this. No Fae alive did this. Everything was tuned to some element and at most some rare individuals would call upon two but never like this.

'What is she?' Keirin asked, terrified that he didn't know how to protect her.

CHAPTER 18

AMARA SANK DOWN ONTO her heels and watched a swirling bead of her blood the size of a golf ball ebb and flow. It shimmered and shook and seemed to be coming together to form a perfect sphere. Where she felt nothing but the pull of the Temple, she now felt like she was being filled up, being made whole in a way she didn't know was possible.

'This is an interesting turn of the worlds.'

Amara looked to her right and saw a woman standing there in light blue clothes. Not just any clothes; a light blue sari covered in embroidery. Gold, bright and warm, covered the woman's arms and torso as if metal flakes had been painted onto her. Then Amara looked up at this woman's lovely face. She had huge almond-shaped dark black eyes, feathered with lashes that brushed against her cheeks when she blinked. Her face was a beautiful oval shape with soft youthful features, creamy yellow skin, and a beautiful soft pink mouth that was in a perfect pout. The final crown to her beauty was the thick locks of smooth jet-black hair that fell in a sheet from her head to just past her waist. Amidst all this beauty, Amara looked down at her arching neck and then screamed and started scurrying backwards across the sand as the woman kept staring at her. Around her neck was a string of ears, all laced along a golden chain.

She knew who this was. She knew in a second of looking at what was almost a childlike face that this wasn't some Fae god come to greet her. This was Kali. Just as she had always envisioned her; but somehow she had not seen the depths of her eyes, the power that lay there.

'Still terrifying young ones?' a smooth voice asked from her left as Amara finished shuffling herself across the sand. Now she was looking at someone as pale as Kali was dark and ominous. He stood seven feet tall in grey robes that pooled around him in a heavy material. Where Kali was shimmering with gold, he was plain, and his long, ash white hair fell past his shoulders. His face was sharp with a pointed chin, and his eyes were also white save for dark irises. His long lips were curved into a smile that made Amara shiver.

He grinned, looking first at the goddess and then at Amara on the floor. 'Well, it is interesting. One of yours and one of mine at the same time? Who would have predicted that would happen?'

'Anyone who sees these creatures mate. How they pretended for so many centuries that they were any different from each other is beyond me.'

'And yet you choose to look like your favourites?' The god

said slyly as he started to circle around the sphere of Amara's blood that still ebbed and flowed on the ground.

'You know this is my favourite body, no one will convince me golden skin isn't the most beautiful there is. The girl was so beautiful, the first one. I wanted such beauty to remain.'

'Well now you have another beautiful one, quite a beauty actually; and rare as they can be in this universe. Didn't we stop making these? Kali, surely neither you nor I is intent on partaking in any more Creation. That would be another several millennia of work, when we have not yet completed this cycle.'

'I had not intended it to be so. But love has found a way,' Kali said with a smile as she looked at the ground, her voice and mind drifting off to things she had long forgotten. She tilted her head, peering at Amara, and started to circle toward the grey god. He was also evaluating the scene and peering in particular at the sphere of blood now spinning unevenly on its axis. Amara's eyes followed Kali, and she panted and went pale, feeling an instinct, a fear where every cell in her body told her that in this game they were the predators and she was the prey.

Kali stopped just inches from her much taller counterpart. Her head barely reached his elbows, which only made her more childlike, her movements vivid and bouncing, the pleats of her dress swaying beautifully with her.

'This is something we both have to pay attention to. I haven't been called into a gifting for so long a time that I cannot even remember. This set of the worlds is supposed to be governed by the Fathain sect. How can they not have recognized her? And to bring her to this place—these ones have forgotten so much. You should see the ones in the sister world.'

Kali huffed as she reached forward, and suddenly Amara's

head curved backward, an unseen hand pulling it back till her neck arched and the whites of her eyes showed as terror fell over her, plunging through her like ice water. *Run, run, run* was all that was streaming through her head, and she started crying. For her whole life she had always considered the world too beautiful, too complicated, and too unique to be an accident of the universe; she had believed in God. But now she felt their presence, felt the gods and their consumption of what is, of an existence that was warping her senses to try and understand. How she wanted to be ignorant of this; how she wished for home and her pink fleece and a flash of her small flat and wondering why she ever left.

'Do not break her. She has a purpose. That is how we have willed it to be. If something has gone towards corruption in this universe, she will be called forth. You know that we will all pay a price were she to fail at her purpose. It was you who demanded that it had to be of flesh and blood.'

'And she is not just yours, so I would suggest you hold back your hands from what is also mine to claim.'

A gentle whisper came from the darkness of the white Temple in the middle of the sand arena. The two gods turned in unison, staring at the lanky figure stalking across the sand. If the others had pressed into the arena with their power, this figure surged in like a storm.

'Krevidian,' the grey god said with a flat tone. 'How is this creature so mixed in its blood alliances? How many sects course through her blood?'

'There is no law against it, Treykilnes,' the newcomer said, standing opposite them and looking at a still-restrained Amara. 'Release her.'

In an instant Amara hit the ground, but then she started screaming in earnest, her chest arched upwards to the sky as she scratched and clawed at the sand around her, legs kicking underneath her to pull away from the force ripping into her chest. There was an echoing crack as her sternum snapped. She screamed like an animal; she voiced such wordless pain that the shock of it coursed with unnatural velocity over the crowd of onlookers.

Erid stood bolt upright in his place, his heart in his throat. She was so small. Witnessing her fear and suffering in this place made him sick to his stomach, he was struggling to stand by the laws of his people and not intervene in arena. In all the millennia that the Fae had been giving themselves to the gods and communing with them, no one had ever heard of a death. Some were shunned, some were left crippled or changed forever, but never this.

Keirin at the advent of her screams had stilled. His horror at what was happening to her was crystallizing and almost froze him to the ground. Then from the depths of his chest he started bellowing and vaulted over the walls of the arena. Theylin and his father didn't try to hold him back, but when they tried to follow, they found themselves catapulted into the stone walls of the Temple with such force that their bodies crushed the stones, cracks emanating from their bodies, bones breaking as they slumped to the ground.

Keirin hit the sand and started running, only to slam into a wall he could not see, finding himself thrown into the air, legs and arms held taut as he was propelled upwards. On instinct he found his will, calling wind and air to him, thrashing out with the inner pool of his magic. He had for centuries kept the true depth of his power in check, but today he unleashed himself. He wrenched himself out of the unseen grip and crashed to the ground. He rolled, and as he turned, all the sand in the arena behind him was blown upwards in a slow wave towards the crowd. Like a tsunami of gravel, sand, and stones, it hurtled forward.

From the other side of the arena Erid with two hands outstretched, pulled backward towards himself, and the wave of sand stopped in midcourse only inches from the first of the onlookers. It stood suspended in a wave several metres tall, stones and sand floating and rotating in the air as Erid took hold of them. It took him only a second; their sudden stillness was jarring. Where Keirin had used the air to bend the ground to his will, Erid could make any form of earth, stone, clay, rock, or metal do his bidding. He grunted for a moment, then after a deep breath he pulled it back, and over some seconds, tonnes upon tonnes of the material pooled downwards like smoke settling. The crowds had already started surging from their seats, screaming and crawling over each other as the mountain of debris started piling into the bottom rows of the seating area.

'Erid, are you allowed to do that?' Ruat nervously asked as his hand slid over his shoulder. Interfering in another's Awakening was one of the most taboo acts that could be done. It was an act of such violation that its punishment was not even known. It had never happened in living memory. Erid was too angry to notice his cousin's concern, too focused on the young woman being torn apart in front of him. The blonde cousins looked at each other behind Erid, who stepped forward still managing the fallout of stone and sand. A chill went through both of them as they saw that Erid was performing this active magic without the smallest signs of his body being taxed. Erid too, had been hiding the true depth of his power.

Keirin came up from his roll and without stopping burst into a run straight for Amara, a wordless bellow rising from him as he barrelled towards her.

'This is a day of surprises,' Krevidian noted with a chuckle. 'A Fae of this strength is intriguing?' Then without looking he again had Keirin held in sway, pulled up from the earth only an arm's length from Amara. She was now gurgling instead of screaming. A trickle of blood started to come from the left side of her mouth, a blood-red drop running slowly towards the ground. Keirin was paralyzed in the air; he was trying to scream but couldn't move. He didn't even think he was breathing; his eyes started going bloodshot, and with his arms and legs held outstretched, he was in the shape of a star.

'That one is the son of Nekheny, you know, incredibly strong,' Krevidian whispered. 'He could even ascend, I think.'

'Enough of this,' Kali said waving an exasperated arm in the air while the other planted itself on her curved hip. She glanced at Keirin in the air, and her eyes narrowed in inspection of him. She threw her left arm towards Amara, as if throwing a ball towards her. Amara gasped and sucked in air, coughed, and spluttered, but she opened her eyes and looked around. She was still helpless and stuck in her compromised position, her head rolling to her left to look at Krevidian. She couldn't see what his face looked like. Every time she tried, it merged and faded and swirled except for an instance when she saw eyes looking right at her. She had seen eyes like that before: the eyes of the green man who guarded the gate. So old and with so much depth and staring straight into her. Where the others had inspired fear in her, she didn't feel like that with this figure. She started keening and her hand went outwards.

Krevidian turned towards her, and for a moment it looked as if he would reach out and take her outstretched hand. 'There, child, the blow was a hard one, but it's the only way to start the process. When your design had been thought up, we gods were young and didn't yet care for your pain.' He took a few steps closer to her, and he stopped himself.

'You started it?' Treykilnes hissed.

'He had to. They have brought about the corruption. You can smell it.'

'Yes. We have been helpless to stop it here,' Treykilnes whispered. 'The Fae are our children, so close to us, so much *of* us, we should have been able to subvert it. But the Starborn laid such a deep wound so long ago, changed their desire too, long ago. They hear us but … not as it once was. It must be the same for you? In this universe? I have long forgotten when I used to venture into the others.'

'A wandering time I do not want to think on,' Kali whispered. 'You are right, when we wished the construct of this creature, it was only to serve its purpose. But they have changed us all. You know the fate you have brought upon her. It will be …' Kali sighed and wrapped her arms around herself. She turned to the grey god.

'She belongs to all of us. A being of three sects. To be this unique in her design deserves recognition. We must gift her, as has been the right of any presenting themselves in this sacred place. Three gifts. I will start.'

Kali walked to the suspended Amara and placed the long pointed index finger of her right hand into the centre of her chest. A deep burgundy glow started emitting from the centre of her chest. Amara writhed and moaned, head thrown back, but what had been pain now seemed to be rolling pleasure.

At almost the same instant four figures in the area were all beginning to gasp and pant, Keirin being the only one who could not be clasp his hands to his chest. One by one, they all fell to their knees and had a matching glow bloom from their chest as warmth and need and desire struck them down. From Venti, who had just reached the temple gates pushing past the hoards of people running form the arena, a deep dark indigo light was emanating like a small star. Even in their terror, people stopped to stare at the magic coming from her. It ebbed and spread out like smoke, but as Venti's arms wrapped around herself, the indigo light stretched out straight with sections breaking off and disappearing as if some unseen wind was pushing them towards Amara.

The same was seen in Erid, who was screaming out in a pleasure so deep he had fallen to his knees and was fumbling to grasp the stone seats of the arena. From his chest poured a deep, rich green glow. Still a mix of light and smoke, it reached out to the girl in the arena, and he knew with utter clarity in that moment that she was the reason this was happening to him.

Agonized gasps came from the ground where Theylin had fallen after being struck down by Keirin. His arm was broken, and though the Fae healed quickly, it would still be several hours. Now mixed with the pain of his aching and battered body, he was twisted with such belonging, such intense pleasure, that he struggled to crawl back against the wall and the rubble behind him, hoping no one would see. But rays of the same great light, a bright glowing rose red, were radiating out of him.

No wisps of wind seemed to move them as they radiated out like great beams of sunshine.

The fourth source of light came from Keirin, hanging still suspended in the air feet from Amara. As they were so close there was no way to miss that the sunflower yellow glow streaming out of him was coursing like smoky ribbons towards the burgundy glow of Amara. In that proximity the beams of colour seemed to reach each other and for moments braided together in great swirling twists.

Kali looked up over her shoulder to see the yellow and burgundy cords of power banding together. 'Now that is a sweet bit of destiny. Four of them, and all here. It is lucky for two of them to find each other, but it appears that she has four.' Kali rose, still smiling at Amara, who had found herself tossing and turning in the sand. Where minutes ago, it had been a struggle, she was now consumed by back-arching pleasure.

'Are you sure you have done that right?' Treykilnes asked with an arching white eyebrow. He folded his arms across his chest and sneered slightly at the glow between Keirin and Amara, now starting to fade from view. The bands of colour still seemed to reach outwards, but they disappeared into transparency.

'Why don't you stop yacking and bestow a gift if you can?' Kali goaded.

'If I can?' he hissed.

'Could we bypass the usual foreplay between you two?' Krevidian walked a tight circle around Amara, not taking his eyes off her. He reached a hand out behind him and slowly lowered Keirin to the ground, gasping and on his knees.

'I have a husband,' Kali said, pouting her lips.

'There are several demigods that would claim otherwise.'

Krevidian spoke aside to her, peering closely at Amara, looking for something in her as she finally started to regain a sense of self, as if she was coming back into her skin. She sat bolt upright covered in a glistening sheen of sweat and saw all three gods standing in a loose circle around her. She looked forward and locked eyes with Keirin. He was on his hands and knees but had looked up just in time to meet her eyes.

Amara saw in him a deep and burning panic. He growled, and his fists hit the sand. He bellowed out a wordless scream that made even the three gods turn and pay attention. Amara scrambled up at that point and stumbled towards Keirin crossing the several feet that separated them and threw herself into him. He caught her in his arms and pulled her in, wrapped as much of himself around her as he could, and then brought his large hands up to cup either side of her face and stared into her grey eyes.

'Are you OK? Are you OK?' he asked over and over, running his hands over her hair and arms, grabbing them while his eyes started filling with tears. He crushed her to him at that point. Almost sobbing now, he spoke one line: 'I swore I would never let it happen again. I swore it, Amara; I swore it. I swore I would never watch it happen again.'

Amara looked at him, confused by his confession. She looked back from him at the three beings still waiting for her. 'Why are they doing this, Keirin?' She turned to them, yelling now. 'What are you doing to me?'

'They? You see more than one?'

'A woman and two men.' She stared at Krevidian and finally started to see his face. There was something so obtuse about him, his chin and his eyes and the way he looked at her. It was like he was a reptile, piercing and intentional movements followed by absolute stillness. His black eyes bored into her, watching her lean into Keirin.

'I can't see them, Amara. Only the person receiving the gifts is able to see the gods.'

'I can feel them. From here I can feel them.' Amara turned in Keirin's arms, looking at the three figures across the arena. She was terrified, but they were as still as stone. She knew they could kill her in a hundred different ways with just a thought. But they hadn't. They had done something to her. She turned, shaking while still pressing Keirin into her back who was now kneeling behind her looking at the empty expanse of sand.

The remnants of the crowd of people were now screaming and rioting out of the arena. Erid was fighting the wave of people crashing against him and was moving closer to the arena floor. He had to know what was happening, and his cousins flanked him like shadows.

'What have you done to me?' Amara asked quietly. She sucked in a breath and then shuffled a step forward with Keirin holding her arm to keep her still and near him. 'What have you done to me?' she bellowed so that the arena was echoing with her scream.

'I always forget how they always have this fire in them,' Krevidian said, smirking and smiling to the ground. 'The next gift will be mine. Something fitting I think, given her station amongst all creation. Let her light shine through.'

'That is a bit much,' Kali simpered as the pleats of her dress blew in the shifting currents of air.

'Well, a candle next to a barrel of gunpowder is rather ironic.'

'What do you know about gunpowder?' Kali asked, nose crinkling.

'More than you know about fidelity,' Treykilnes teased and Kali laughed. Chaos was extending around her, and it was simply intoxicating.

'And you?' Krevidian asked. 'What will your gift be. She is maybe more human than anything else. The smell of them swamps her. What will you give this daughter?'

'I think the presence of so many close to ascending is a clear sign of what she must be given.'

'You want more to your number? New gods are not easily born into the world.'

'We have been stagnant and dwindling in this world and are almost long dead in the sister world. I hear them cry out at times, their agony at the death of what was a paradise. It was the Gates that led to this, the partition of what should have been two worlds in balance. It was the Fae who brought this about. Let them be given the power to correct their mistakes or be consumed with the corruption they have rendered.'

'So you will make her a god-maker.'

'She is the only being capable of holding this power besides a god.' He looked at Kali, who was one of the oldest of them. 'It would seem the threads of destiny you wove into this universe so long ago are coming together, beautiful one.'

'I regret what she will endure to make this happen. I cared so little for them in the beginning. But over the eons … their love is something to behold, when it occurs. She will need the help of gods.' She glanced across the arena at Keirin, who was struggling to get to his feet. 'Let them be new and eager.'

'Your gift will ensure that they love her, beyond anything

human or Fae. That power was considered a curse by many.' Krevidian turned his head up to the sky, his mouth moving with silent words; he suddenly appeared tired and weary. 'I am glad to have never known it, for all I have seen is eons of pain and suffering from it.'

'You should both go, while I pass on what I can. I will be weak after and will not linger here.'

Kali rested her hand on Treykilnes's arm and turned towards him with a questioning look. 'Do you not have the strength? We could do it together.' He smiled at her and wrapped his arms around her, pulling her small frame towards him. His head swept down, and he kissed her with the familiarity of old lovers. Krevidian sneered and in an instant vanished from the arena.

'You never know what he truly wants.' Kali said quietly as she stared around the arena, surveying the thrilling chaos that was fuelling her. She started to radiate red plumes of electrical energy. She started crackling and when she finally turned her attentions back to Amara, her eyes had transformed from the liquid honey brown to a radiant red.

From the side of the arena a crackling began, the sound matched the snapping electrical chorus coming from the goddess Kali. Theylin was holding a broken arm against the side of his body, bleeding from the side of his face, he was on fire. He had walked, limping into the arena space towards Keirin and Amara.

'Keirin!' Theylin bellowed as a sharp blue and orange blade of flames exploded from his left hand, the tip sizzling across the unsettled stone and rocks, the scraping noise joining the crackling snaps of fire. 'Take her from here.'

For a moment Keirin hesitated, but then he knew what

Theylin was asking for. Keirin had only tried once to Nix with a passenger; he had almost killed them both and had sworn never to try again. But now he knew there was no other option; he had to get Amara to safety. He pulled her towards him and wrapped his arms around her so that she was swallowed by his height and he towered over her. She bent her head backwards looking up at him, and with a shout she was about to ask what was happening.

Treykilnes, who had been standing with his eyes closed, was concentrating deeply inward. Then a glowing bright cord released from the centre of his chest. The string-thin strand of glowing light was spitting and releasing glowing balls of orange-gold liquid that floated momentarily and reattached themselves. It looked like molten lava burning from his chest, and after three misdirected twists, it shot like a guided missile towards Amara. In the same moment that Keirin had pulled Amara next to his body, the golden bolt almost reached her spine and glanced off of her. Blue shades of power exploded outwards in all directions from Amara and Keirin, who were untouched but cowering in the centre.

'No,' Kali whispered in horror as she raised both her hands to protect herself. Blue power crashed against a gossamer thin wall of red transparent light that now danced around Kali and her fellow god, who was on his knees screaming in agony, clutching his chest where the golden light had first erupted from him. Through his hands copper brown liquid was dripping between his fingers, staining the grey robes. He clawed at himself as Kali watched in horror and started edging away from him, bringing herself against the wall of the bubble of protection she had created. She started to breathe heavily, skirts swirling around her as she stared up, waiting for the blue burst of power to stop washing over them like a torrent of waves.

As soon as the blue waves of power had died down, Kali Nixed without being seen to the other side of the arena, leaving Treykilnes keening on the ground.

'What have you done? What have you done?' he screamed in ragged breaths as he dragged himself across the arena sands.

Being the only one who could still see them, Amara looked in horror at the creature scrambling along the sands. He was in agony. Where her chest had been split open pouring red blood, his was pouring metallic copper brown liquid. She glanced to see Kali standing stone still, staring at Treykilnes, but there was no sympathy there, just cold calculation.

'Help him, help him!' Amara bellowed as she struggled to her feet, moving towards him.

From one side of the arena door a small blue streak appeared, running flat out along the sands in a blur straight for Amara.

'It was you! It stinks of you! You maggot of a creature, the power was yours, and it's ripped me asunder.' There was an animal-like moan as the god started sobbing. 'You did this. How dare you interfere? How can this have happened?'

Ribben stopped running for a second, hearing the god's plea towards him. He stood just inches from Theylin and his burning sword, and then he attempted to Nix to where Amara was.

'No, I don't think so, little maggot.' Treykilnes pulled the air towards him, and Ribben was pulled out of that hidden space in which he travelled and was struck down on the dirt of the arena. He was only an arm's length away from Amara, and he was scratching and clawing at his neck trying to release unseen hands, choking and gurgling as he tried to scream.

Amara turned to see the small creature being tortured, saw the intent to kill on Treykilnes' face, who growled against the pain he was still experiencing. Ribben was so small; amidst all the carnage and chaos, he was so small. Something erupted in Amara; at the same moment she experienced what she had so many times in life. She was desperate to stop what was happening in front of her. The force of her revulsion, for the suffering she was seeing in Ribben and what she had endured, burned out of her stomach and started upwards. She thought for a moment she would vomit, seeing and hearing Ribben's arm snap as the bone broke and he screamed wordlessly.

Rage burned in her. This was not a new rage. This was the rage of a lifetime—a lifetime of seeing in countless ways that the strong will prey upon the weak because they can, for sport, for cruel pleasure, or simply because they do not care about the life in front of them. How many times had she been made to feel helpless in this life? Even standing here in this arena had not been her choice.

She was choosing now. She was screaming out against what she was seeing. She turned and stretched her arms towards Ribben, trying to get herself between the Fae god and the small Pixie Cobalt. As she did so, shards of white sliced from her hand landing in succession, hit after hit, into the ground inches from the Fae god's feet.

Ribben could suddenly breathe as he clutched his arm but fell onto his side in the arena, puffing out and unable to move in his pain. The sand was softly spraying in front of his mouth as he cried.

The blades of white flickered and crackled in the ground. The god was still bleeding from his chest. Now rivers of the copper ooze were drenching through the robes he wore, soaking into the sands below. If he had been human or Fae, he would have been dead.

He looked down at the shards of what appeared to be pure glowing light and backed a few stumbling steps away. He was losing consciousness.

He looked over and begged with his eyes to Kali. 'Please take me from here. I don't have the strength.'

Kali still stood watching the events unfold without moving, so statue still she didn't look like she was part of the living world anymore. In a moment she stood inches from the bleeding god. 'I can send you, but I can't go with you. You know what is going to happen. Where do you want your soul to reside when it loses this form?'

'The mountains, the blue and peaceful mountains to the East.'

'Then let it be there.' She sighed and pushed her two hands forward as if she was moving something of great weight away from her. Treykilnes started to smoke and swirl, he started to fade from something solid and looked for a moment like one of the Djinn. With one final push he faded and vanished.

With this Kali turned and looked at the blades of light still crackling in the sand. The earth where they sat was starting to burn, the stone melting around them. She stared at them a long moment, her curling locks of hair blowing in the wind. 'Just beautiful,' she finally whispered.

In the seconds it had taken her to cast Treykilnes away, Amara had crouched and scooped Ribben into her arms. Keirin was next to her, trying to see exactly where the damage was.

Kali smiled at the dark-haired girl clutching a Pixie Cobalt and vanished.

CHAPTER 19

THE SCREAMING IN THE arena had not stopped, and now it was Risa whose tiny form was running out onto the sands where her brother was, running full tilt to get to Ribben, who was part of her earliest memories. Hair flowing behind her, she ran in swift long strides right past a hobbling Theylin, who was also making his way to them.

'Get out of the way. I can help,' she yelled as she slid to her knees across the gravel and shoved Keirin out of the way. He didn't put up a fight and fell back onto the ground, scooting backwards. Risa's hands went out and made sure skin was touching skin.

'There now, there. It's OK. It's not hurting.'

Ribben's head lolled to the side, turning towards Amara, who had him cuddled to her chest like a small child. Amara was trying to get up with him, trying to move him from the dust settling around them. Ribben finally breathed out, and his muscles relaxed, his large eyelids finally dropped down. 'Thank you, Risa.'

Amara was looking at Risa's delicate hands and realizing that she was taking Ribben's pain away. She was walking as fast as she could, instinct telling her that she had to get away from this spot. She didn't care where, as long as she wasn't in this place that was swamped with unsettling power.

Theylin saw her go past him, but he kept walking forward, seeing that Keirin was still sitting on the ground, looking shell-shocked. As Theylin moved closer, he realized that Keirin was staring at the crackling blades of light that were still sitting in a half circle in the ground. The stone and earth around them glowed red, steaming and sizzling, showing that the heat was so strong it was melting the sand and rocks around it.

Theylin finally stood next to Keirin and put down one dirt- and sweat-covered arm, offering to pull him up. Without looking away from the glowing forms, Keirin reached up, gripping his elbow, and pulling himself up. Once he was standing, he took a few steps towards them.

'They came from her.'

'I saw it.'

'Can you change them? Is the power like yours?'

Theylin held out his one good arm and concentrated on the curved blade of light closest to him. After a few seconds nothing happened. 'No, it's not fire.'

As they turned to each other sharing a look of shock, the earth around one of the blades started to shake and move, it crumbled and swelled, pushing the blade upwards till it started to teeter from side to side. The ground started to move underneath it, and a large slab of rock appeared to erupt slowly from the ground, the blade falling to the side and resting on the flat stone surface.

They both looked past the stone to see Erid and his cousins walking towards them and the now floating item of power. Keirin and Theylin had of course heard of the Evandrus heir. In hundreds of years the men had crossed paths on a handful of occasions, but with the associations of Keirin's once-human father and Theylin's abdication of his family title, Erid had not spoken more than a few words to either of them. His family and titles often kept him with the more pretentious and loftier elite. While no one could deny their power, the two men were often set apart.

Erid's cousins cautiously flanked him. Anxious at all that had transpired, they looked all around the arena for any new threats that could occur. Many of the Evandrus line would be born with affinities to the earth. The cousins were certainly not the strongest of their line, but even making a small pebble move swiftly through the air could have untold uses, especially when they had sniper-like accuracy.

'It's obviously not a gift aligned with the Earth,' Erid said to them, glancing from the rotating suspended blade to the other half dozen that still sat in the ground. He turned his head to see Amara running to the open arena doors. Two high Fae with beautiful white hair were running to meet them. It was quite a sight. Two beautiful dark-haired petite women with an almost matching set of tall fair women. And while he stood with the men focusing on what was a new and unusual display of power, the source of this power was only concerned with what was to become of a tiny Pixie Cobalt. She might have been granted powers like one of the high Fae, but her behaviour was distinctly other. Erid found that he more than liked her choice of priorities; he respected it.

'So it's true. You brought a human here to be Awakened.'

'I don't know what I brought her here for. Not this, never this.' Keirin began to look around him at the buried seats, the empty theatre. Outside there were still shouts and screaming. Distantly they could all hear and feel the voices and fear coursing through the common telepathic channels. Within the hour, the whole of the continent would know what had happened here.

'Something happened to me.' Erid looked at the men directly, while his cousins turned to him. Without giving away their own ignorance, their eyes flicked to one another. 'It was ... I don't know what it was.' There were few true powerful spell casters anymore, anywhere in Beluvial. High Fae who were gifted could always identify what kind of magic they were encountering, easily if it was similar to their own. Active magic was always aligned to an element. But none of them knew what this was.

In an instant Keirin turned. There was someone who knew. Rage burned in him anew as he turned on his heel and ran towards the walled-off box where he had left his father. Theylin had left Mehkar hunched against the wall where he had been slammed. He was still unconscious, leaning against the cracked stone behind him.

The high Fae were strong, blows that would kill a human would only leave an ugly bruise that would heal in hours. The fact that Mehkar was still unconscious spoke of the force with which Keirin had thrown him against the wall. Keirin leaned down and checked his father's pulse. He was relieved to feel it strong and steady.

He started to gently smack his father's face. 'Wake up.'

'Gods, what in twelve hells?' His father shook his head, clearing his vision and looking around. 'No.' He started to see the heaps of earth and the empty arena seats. 'No, what happened to her? Where is she?' He started to get up but winced and put a hand to the back of his head and brought his fingers away smeared with blood. 'You really know how to get your way when you want it, my boy,' he said with a grimace.

'I wonder who I got that from,' Keirin said rising from his squat to look down on his father. 'The truth now. What do you know about her? You owe both of us that much.'

'Keirin, is she OK?' Mehkar asked, slowly getting to his feet, seeing Theylin also looking grim. 'At least let me know that much.'

'Ok? Is she OK? Three gods just tried to rip her in half; she's currently trying to save Ribben's life, and I'm pretty sure that she was spelled. And I'm not entirely sure that I wasn't spelled with her.'

'That makes two of us,' Theylin chimed in from behind them, rotating his broken arm and sensing that the bone had already started mending.

'Three of us,' Erid called from even further back.

'Spelled? Was she given an active power or not?'

'You are supposed to be supplying us with answers!' Keirin shouted, and his father winced at the force of it, air brushing past him, so that he was almost for the second time thrown into a marble wall.

'Enough, enough! By Isis. Enough,' Mehkar said, shielding his face. 'I suspected a truth about her families' line. A hundred years ago I was searching for a way to gain my own gifts. I know that becoming Fae had been a gift, life immortal is not something I take for granted. But I missed it. I missed the powers I had when I was human, the magics of my time. In the beginning it was about power, but now she may make us strong enough to fight what is coming for us. Something is coming for us from the darkness.'

'Humans with powers?' Erid asked in the background.

'Oh yes. It was different then of course; there were so many rituals and objects of power to help you manifest. It was after meeting one of your golden kind, masked with the golden head crest of Horus, that I sought you out. And it's been wonderful Keirin. Your mother, you, and your sister. All wonderful.'

'Why do I hear an arrogant "but" coming up?' Theylin said, leaning heavily against one of the stone walls.

'I just wanted active powers like my children.'

'How? How would bringing her here give you powers?'

'Her line come from Danu herself.'

'From who? Is this a goddess from Earth?'

'Maybe from before there was a Beluvial or an Earth.' Mehkar turned and saw Amara hunched with Risa in a protective circle around Ribben.

'Why did you want her here?' Keirin asked.

'Because her line can force the gifted to be Awakened and the Awakened to become gods,' Mehkar snapped back.

Silence fell over all the men. Ruat gave out a derisive bark of laughter, and the other men simply looked at each other, not able to process what they were hearing. Nothing could force a person to manifest their powers. If that were the case, there would have been hundreds Awakening. The centuries-long concern over their dwindling births, their lack of power, even the treaty made with the Orchidru, all indicated that there was no true or known way to force a Fae to Awaken.

'It would be insanity enough to suggest that she could make someone Awaken. But make a god?'

Erid had heard enough. He turned his attention to the woman who seemed to be at the centre of hunt for power. 'When she was being attacked, I felt like I was being spelled, but it was nothing I've ever known, it went through me like a rush and settled in my chest, and all I felt was—' Erid paused, feeling uncomfortable admitting to strangers what had happened. 'All I felt was pleasure. There was no taste of an element with the power, and I can usually tell; there's a copper taste or acid or sweetness depending on the spell.'

The earth-aligned Fae often had a better affinity to spell casting than others. Some could see the spells as colours; some could hear them. Others would sense the spells as an aftertaste. Erid had not trained or had any interest in spell casting. It was an arduous undertaking, and in truth he was already afraid of the true depth of his active powers.

Erid was still looking at the women huddled around a pixie, who was lying on the stone floor of the gateway but appeared to be better. Erid could feel another earth-aligned Fae spell casting— with great skill, from what he could tell. He was struck by the mix of this spell; lavender and peat were rolling around his mouth.

He stared at Amara who seemed anchored to the ground next to Ribben. He had hidden the power he had been given, feeling alone with that power. He turned back to the see the shards of light, one still floating on a slowly rotating piece of rock and realized he may no longer be the strongest Fae on the continent.

Venti was stumbling through the doors to the Temple arena. She wasn't sure what had happened to her. One minute she had been trying to get to the viewing galleries, and the next she had felt struck down. She thought it was a spell. She had only learnt about them in her adolescence. When her family had thought she would show some signs of Awakening, they had paid for the best tutors in preparation. It became clear that she was to have no access to any power, barely even able to practice the commons magics.

She had grabbed someone running outside to ask them what was happening. What they described couldn't be true, but she had given the young girl directions to a powerful healer. The healer used to live in the Aperath, the poorest sections of Rehna, and had helped both Theylin and herself when they had travelled south. If she could manage the bloodied pulp that was Theylin after he defended Astian, then she could manage whatever was waiting in the arena.

She felt she was getting her bearings again when she saw Risa and Amara running towards them carrying a pixie. The Fae Boron's pixie, if she remembered correctly.

'I've sent for a healer already, though I think with all the turmoil being broadcast on the channels we will see more than one healer arriving at these doors. How is he?'

'His arm is broken,' Risa said, 'and I think his neck was damaged. Venti, I've never seen a pixie hurt this badly. They aren't like us. Can he heal from this? I'm taking away his pain the best I can, but I can't keep this up.'

'I'm here!' yelled a sharp voice from the main Temple doors.

'Astrellix here! We are here!' responded a relieved Venti, who only knew the barest of field medicine and had no idea what to do with the small body in front of her. They laid Ribben gently on the ground, Amara hadn't spoken and was holding his hand and talking to him softly. Ribben's large eyes were watering, and he was trying to give her as much of a smile as his thin Pixie mouth could muster.

Oriad Fae Astrellix dropped to one knee by the pixie and heaved a large blue cloth satchel onto the ground next to him. She was of a Southern people, even beyond the waters of the Pes kingdom. Her skin was a brown that left her with a deep red appearance, and her hair was silken white. Topped off with vivid green eyes, even among the Fae, she was striking. She started to cast as soon as her hands were above Ribben, with rapid movements of her hands; her fingers artfully and carefully creating shapes, she called forth a healing orb.

Water-aligned Fae were known for their ability to create barriers, but Oriad had the ability to change the function of that sheet of magic-imbued water. It could be asked to mimic that shape of the water held within the cells and body of whatever object she wanted to interpret. The small fluctuating orb was a turquoise blue, rotating and changing shape. Oriad pushed the ball over various portions the pixie's body, starting from the head, moving down over the neck and chest, then over the limb that she already knew was broken. Luckily it was a clean break, straight through the bone without any shards. She pushed down on the orb then, asking it to show her the blood vessels surrounding the bone. The water pulsed outwards and reformed a glistening network of tubes, a diagram of all the veins and arteries.

'He's lucky I can fix this. Well, I can start the process. Pixie physiology is frailer that we are. It will take him several weeks to heal, but I can start the bone callus to stabilize the fracture.

The swelling around his neck I can relieve as well. But he has to rest. They don't have the same constitution as we do. If he tries to Nix or use his magic in the next couple weeks, he could trigger his body's ability to fade.'

'He won't be allowed to move from my bed,' Risa said. 'I swear it. Do you need me to stop taking his pain?'

Oriad stared at Risa with a new appreciation. 'A handy gift, that.' She glanced down at the pixie, running her hand over his small blue cheek to get his attention, as he had been focused on the whispering Amara, who had picked him up again. No one else could hear what was being said.

'Little one, I believe the forms of pain relief I have will not be safe in your kind. I'm going to ask the Fae Boron to leave you conscious.' She glanced at Risa, asking with her eyes if this was possible. Risa's eyes went wide, but she nodded in agreement.

'Risa is good. She will make it not hurt. Always a good high Fae.'

Risa's eyes brimmed with tears. She gave one quick nod and then touched her finger to his forehead, and he slumped into Amara's arms, dazed but still awake.

'I hope you know what you are doing,' Amara said, looking at the healer.

'Well, I can heal his body. But he is more fortunate than most, that he has a Fae with Risa's abilities to ensure that the scars no one can see heal as well. That is part of your gift? To take pain?'

Risa nodded her head in agreement.

Amara turned to her. 'Any pain? Can you take …. take this? Make this go away?'

'Fear?' Risa asked, knowing from the tone of her voice that Amara was dancing at the edge again.

'I really don't want to faint again,' she whispered.

Risa chuckled and brushed her hand against Amara's. 'You will be fine. What you feel now is natural and to be expected. I learnt a long time ago that I have to be careful, fear and pain are there for a reason. You are not doing anything wrong; in fact the rest of us would not be so … brave … had we been through what I just witnessed.'

'I'm running on instinct and adrenaline.'

'Things that keep us alive, that is not weakness.' Venti offered, nodding in approval.

Oriad began spell casting on Ribben. Healing spells were always very personal, unique to the abilities, personality, and empathy of the caster. Oriad also had the unique distinction of being aligned with not just water but also earth.

As she called on her own earth powers to start the mending process of the bones, she could feel immense power pressing outside of hers. Years of attuning herself to the electrical energies of bodies to make herself a better healer had also made her sensitive to the magic of others. When she reached out, it felt like she was a small ship floating on top of an ocean of power. She couldn't believe what she was seeing or feeling; she had encountered nothing like it in centuries.

Ribben was making a slight hissing noise, turning to Amara, clearly experiencing discomfort as his bones welded together. Risa's eyebrows came together, and she exerted more of her power. At once Ribben proceeded to go limp and started to giggle in Amara's arms.

'Hey, go easy over there, Empath.' Oriad struggled to concentrate with a now shuffling patient.

Ribben made a hissy squeal and ran a finger over Amara's chin. 'Amara bobara somara … Boo yah!'

'That is way too much happy juice you are pouring into his brain. Mind pulling back?' Oriad asked while raising an eyebrow. Amara shed a few tears of relief and she giggled with him.

'Was one of those your name?' Oriad asked

'Yeah, actually all of them. My dad used to sing that song to me when I was hurt. When I was little, to make me laugh.'

'Quite a history then.' Oriad was pushing the final casts of strength into her work. She was going to be winded after this; no doubt there were other injuries around the Temple grounds to attend to. 'What would you like me to call you?' Oriad asked, finally dropping her hands and watching the turquoise glowing ball of power fade into nothing. 'There are not a lot of high Fae who would have concerned themselves with a Pixie Cobalt.'

'I don't think that's true.' Amara glanced at Risa, who had taken her hands off Ribben and was barking orders at someone running up to the gates. She then looked to her side at Venti, who had stood up and remained above them, watching the healing process without saying a single word. *Gods, she is tall and beautiful*, Amara thought. She seemed to stand there like stone, looking powerful with vambrances shining on her forearms and a bow at her back. Without having to ask, Amara knew she would have stopped anyone from interfering.

'So, he's going to be OK, right? You magically did some hoodoo, and he's going to be all right?'

'What is "hoodoo"?' Oriad asked,

'I heard "hidoha,"' Venti offered.

'Damn intention spell on the blitz,' Risa whispered, as she took Ribben slowly from Amara's grip.

Amara finally stood up. Deep indigo blood was now smeared over her hands and her clothing. She started to rub her hands over her dress, no longer caring if there was more dirt and filth on her; she was covered in arena dirt. But she was covered in much more than that. There was that taint, that film of violence that was too familiar.

Amara turned and squared her shoulders. She stared at Keirin yelling at his father. Venti watched Amara carefully, strangely entranced by the petite woman, having only met her moments ago. She followed Amara's steel grey eyes, watching the light and sympathy drain from them. The look on her face could be understood by any being, fae or human, god or deity. The woman was furious.

Amara started walking in a beeline towards Keirin. She was thundering towards him, moving faster than even she expected, and slipped past Erid and the cousins so that she was just inches away from Keirin's face.

Keirin started. *Damn it when did she become so fast?* 'Gods, Amara. How is Ribben? Have you been seen by a healer?' he said while putting out a hand to take hold of her shoulder.

Amara smacked his hand away, shocking him. He was confused but didn't get angry, he couldn't imagine what she must be thinking or feeling. 'Hey, hey. It's OK. Whatever has happened, we are going to fix it.'

'Are you now?' she quipped, still staring at him, grey eyes boring into him. 'What did you mean by "I swore I wouldn't let it happen again"?' she asked, going incredibly still. 'And if you lie to me, I swear, I will know it.'

Keirin abruptly froze. He hadn't been thinking when he made the admission. She was being used again, like some small toy, and he just let his emotions and feelings run through him without checks or protections. But now she knew; she knew what he had done.

'Explain. To. Me. What. You. Meant.' Every word came out clipped. Amara took a step forward, and Keirin hovered back a few steps. Still struggling for words. Struggling to explain. The silence between them was stretching on, and he could see her getting angrier by the second, his silence confirming what she already suspected. 'You were there. You were there the night Derek was there.'

'Amara, please.' The look on Keirin's face was devastating as he begged for her to stop, to let him explain.

'Deny it. Say you weren't there. Say you didn't watch what he did to me.'

'What is she talking about, Fae Boron?' Erid spoke up, his hackles rising as he heard the trauma in her voice, feeling anguish and shame taint every word. Theylin had turned so he was squarely looking at Keirin, green eyes starting to glow at their orange centres as his own frustrations over the events of the Awakening came to the surface. His friend had attacked him, and hearing Amara's accusations brought about a fresh wave of anger.

'You had better explain to all of us what she is saying,' Theylin said, starting to heat the air around him. 'And brother, if it is what I fear, if something … happened to her, I'm going to kill you.'

'No. No this isn't happening. No, it wasn't like that, Amara.'

'Do you think I'm stupid?' she spat. 'I find out you and

Ribben have been spying on me—oh wait, that's right, *protecting me* my whole life, and you think I haven't wondered where you were? But I told myself that you couldn't have been there. You couldn't have watched that man break into my home. You couldn't have seen him destroy everything, destroy me.'

Keirin helplessly shook his head. He looked down, shutting his eyes, not wanting to see it again. But Amara saw it, saw the confirmation that he had been there.

'You *were* there.' She was surprised, even though she had suspected the answer. 'So, what, you just watched me, great protector? You didn't feel that a man holding a knife to my throat, as he told me that he'd rather I was dead than not his, was reason enough to get involved? You think that because he wasn't raping me, you didn't have to step in?' She yelled the last at him.

'Amara, there are rules,' Keirin pined at her.

'Oh, gods help you, Keirin,' Theylin said through gritted teeth, 'because if she wants to kill you, I'm going to help her.'

'I couldn't interfere. There are laws. If the Fae are involved I can, but he was human. What was happening to you, it was a human affair. I couldn't.' Keirin sounded as if he knew he had lost any defensible ground with Amara or the men standing behind her.

'And if he had? If he had tried, what would you have done?' Amara asked. 'You know what? It doesn't matter. Not to me. Because I will never forget. He didn't rape me, but he still took from me.' She was nearly vibrating with rage. 'I won't ever forget the hatred that I could see in his eyes, rolling behind all his pretty words of loving me. He loathed me, loathed wanting me. I won't forget the look in his eyes as he enjoyed my heartbreak. But I was supposed to move on, supposed to be fine because apparently nothing actually happened to me.'

Keirin was standing stark still, letting her rage wash over him. His eyes welled up with tears, starting to brim over as he remembered the inaction that was the single deepest regret of his life. Part of him had wished a thousand times that it had gone differently, wished he had arrived earlier. In his most shameful moments, he wished that he hadn't even been there, hadn't seen and heard all that happened, the breaking glass or her screams and pleas. It had taken everything in him not to suck the air from Derek's lungs.

'How could you, how could you stand there?' she asked as small sparks of white light started crackling from her fingertips. They danced like lighting, snaking and arching as they hit the ground around her. 'How could you let me live day after day, while nobody else in the world understood, how changed I was, how lost I was.' She stepped towards Keirin, who, to his credit, did not move an inch.

There was a moment where her anger burned away. Keirin's power was slipping away from him, and he stood dirty and exhausted, and his usual strong hold was slipping. The air started to become thick around them. Amara looked at him with more questions than answers, pleading with her eyes as her grief rose up anew. She always told therapists and family and friends that she was OK. But she was never OK. The pain of the event was just tightly packed away, in a paper-thin box that she skirted around every day. Once in a while she'd knock the box and feel the festering memories leak out. Those days were hard. Today it felt like someone had crushed the box.

But then she was looking down at her arms, at her hands. She kept seeing flashes of light, and the smell of ozone had risen around them, like air before a storm. Her eyes went wide, and she started seeing the thin dancing lines of light, now going turquoise green and as she started to panic a hot acid pink. She stumbled backwards, turning quickly, and another spray of now pink shards of light hit the ground around her. Her eyes were wide, her hair started floating around her, and she was suddenly a deer caught in headlights.

'What is happening right now?'

'Amara, you need to stay still and take some deep breaths. Stay calm.'

'What are those?' As she squealed, she put her hands up, and more turquoise blades of light hit the ground inches from Erid's feet. His two cousins stepped back immediately, and a film of dust and stone sprung up between them like a shield. Erid, instead of backing away, stared straight at Amara, he wanted to get her attention, her focus. He stepped over one of the blackened smoke-filled craters left from where light and sand had combined, melting into what looked like a glass puddle.

He walked up to her slowly, and he could see her tensing, not at his approach, but with clear worry that she was going to hurt someone. He knew that terror, when your body suddenly wasn't the one you knew. 'Take a deep breath with me. Your power does appear very linked to your emotions. So a nice, deep long breath. My name is Erid Fae Evandrus. My favourite sweet is Treta, and I used to run with my cousins from our home to the nearest village to buy them. Ruat was always faster than me, he's on my left.' Ruat lifted two fingers and smiled at her, saluting his hello. 'Mesvana can eat his body weight in Treta, and never even has to loosen one notch on his belt. He is to my right.'

Amara turned to the other man with blonde hair, who looked so different from the man in front of her, but caught herself looking at the bustling swirling cloud of dust and sand that Mesvana was churning up on instinct. Erid turned his head and looked over his shoulder at Mesvana. After a painful few seconds, the winner of a battle of wills was Erid. The dust fell to the floor and stayed still.

While Amara was watching the dust settle, suddenly Erid's hands were hovering above hers, his face was inches from hers, and his hands were just brushing over her own. She sucked in a breath of what smelt like cinnamon and rust mixed together, a crisp heady mixture.

'I need your permission. I just want to bring your hands together. We will do it together, slowly. You are not alone in this.'

Amara was only a few inches shorter than him, but it felt as though he was drawing closer to her than anyone had in her whole life. She nodded rapidly; she wanted help. She needed someone to help her, and as far as she knew, this man wasn't asking anything of her.

'Close your eyes; it helps.'

Amara felt cool hands skim over hers. They gently circled her wrists and slowly turned them inwards. He brought her hands together so that the palms were touching, and the air stopped pulsing. Amara breathed a sigh of relief when her hands touched.

'It seems you have been under the care of these men, Fae Marcus and Fae Boron, yes?'

'That's not what I would call it,' Amara replied under her breath with a growl.

'I can offer you my home. I can offer you my care, my protection if you don't want to be with these men anymore.' He cupped his hands around her hands gently.

'This isn't your place. You have no right to do this,' Keirin cried out behind Amara. She turned to look over her shoulder at him. He was about to step towards her when a wall of flame burst into life from a single spark on the floor, exploding to a square burning piece of magic that was taller than anyone present.

'Theylin, stop pissing around!'

'Oh, that's not me.'

'What?' Keirin yelled, standing back as the heat was forcing him backwards.

'You are lucky she isn't killing you,' Theylin said with little inflection. He was listening intently as Seraf walked through the arena doors. Theylin tipped his head toward her. 'She said it's not your choice, that Amara can choose.'

'She says … Amara isn't Fae, and she isn't human, and she isn't Deity but she sure as shit doesn't have to listen to you. That's a direct quote.'

Amara was looking at the wall of fire that was now curving around a very nervous Keirin, with beads of sweat starting to form on his forehead. She might have calmed down, but she wanted to leave this place. She wanted to crawl into a ball and eat ice cream while she hid under her duvet watching reruns of her favourite shows—to pretend none of this had ever happened. She wanted Jess and home and Dad's border collie, Grey.

'Can you take me to the gate?' she asked Erid. 'So I can go home?'

A look came over Erid's face that was worried and sad. He rubbed his thumb over her hand, and his eyebrows creased together. Erid was known to break the rules when needed and had made it an artform to justify his needs when breaking them, but even he knew that what she was asking wasn't possible.

Given that she was displaying powers that had not been seen by anyone, going back to her human life as an untrained magic-wielding creature was a recipe for disaster. Continental, world-altering disaster. She couldn't go back.

Erid was about to snap out a curse, but he licked his lips and returned his focus to the woman he was trying to keep calm. He'd never seen such cool grey eyes, like a summer storm cloud or ash from a fire. It was the most beautiful colour.

'Amara, once you are trained, once you have even the most basic control of the powers that are coursing through your body now, I will take you to the Gates. I will even take you home to the other world if you ask it. I swear it; on Meradia of the earth and Hercator of the Underworld I swear it, or my life is theirs.'

Amara sighed; this again. What was it with these Fae men and making promises? She couldn't turn around in this world without one of them promising to provide for her, like she wasn't just as capable as them of finding her way back. Did she really need escorting? Really, it was just Fae-infested woods around this city. She had lived in London, she had lived in Soho, she had conquered cities. Well, at least some dodgy bars.

'I don't want your promises.'

Now Venti was smirking next to Theylin. This was too good. Finally, someone else who didn't fall swooning over these power-filled men.

'What?' Erid asked, incredulous.

'I do not want your promises. How stupid and helpless do you people think I am?' She pulled her arms away and pointed towards Keirin, who at last was not standing in a circle of fire. 'That one says he has been watching me my whole life, and he stood by and watched me be emotionally and verbally brutalized by another man. So—you seem lovely, but no. I'm going to figure this out. I figured it out when Derek was there; I saved myself when Derek was there. I'm gonna figure this out too.'

'They don't give powers that aren't suitable to you,' Venti said softly behind her. 'They were meant for you, and you alone.'

Amara gave the woman a hopeful nod of acknowledgement, but her face remained grim. She turned in a circle looking at the group of people surrounding her. Keirin was silent, unwilling to bring up the memories that Amara was managing to move past again. He knew she would not forget this. How had he thought he would get away with it, that he would never tell her?

Amara scowled in frustration. She turned and squared her shoulders to walk towards Keirin again. He looked defeated and worn out, and he flinched as she finally stood before him, closer than before when she was in a rage. He looked straight into her eyes. He was full of regret and shame at what had happened.

'I can't stay with you or be with you anymore. I won't,' Amara said quietly. Keirin's eyes blazed open. He had thought her anger minutes ago had been hard to bear, but her soft voice might as well have sliced through his ribs and straight into his heart. She was leaving, and he wondered if this would be the end. Would she ever forgive him or speak to him again? His stomach rolled at the prospect of something he hadn't imagined: Amara not being in his life, not knowing her anymore.

But when he looked at her still-stricken face, streaked in blue blood from Ribben, dishevelled and dirty, a woman almost ripped apart by the gods, who was changed in ways they still didn't understand, he could not find the words. Tears ran down his face, but he nodded. It wasn't permission, as he didn't have any right to offer it; it was the only movement he could muster.

Amara too looked at him for a moment. She opened her mouth, but silence overcame her as well. She glanced briefly over her shoulder at Theylin. He was already saying with his own anguished expression that he was sorry, that he also would let her go, if that was what she wanted. Amara nodded at him and then turned and walked away from the whole group of them. She saw the gate opening out onto the streets. The light was dim now; the sky above them had faded to a soft peach glow at the horizon, but a dark blue sky was above it, full of stars that Amara did not know.

She saw her duffel bag on the floor and, through the lattice walls of the Temple entrance, Seraf outside pacing and nickering. She grabbed her bag and walked up to the great horse. Amara had enjoyed Seraf before, but now it was different, she could feel Seraf's power; she could hear it like a chime in her ears, a soothing, soft note. She put her hands along her great muscular neck.

'I need a favour. I know you are Theylin's, but I need your help.' Amara said this leaning her forehead against the great horse. She was immensely tired. 'Take me somewhere safe. Anywhere but here. I just need a little time. Just to think, to be. To figure this out.'

A silken voice danced through her mind. *'I know just the place, sister Witch.'*

I T HAD BEEN TWO days since the Awakening ceremony in Rehna. The smoke from the fires had lingered in the air, causing an ash and tinder smell to permeate even as far as the northern cliffs. Beraphon had tried to avoid news of the event and stay focused on his work and the Gryffin herd on his families lands. The staff whispered constantly, slipped from the room to take stolen glances at their mirrors. Many were relieved to find out their loved ones were well. Several Fae had been injured in the panicked stampede out the Temple.

Beraphon had heard many rumours as the hours passed. But he had no taste for the politics and power that the rest of his family craved.

The herd of Gryffins were here on their yearly migration. As the winters grew cold they would come down from the north, hunting the game that had grown plump from lush summer growth. Their thick pelts were lined with golden guard hairs that kept out the snow, and crisp gold and white feathers spread from their eagle heads to the tips of their wings. Beraphon had always been fascinated by them as a child. Onyx House always saw a wild herd of hundreds flock and land onto the uneven cliffs surrounding their mountain farm. His father Darius had in the past always come with him to try and find a large black bull, whose feathers were prized and coveted.

The herd had flown in days earlier than expected. This year had seen a particularly large male arrive. His eagle head was jet black and vivid yellow eyes glowed amongst ebony feathers. Beraphon had marvelled watching them in the morning mist, the creature shook his wings and furred body, water spraying off him in the streaming sunlight. They towered over him as he walked amongst them. Gryffins did not speak in a dialect any of the high Fae could understand, but they were intelligent. And, fortunately, high Fae were reported to be stringy and not to their tastes.

This morning one of the small folk, a green Spraxa had flown in a panic into the front courtyard, his velvet butterfly wings flashing red as his fear coursed through him, making the transclucent wings flush blood red. The servants had rushed out to help the terrified and exhausted creature. He was chattering so quickly people could barely understand his words. Beraphon had only been able to hear a few of them through the spell of intention as fear overpowered reason.

'Killed the herd. It killed the herd.'

Beraphon already in a cream heavy knitted jumper and riding boots had started running out of the farmhouse and over fences to get to the last field where he had encountered the herd. Gryffins were strong beasts, immensely strong with few natural predators this far south. The herd this year was over two hundred in number. He couldn't believe what the Spraxa had said, but he had been so scared. No one could feign that kind of terror, why would he lie?

Running at full speed he rounded the corner of a grove of conifer trees. The trees were separated by a long metal gate; he bent down to quickly pass under and between the bars. Beraphon's short black hair and olive skin was beaded with perspiration. He looked out over the field and nearly tripped as he swerved to try and not run over a body. A large golden red Griffon body. A female that had been ready to birth here, in the safety of the south. He rushed around her large padded hindfeet to lean his head against her large furred abdomen, his hands running through and gripping the coarse fur. Would he be able to hear the heartbeat of the foal? He pressed his ear to the body but could already feel how cold she was. Rigor had set in. There was silence from her and no movement inside her. The foal was long since dead.

From above him came a shrieking cry. He looked up as the shadow passed over him, in time to see large black talons wrap around the limbs of the female's body in front of him, dragging the huge and rigid creature away. Tossing it back and shrieking and lunging at Beraphon, talons clawing at the ground just in front of him so that grass and dirt sprayed everywhere, spread even further by the beating of black wings.

It was then that Beraphon turned and looked out over the field, past the bloated body of the female to see more, many more. All of them. There was body after body, mangled and stretched. Feathers flickered in the wind as the smell of rot suddenly hit Beraphon and he was brought to his knees at the sight of them.

What could have killed all of them? He looked up, honey brown eyes shining with tears at the single large black male Gryffin that was a still shrieking above him. To his horror it landed on the body of the female, his heavy weight crushing her as his clawed front feet ripped into her, a wet sound accompanied a loop of intestine that spilled out of her torn stomach. Beraphon gave a drive heave as a rancid smell hit him anew on the strong winds.

Turning he heaved the contents of his breakfast on the ground beside him. When he turned forward again, wiping his mouth with the back of his hand, the Gryffin had turned one large yellow glassy eye towards him. It charged at him a moment later, four limbs moving as wings beat downwards and he flinched as he steeled himself for death. He closed his eyes and called out to the goddess Meradia that she would welcome him to the next plane, and he felt as if his insides were being ripped apart. He screamed in agony and looked down to see that the Gryffin had rammed his stomach with a dark beak. The Gryffin was looking up at him with his head titlted to the side, the wrinkled yellow skin surrounding its dish sized eye filling with water, almost as if the creature was weeping.

'*Finally a place.*' Whispered through his head

'*Who are you?*' Beraphon shouted out in his mind unable to pinpoint the source of the whispered voice.

'*Pain. So much pain. I don't understand why they all hurt. They all hurt, so I had to kill them, but it kept hurting.*' The voice pleaded.

'*What are you?*

'*Soul. Soul without a place. But I can feel the empty. I have to go to the empty.*'

'*I don't understand. What is the empty?*'

'You are different. All the others hurt but you are different. You can burn.'

Beraphon had only heard of possession, spirits did not linger in Beluvial. But there was no denying that he was not alone with his thoughts.

'Are you a ghost? Do you need a Priestess?' Beraphon asked, hoping that he could reason with whatever was inside of him.

Before him the Gryffin that the voice had left was running manically from body to body, pushing and prodding, crying out in desperation. An agonizing cry was ripped from the creature's throat. Fear coursed through Beraphon as he realized the truth. It, the voice in his head, had made the black Gryffin kill his entire herd.

'You can make it burn.' A more sure and steady voice replied to him.

Beraphon couldn't stop what was happening to him. He started walking towards the body closest to him and his hand pressed against the cold wet fur. Without any control, his hand heated and glowed as his families power came coursing through his fingers. He couldn't call fire, but he could melt and burn anything he touched at will. He had sworn the gift would never be used for death. Sworn to the goddess that had gifted him that he would only make beautiful things.

The body of the creature started to collapse and burn in front of him. Red heat pooling inwards and making the flesh burn. The smoke began to stink of charred flesh. The male Gryffin screeched in panic, wings beating him backwards as he took one last look at his murdered herd before he shot into the air. Grief and anguish filled his cries as he ascended upwards.

'You have to make them burn. And then we will go to the empty.

You are different and you will take me to the empty.' The voice said in slithered tones.

'You can't do this, you can't take me anywhere. Stop this! Stop this, get out, get out of me now!' Beraphon shouted as his body kept walking forward, burning bodies as he went, till the green field was filled with smoke and crackling fire.

'We have to go where the souls are vanishing. The empty space. That is where a strong one will house me. That is where it will not hurt anymore.'

'What in the name of the gods are you?'

'God soul stupid creature. God soul that needs a place that doesn't hurt.'

Lightning Source UK Ltd.
Milton Keynes UK
UKHW012059271121
394710UK00003B/10/J

9 781665 593182